LONDON UNDONE

Visit us at www.boldstrokesbooks.com

LONDON UNDONE

by
Nan Higgins

2019

ISBN 13: 978-1-63555-562-2

This Trade Paperback Original Is Published By
Bold Strokes Books, Inc.
P.O. Box 249
Valley Falls, NY 12185

First Edition: December 2019

CREDITS
Editor: Barbara Ann Wright
Production Design: Stacia Seaman
Cover Design by Tammy Seidick

Acknowledgments

A vast community of readers, writers, and editors put a lot of work into this book. They are all uniquely equipped to either extinguish a fire I'd left unsupervised, light a fire under my butt, or as was often the case, perform both tasks at the same time.

When I finished the rough draft of *London Undone* and wasn't sure what to do with it, I asked for beta readers and was overwhelmed at how many people reached out to me. Those who saw London at her most disheveled helped me take a few steps back and see the big picture: Jason Cox, Paul Evans, Cynthia Kazaroff, Courtney Sellers, Misti Simmons, Heidi Steiber, Jaime Winkel, and Malikah Woody— I'm so grateful to you all.

Erin Sweet-Al Mehairi edited my rough manuscript. Her kindness, professionalism, and perfect blend of tough feedback and gracious encouragement were invaluable to me.

After all the work that went into writing *London Undone*, I almost didn't send it out into the world because of my fear of the dreaded query letter and synopsis. Octavia Reese helped me get out of my own way and gave me the resources and, more importantly, the kick in the pants I needed to get the damn thing done.

Finally, I am incredibly thankful for all the fantastic folks at Bold Strokes Books, who have been knowledgeable and generous. I especially want to thank Sandy Lowe for answering my endless questions and my editor, Barbara Ann Wright, who guided me through this process with skill, humor, and more than a healthy serving of patience.

For Misti, who inspired me to start writing again, and for Ben and Edison, who are proud of this book, even though there are no zombies or dinosaurs in it.

CHAPTER ONE

N, fifty-eight," Lotta Lays shouted, licking her brightly painted lips. "We're looking for an N, fifty-eight!"

"Bingo!"

London and her friends groaned and moved the tabs on their wooden bingo boards so they were blank again. They only had one more chance to win tonight.

"I thought someone was gonna tell Lotta it's my birthday so she'd make sure I'd win," said Reggie, tucking her mini-braids behind her ears. Her eyes, the same color as the whiskey she sipped, focused on her now blank bingo board.

Thomas shrugged. "We did tell her, but she has to use that bingo app on her phone so there's no way to cheat the system."

London kissed her girlfriend on the cheek. "It's okay, Reggie. I'll make sure you win big when we get home." Regina Williams ran her fingers through London's mane of blue hair—hair London achieved with a color called Royal Sky—and kissed her, the sad bingo board forgotten.

"And I'm sure what you win in the bedroom will be better than the DVD box set of *Facts of Life*, season two." Grant took a swig of beer. "Where the hell is Tate with our drinks? He went up for the next round ten minutes ago."

London tried to see the bar, but even from her high stool, she couldn't get a glimpse. Cavan, their favorite hangout, was packed this evening. Every dark corner—and with the oak-paneled walls, there were a lot of dark corners—was crowded with enthusiastic patrons. Normally, she knew at least half the customers by face if not by name, and she liked to think of it as Columbus's gay version of *Cheers*, but Lotta Lays had been bringing in drag queens from other clubs to perform between bingo sets, and it turned their low-key weekly tradition into more of a production than usual.

"I don't see Tate," said Thomas, "but here comes Lotta."

The glittering drag queen was making her way to their spot at the back of the bar, microphone in hand, chatting with the clientele at each table as she went. "Are you two leaving together tonight?" Lotta asked two men who looked so young, this might have been one of their first experiences inside a bar. The fairer of the two blushed and looked at his companion, who grinned but did not speak. "That's a yes!" Lotta guffawed.

She moved on to a group of boisterous women who'd been heckling her all night. "How are you broads?"

"I love your dress," slurred one.

"Thank you, honey," said Lotta. "You won't find this at the Big & Tall Men's Shop." She straightened her blond Marilyn Monroe wig and batted her false eyelashes.

Tate arrived with a fresh round of drinks just before Lotta got to their table. His normally pale skin was a deep strawberry red from the heat of the crowded bar, and a few tendrils of his dark blond hair had tightened into corkscrew curls.

"It's a madhouse in here tonight," he said.

"No kidding," said Reggie. "You were gone so long, I was afraid one of Lotta's queens ate you alive."

"Would I let that happen?" demanded Lotta, arriving at Reggie's side. "No," she said, almost to herself. "If anyone's gonna eat this fine specimen, it's gonna be me!" She pinched Tate's cheek, and he laughed. "This man just brings out the beast in me!" Lotta put her mouth closer to the microphone and purred, and the customers of Cavan hooted and clapped.

"Seriously, folks," Lotta said when the cheers died down, "I want everyone to give a hand to the people at this table. They are so regular here at Cavan, you'd think we put liquid fiber in their drinks." While the patrons clapped, Tate whispered something in Lotta's ear. "Oh, say that again out loud, sugar." She pushed the microphone up to his mouth.

"Uh, it's our friend Reggie's birthday today," Tate said.

"That's right," Lotta said. "That's right. I haven't forgotten you, Reggie. We'll be getting you up on stage after the next bingo set for your shot of birthday Fireball."

Reggie laughed and nodded, and Lotta walked back to the front of the club to introduce Honey Pot, the next drag queen, performing "Hit Me Baby, One More Time."

"Anybody wanna go smoke?" asked Tate.

London gave him a playful pop to the belly. "Nobody smokes but you."

"Yeah, but you could come out and breathe fresh air before the next bingo game," he said. "It's hot in here. Please?"

Five minutes later, they were all on the patio. Surprisingly, given the size of the crowd inside, it was deserted. Two of the drag queens who'd performed earlier sat at a corner table, and one of them had her size twelve stilettoed feet up on the table.

"I can't believe you wanted to come to Cavan for your birthday, Reg," said Grant. "No city besides San Fran has more gay clubs than the 'Bus, and you decided to come to our usual place."

Reggie shrugged. "I like it here."

London smiled. If it had been her birthday, it would have been an extravaganza of club after club, with dancing and drag shows, pageantry and debauchery. Her girlfriend wanted to play bingo with her friends, drink some beers, visit with their favorite drag queen in town, and call it a night. She loved her for it.

"Do you guys want to do brunch tomorrow?" asked Thomas. He sipped his Scotch on the rocks and wrapped his light jacket around his slight frame. "Tip Top's mimosas are calling me."

Grant chuckled and looped his arms around Thomas's waist. "I love my little lush." Grant was always described as a teddy bear, which he hated. "Might as well just slap a sticker on my forehead that says, 'hairy and chubby,'" he'd mutter whenever someone made the comparison.

Thomas arched an eyebrow. "You're one to talk."

"Oh, I know," said Grant, who slipped the Scotch from Thomas's fingers, took a long swig, and kissed his boyfriend.

"Awkwardly single, party of one," Tate muttered.

"Please." London rolled her eyes. "Nobody feels bad for you. You get hit on twenty times a day."

"Yeah, mostly by men," said Tate. "Not that I'm not flattered, of course. If I liked dick, I'd be all set. Alas, I've always preferred donuts to bananas."

"That's a real shame," Grant said. "Bananas are much healthier for you."

"Speak for yourself," said Reggie.

"Anyway," Thomas said, "brunch?"

"I'm not sure," said London. "I may have to stop in at the store in the morning."

Reggie frowned. "What? You didn't tell me that."

"I'm sorry. With the holidays coming up, I really need to organize the inventory."

"The holidays? It's September," said Reggie. "And isn't this why you hired Jasmine as a co-manager? So you wouldn't have to be in the store on Sundays? And after all these years, doesn't Jasmine basically run the store?"

"I just want to make sure we're prepared." London stared at Reggie's perplexed face. "Baby, what's the big deal? It would just be for a few hours."

"I…I had plans for us tomorrow."

Before London could express her surprise, a deep voice called from the doorway into Cavan. "Hey, guys, before the next queen starts her set, I'm gonna bring Reggie up on stage for her birthday shot." Marcus, aka Lotta Lays, fastened a clip-on to her ear. She picked up the microphone from the table at the entrance, and in her Lotta voice, said, "Before we hear from Ms. Sugar Pants, we're going to bring our birthday girl up here!"

The group shuffled inside to stand beneath the stage as Lotta climbed the stairs with her tumbler of amber-colored liquid and raised her glass. The stage at Cavan wasn't even as big as a parking space, but the performers made the best of it.

"You know, I have a tradition here at Cavan to bring the birthday boys and girls forward to do a shot of Fireball with me. I'd like to ask Regina Williams to come up on stage." As Reggie made her way up the few steep steps, Lotta continued. "Reggie is a good friend to us here at Cavan, and if you're a part of the queer community in Columbus, Ohio, chances are she's a good friend to you too. A director and spokesperson for Stonewall Columbus, Reggie works hard every day to advocate for equality and freedom for all of us. It's a pleasure to have her on this stage tonight."

Lotta reached down to the server's outstretched hand, took the shot glass filled to the brim with Fireball, and carefully handed it to Reggie.

"Happy birthday!" She tapped their glasses together. The crowd echoed the sentiment as Reggie and Lotta did their shots.

"Now," Lotta said, handing their empty glasses back to her husband, "we are going to do something a little different. Reggie has asked to say a few words, and since it's her birthday, and she's so special to us, I've agreed to give up my precious microphone for a few minutes."

Confused, London looked at her friends, her brow furrowed.

"I take it you didn't know anything about this?" asked Tate.

"Not at all."

Reggie took the microphone and cleared her throat, twisting her braids through the fingers of her free hand.

"Hi, everyone," she said and cleared her throat once more. "As Lotta said, tonight is my birthday, and on your birthday, you get to make a wish. Wishes aren't usually my thing. My girlfriend is the one who makes the wishes." Reggie paused to look at London and smile. "She's an expert. She wishes on stars, she wishes on candles, on pennies she throws into a fountain; she even wishes when she notices the clock says 11:11. And she won't ever tell me what she's wishing for, either, because, of course, that means the wish won't come true.

"This year, months before my birthday, I started wondering what I would wish for when this night rolled around. When I stood up here and did my birthday shot with Lotta, what would be my wish? For inspiration, I pictured London every time she makes a wish. She closes her eyes, crosses both hands over her heart, and breathes really deep. When she opens her eyes, she nods her head and says, 'It's done.'

"The funny thing is, even though I never know what the hell she's wishing for, I always believe in it. I believe it's going to come true." Reggie closed her eyes, put her hands on her heart, and took a deep breath. When she opened them, she looked directly at London and got down on one knee.

"London," Reggie said, her voice wavering but strong, "somehow, you make me believe in wishes so much that I even want to make one for myself. The only possible wish I could make, the only one that would truly matter, is for you to be my wife. So tonight, I'm making my first wish since I was seven years old. And I'm asking you now: London Craft, will you marry me?"

London could see people cheering and clapping, but all she could hear was a deafening ring in her ears. She stood, paralyzed by the weight of this unexpected question, staring at Reggie: her expectant and hopeful face—that face with the enormous brown eyes and wide lips that she loved—turned first confused, then hurt, and then angry. A bitter taste filled London's mouth, as if the guilt and anxiety coursing through her had bubbled up and landed on her tongue. She didn't know how much time passed before Reggie got up, scrambled off stage, and out toward the patio. When London ran after her, she noticed her cell phone was ringing but ignored it.

How had this happened? The only times they'd spoken about marriage were early in their relationship, when London explained it wasn't something she wanted. As much as she was devastated for Reggie, there was an undercurrent of resentment that Reggie had made such a public proposal without checking in to see if her feelings on the matter had changed.

"Reggie!" London yelled. She saw her striding to the side gate toward the parking lot. "Reggie, wait!"

Reggie whirled around "What for? So you can further humiliate me?"

"Please, I'm sorry," London said. "It was a shock, I just…I just wasn't expecting this."

Reggie gaped. "You weren't? Almost six years together, and you've never even considered marriage?"

London swallowed hard, and the bitterness burned her throat. "No," she said, almost in a whisper.

"That's great, London. That's just great. All this time, I'm thinking we're going to spend the rest of our lives together, and you haven't even thought about it."

"Wait a minute. I *do* want to spend the rest of my life with you. I want to be with you forever. But you know how I feel about marriage, Reg. It's an archaic institution created by the patriarchy, to—"

"Please, don't talk about the fucking patriarchy right now," said Reggie. "You just rejected me in front of a bunch of people."

The resentment that had been an undercurrent flashed to the surface. London's phone began ringing again, and when she declined the call, she saw it was an unknown number. "I didn't reject you. This doesn't have to change anything."

"Doesn't have to…" Tears streaked Reggie's face. "This changes everything."

"Why?" London grabbed for Reggie's hands, and Reggie jerked away, backing up. "Baby, I love you, and I want to spend forever with you. We don't need to get married."

"I do. I need it."

"Since when?"

"You know," Reggie said, choking on tears, "I remember when the Supreme Court struck down DOMA, and we got national marriage equality. You and I danced in the streets all night together. I thought we were building to this moment."

"But…I thought you knew how I felt about marriage. When we talked about being together always, I didn't know you meant getting married. How could I have expected this? We haven't talked about it in five years."

Reggie used her balled-up fist to wipe tears from her face. "I guess that's my mistake, then." She turned and opened the gate.

London grabbed her shoulder. "Please don't go," London said. Her voice was thick with the tears that couldn't fall, tears that felt lodged in her throat.

Reggie took her hand and squeezed before pushing it away. "I have to."

London watched her walk away, and all the emotions from the argument—confusion, shame, anger, resentment—collected in her chest. "Happy birthday."

❖

"Maybe I should have said yes when she was on stage and no when we were alone." London stared into her vodka and soda. "At least then there wouldn't be the public embarrassment factor."

"Sweetie, you were in shock," Grant said. "Hell, we all were."

London had collapsed into a chair on the patio after Reggie left, and the guys swiftly pulled a table over and joined her. Her phone rang, and she lifted it to see if it was Reggie calling, but again, it was an unknown number. She let the phone drop on the table with a clatter.

"What I don't understand is why Reggie thought you'd even want to get married," Tate said through a puff of smoke. "You've never wanted traditional *anything*, let alone something as huge as that."

"You don't ever want to get married?" asked Thomas.

"Not really," said London.

"Why?"

"It's just not my gig. I love Reggie, and I'm committed to her, but that doesn't mean I want the government involved in our relationship. And I'm not particularly religious, so I don't need the holy matrimony aspect."

"Ah," Thomas said, "so you're a cynic."

"Not at all. I believe in love, but I'm ambivalent about marriage. It's too big a thing to do unless you feel strongly about it."

"That's true," said Thomas. He leaned his head against Grant's shoulder.

London's phone rang again, and she glanced at it and sighed.

"You gonna get that?" asked Grant.

"No. It's an unknown number. Probably somebody selling something."

"At midnight?" Tate asked. He grabbed London's phone. "Hello? Yes, she is; who's this?" He frowned and handed the phone to London. "It's your sister."

"What? There's no way it's my twin. She doesn't even have my phone number."

Tate put the phone in London's hand. "I think it's really her."

London hesitated, then put the phone to her ear. "Diana?"

"London, is that you?" She sounded hoarse.

"Yeah, it's me."

"London." Diana gulped. "It's Mom. She died today."

CHAPTER TWO

London woke the next morning to the smell of coffee and felt the bed shift under the weight of someone sitting down. She thought of Reggie, but when she opened her eyes, it was Tate on the edge of the bed. The mug he held had steam rising from it, and he offered it with a gentle smile. She sat up and peered around the room in a dull daze that she mistook for a hangover. Something was off, but in the moments before she fully shook sleep away, she didn't know what. When her eyes rested on the open door of the closet, she noticed it looked emptier than usual, and the previous night flooded back.

She couldn't take her eyes away from the closet. It mirrored the slightly empty, mixed up way she was feeling. Her mother was dead, and Reggie was gone, and she couldn't shake the sense that she was displaced in her own home.

Warmth filled her hands; Tate was holding the steaming mug to them.

London took a sip. "Thanks for the coffee."

"No problem."

"Wanna go over to Hell with me? I just need a quick shower first."

Tate's eyebrows furrowed, and he rested a hand on London's back. "Do you really think you need to go to the shop today?"

"Yes," London said. "Before I leave for Keys Crossing, I have to make sure things are settled here. I'm not sure how long…you know, how long things will take."

She knew next to nothing about the circumstances of her mother's death. Aside from details surrounding the day and time of the service, Diana hadn't given her a lot of information. They'd both been distraught. It hadn't occurred to London until after they hung up that she didn't even know how Grace Craft had died, and in the too bright light of the morning, that realization made her lungs feel thick, and she concentrated solely on her breathing for several seconds.

In the moments she'd allowed her thoughts to linger on her estranged family throughout the last few decades, she always fantasized about a phone call from her mother saying she'd been wrong, that she didn't care about London's sexuality; all she wanted was to have her daughter back. The daydreams ended with tearful reconciliations and promises to make up for lost time. As much as London knew it would never happen, she'd loved the fantasy. Now it was gone.

What was almost as painful as that loss was the fact that she couldn't turn to Reggie for comfort. How could things have gone so terribly wrong last night?

"Well, one of the benefits of being self-employed is that I can go with you." Tate blessedly interrupted her sad reverie. "Not only to Hell but to Keys Crossing too, if you like. Provided we're taking your car, of course." Tate's career as a freelance web developer allowed him to take his work wherever he went. Strangely enough, most of the places Tate went, he visited on his bicycle. Part fitness buff, part minimalist, and part environmentalist meant he didn't own a car.

"Of course." London looked again at the open closet and wondered what other empty spaces she might find around the condo.

"Reggie texted me," Tate said. "She said to tell you she's at her parents' house for a while."

The coffee curdled in London's stomach, and she set her mug on the nightstand with a thud. Reggie had texted Tate. She was reminded of the time when she and Tate were in first grade, and Holly Davis passed a note to Tate explaining that she didn't want to be friends with London anymore because London thought dogs were cooler than cats.

"That's big of her. Did she also break up with me through a text to you, or is she waiting until after the funeral?" London threw the covers back, got out of bed, and stalked toward the bathroom. When she opened the door, she noticed Tate had followed. "Do you mind?"

"For what it's worth," he said, "I don't think this is a breakup. She just needs some time."

London felt tears sting her eyes and blinked them back.

"Sweetie, are you sure you want to do this? We can pack a couple bags, swing by my place and grab a few things, and be on the road. Things will be fine at the store while you're gone."

"No." London shook her head. "This is the way I want to do it. First Hell, then Keys Crossing."

❖

The Hell in a Handbasket sign was printed in large, cross-stitch letters in black with a red background. The logo emblazoned on the sign was a skull with knitting needles underneath in the place of crossbones. London and Tate entered through the customer entrance, and from halfway back in the store, Jasmine yelled, "Welcome to Hell!" She popped up from behind a display and laughed. "Oh, it's you. I wondered who was coming in so early. We don't normally see any customers in here on Sunday until after brunch, and I..." Jasmine's voice trailed off as she moved closer. "What's wrong?"

London glanced at Tate, who took Jasmine's elbow and guided her outside. Jasmine was barely five feet tall and probably ninety-five pounds after a large meal. Still, anyone who assumed she was frail ended up sorry. London watched them through the front windows. When she saw Jasmine cover her mouth and shake her head, she turned away and looked around the store to distract herself. It wasn't in too bad a shape for Sunday morning.

She looked down at the display Jasmine had been working on. It contained one of London's favorite pieces she'd created this year: a small satin knapsack with the hand-embroidered words "Bag of Dicks" on it. Inside were a dozen individually wrapped gourmet chocolates in the shape of penises. She'd gotten the idea when she'd jokingly told Grant he could eat a bag of dicks.

The shop was her baby. Long before she'd known the kind of success she'd have expanding, first to a huge online presence, then to some celebrities who ordered her handmade items for gifts and party favors, she'd had a dream to open this store in the Short North, Columbus's edgy art district. People told her she'd be out of business in a year because there wasn't a market for raunchy crafts. That was five years ago.

London startled when she heard the door open. Jasmine opened her arms and folded London into a tight hug.

"I'm so sorry, sugar," Jasmine said, her voice muffled against London's shoulder.

"Thank you," said London. She embraced the tiny woman and let herself be held for several minutes. It wasn't until she felt a sharp pain in her lip that she realized she was biting it to keep from breaking down.

"Now," Jasmine said, pulling back, "what can I do?"

"I need you to run the store." London felt foolish. She'd come here under the guise of putting everything in place so she could leave town, but now that she was here, she just wanted some love from Jasmine before dealing with her estranged family.

"You got it," Jasmine said. "I'll keep everything under control. I might bring Diego in to help me take pictures and post things to the online store, if that's okay?" Diego was Jasmine's son. He went to the Ohio State University and helped out sometimes for pizza and beer money.

"Of course it's okay," London said "How are his classes going?"

"Fine. They'd go better if he could leave the girls alone, but what do I know? I'm just his mother." She shook her head.

"Even if he left the girls alone, they'd never stay away from him," Tate said.

"Don't I know it!"

"He's lucky to have you as his mother," London said.

Jasmine took both London's hands in hers. "I am so, so sorry, London."

"It's okay," London said, blinking hard. "She stopped loving me a long time ago." Her voice broke, and she wrapped her arms around herself. She could use another Jasmine hug, but she felt too vulnerable to ask.

"I don't believe that," Jasmine said. "Mothers don't stop loving, even when they don't know how to talk to their children."

"Not all mothers are like you," said London.

"You trust what your Jasmine tells you," she said and pulled London into another tight hug, as if she knew. Maybe she did.

"I'll try," London said, knowing better than to argue, and acknowledging, if only to herself, that Jasmine was probably right.

"And you," Jasmine said, putting her hands on Tate's cheeks. "You take care of her."

"Always."

❖

Tate looked out the window of the Holiday Inn and surveyed their view of the east end of Keys Crossing. "Jesus," he muttered. "This place is like a giant, sealed-off time capsule. Nothing ever changes around here."

"Oh, that's not true." London folded her clothes and put them in the shallow drawers of the cheaply made dresser. "I heard Becky finally took over for her mom at Shelly's Deli."

"Becky's Deli? That doesn't have the same ring to it."

"True. But I'm starving. Wanna go over and see if the sandwiches are still good?"

"Sure."

Shelly's Deli was two blocks away, so they walked. Tate was right; nothing ever changed in Keys Crossing. Hole in One Bagels was still there with its ratty sign, as was Brothers' Barbers. They crossed Main Street with the same flashing yellow traffic light; there wasn't enough traffic to warrant a light that also turned red and green.

"These are the same menus," Tate said after they sat at their table.

"Honestly, I'm relieved," London said. "Remember when Becky took home ec and almost burned down the school when she made that devil's food cake?"

"Now I do." Tate laughed. "You're right, it's probably for the best if Shelly's recipes stay intact."

After they ordered—a club sandwich and chips for Tate, a tuna melt and fries for London—Tate drummed his fingers on the table. "Have you talked to Diana since we got here?"

"I called to let her know we made it to town, yeah."

"What about your dad?"

London crossed her arms. "No, I haven't talked to him yet." Her already tender heart couldn't endure what she suspected would be another blow after facing her unapproving father.

"Okay. So are we just gonna wing it tomorrow when we show up at the wake?"

"I don't know what else to do. I haven't seen anyone in my family in almost twenty years. Diana made it clear she doesn't want me involved in the service or the planning. I'm kind of surprised she even told me Mom died at all." London paused when she realized how loudly she was speaking. "I don't even know why I came."

Her conversation with Diana upon her arrival in Keys Crossing revealed that their mother died after years of battling cancer that began in her right breast and traveled to her lungs. When London asked why she hadn't learned of their mother's illness earlier, Diana's brittle answer came after a long pause. "You know why." And London supposed she did. Who knew, Grace might have made requests to keep London in the dark.

She had to push that thought aside because it made her want to run back to the safety of Columbus and the people who actually wanted her in their lives.

"You came because your mother is dead, and it's time to say good-bye."

"Good-bye." London spat the word. "That's all my family and I know how to say to each other."

"I know, honey. But this could finally give you some closure. You've mourned the loss of your mother for years. Maybe now you can mourn in a productive way and heal a little from all of this. It's worth being here to at least try."

"London! Is that you?" Tate and London turned to the freckled, fair-skinned woman approaching their table. "It *is* you! My God, I barely recognized you with all that blue hair. Is that a wig?"

"Hey, Becky. Uh, no, this my real hair."

Becky scanned London's tattoo-covered arms and shoulders. Her gaze rested for a moment on the nose piercing before settling on her eyes. "Well, my goodness, aren't you...colorful."

"Yes, I guess I am."

"I was so sorry to hear your mom passed," Becky said. "She was such a great lady, just sweet as could be."

London's face felt frozen. "Thank you." She wasn't absolutely certain Becky knew she'd been estranged from her family, but she had a pretty good hunch most people in Keys Crossing knew. It would have been big news in this small town.

"Who's your friend?" Becky had turned her attention to Tate, who paled a little.

"Uh...this is my best friend, Tate."

"Have you been in here before? You look awfully familiar." She said the last word as if it was spelled "fermilyer."

"I have," Tate said, "but it's been a long time. Years."

"I see. Well, I hope you come back again before more years go by. I'll see you tomorrow at the wake, London." As quickly as she came, Becky bustled away.

"Jesus, Tate, I feel like such a shit," London said. "I didn't even think about how it would be for you coming back here or that you'd have to reintroduce yourself to people. I'm so sorry."

"It's not your fault. I didn't say anything because I didn't want you to worry about it. I still don't."

"But—"

"No buts. Let's get you through these next few days. I'm fine. I don't care if Becky recognizes me or if anyone else does, for that matter."

"You're amazing, you know that? I think I'll keep you around."

Tate grinned. "Lucky me."

❖

Standing outside the funeral home when London and Tate arrived were Grant, Thomas, and to London's surprise, Reggie. After London took a moment to hug them all, they stood together in a circle, giving London a chance to gather herself before going inside.

"Tate, can I have a smoke?"

"Sure," he said, exchanging concerned glances with the others. "If that's what you want."

"What I want?" London mused, taking a deep drag and coughing a little. She didn't even know what that was anymore, but it was feeling more and more like something she couldn't have. She felt deflated, like a balloon with a slow leak. The more she tried to gather herself to deal with what was happening, the more she felt as if she was losing her grasp on everything in her life.

"I didn't know you smoked," Thomas said.

Grant shook his head. "She doesn't."

"Excuse me! You can't smoke here." A squat man in a black suit had come outside and was pointing to a No Smoking sign just above their heads.

"Sorry," London said.

The man folded his hands and said nothing as he watched her put out her cigarette on the bottom of her shoe.

"Well," London said, "I guess it's time." She was surprised when Reggie took her hand. Their fingers intertwined, and London gave a grateful smile when Reggie gave her a reassuring squeeze.

London wasn't sure what she had expected the inside of Fullerton-Rowe Funeral Home to look like, but it definitely wasn't pale yellow walls and leafy green curtains. It seemed wrong for the place to look like springtime, the season of new life.

"London?" A wispy woman in a charcoal gray pantsuit stood a few feet away. Two deep creases slashed the space between her eyebrows, and London imagined those were created from wearing many frowns, much like the one on her twin sister's face right now.

"Diana."

"That's what you wear to your mother's service?" Diana hissed as she marched toward them. "Blue hair and a dress with *combat boots*?"

"And that's what you say to me when our mother just died, and it's the first time we've seen each other in almost two decades?" She shouldn't have been surprised that this was how their reunion was starting, but her skin prickled, and her fists balled with shock and anger. How dared she?

"That was your choice, London."

"No, Diana, it wasn't. I didn't choose to be gay, for the thousandth time. God, are we really having this conversation again, here, today? And why am I even a little bit surprised?"

"Girls." Frederick Craft's voice broke through the argument, as it had so many times when they were children. "Let's take a moment in private before people arrive to pay their respects."

As if he'd been anticipating this moment, the dark-suited man appeared and ushered the three remaining Craft family members into a small room adjoining the main space. London felt like a prisoner being taken away from her loved ones and into life behind bars as she caught a glimpse of her friends huddled outside the door. She hadn't felt this vulnerable since, well, since the last time she'd seen these people who shared her blood and her name. As the door clicked softly, barring her from her friends, she was struck by the knowledge that she'd never felt at home with the people on this side of the door the way she did with the people on the other side.

"Take a seat," their father said, gesturing to two folding chairs. London and Diana paused to exchange a glance and sat. London felt more and more like a teenager. Their dad leaned against the Formica countertop and gazed at them. "Many words have gone unspoken for many years. Perhaps we will discuss pertinent matters over the next few days, and perhaps we won't. But let me be clear: we will not be speaking of anything today except your mother, her memory, and her legacy. That is all that matters right now. Is that understood?"

It was all London could do to keep from rolling her eyes. He wanted them to only talk about their mother? Perfect. How about the fact that Grace Craft had been battling cancer for years, and nobody had bothered to tell London? They could have at least given her a chance to say good-bye at the end, but no. She'd been notified only after her mother was gone, and she'd love to talk about that.

"Girls," their dad grumbled, "is that understood?"

"Yes," Diana said. London gave a curt nod.

"Good. It's going to be a long day. Two hours for the wake, a short break, and the funeral. London, you may want to take a moment or two with your mother before the wake begins. You have only a few minutes." He turned, opened the door, and stepped aside.

London followed her sister back into the plush main area. Reggie took her hand again as soon as she exited the tiny room.

"Are you okay?"

"Yeah."

"Really?"

"No, but I'm dealing. Where are the others?"

"They said they had an errand to run."

"An errand?"

"That's all they told me," Reggie said. "They said they'd be back in twenty minutes, tops."

"Okay. I'm going to go look…go see my mother. Will you come with me?" Reggie nodded and put an arm around her shoulders.

Grace Craft looked small in the dignified, dark wood casket. That was strange because she'd been nearly six feet tall. It must have been an optical illusion brought on by death. London stood over her mother with her arms crossed. She hadn't seen this woman in nineteen years, and after today, she'd never see her again. London touched her icy, rouged cheek, stroking it for a moment before taking a step back.

To the left stood a collage of pictures from Grace's life. London felt the reassuring pressure of Reggie's hand on her lower back as she crossed to the display. There was Grace as a teenager on the way to the prom with her handsome date. Another showed her graduating from college and yet another on her wedding day, gazing up at her husband. There were photos of Grace and Diana in front of Niagara Falls. London remembered that trip well; she and Diana had snuck out of their hotel room that night and got drunk on Boone's Farm. A picture of Grace, Diana, and their dad sitting at a picnic table looked more recent, maybe within the last five years. There was a picture of Grace handing Diana car keys while Diana proudly held her newly acquired driver's license up to the camera.

What London didn't see was any pictures that included her, and while she wasn't entirely surprised, she was hurt. She'd been completely erased from her family's history.

"We can fix this." Tate, Grant, and Thomas appeared beside her. Tate moved between London and the collage and bent down. She looked at Thomas and Grant for clues but they only smiled. When Tate moved, she saw that he'd taped two photos of London and her mother to the bottom of the display. In one, they were feeding each other cotton candy at the state fair when London was about sixteen. In the other, they were standing on top of the Empire State Building with the New York City skyline in the background. It was just after London had graduated from high school.

"How did you do this?" London asked, feeling the pinprick sensation of tears in her eyes.

"I have all those photos from when I went on vacation with your family," Tate said. "Remember a few years ago when I was obsessed with uploading every picture from my past on Instagram?" London nodded, not able to tear her eyes away from the photos.

"We went to the Walgreens down the street and uploaded the photos on to a thumb drive so we could print them for you," said Grant.

Finally, London looked at her friends. These were the people she'd chosen to be her family, and never had she been more grateful for that. They were the family she'd always wanted. "I don't know what to say. Thank you."

"Anything for you," Tate said.

"London, it's time." Diana stood at the entrance of the room. "People are starting to arrive."

London shook hands of people she'd either known as a child or people she didn't know at all, who had no idea Frederick and Grace had two daughters.

"London and Diana," mused a man with slicked back hair. "Your mother liked Great Britain, did she?"

Diana chirped, "She was very knowledgeable about the monarchy. She traced our family tree back to British royalty."

"I thought the *Keys Crossing Bulletin* made a misprint in Grace's obituary when it said she was survived by two daughters," said one overly perfumed woman. "But here you are!"

London agreed that she was, in fact, there. It was odd and surreal, but she was making it through. There were just a few minutes left before they'd be done with the wake. Only a handful of guests stood near the alcove where the Crafts greeted mourners.

"Do you need anything?" Reggie asked. She had brought London a few cups of water already.

"No, I'm okay," London said. Reggie kissed her on the cheek before joining the guys in the corner on the opposite side of the room.

With that kiss, London felt the bond she and Reggie shared, so strong and sturdy. Despite their recent troubles, London was confident their connection would carry them through much worse than the awkward marriage proposal.

"Disrespectful," Diana muttered.

"Excuse me?"

"I said you're being disrespectful," Diana said, still speaking in a low whisper. "Bringing that person here. And it couldn't *just* be a woman or *just* a black person; it had to be both, didn't it?"

"That *person* is my partner," London said, matching Diana's low tone. "She's not a political statement. She's the woman I love."

Diana snorted. "Everything you do is a political statement."

"Girls." Their father's voice was hushed, but his warning was clear. London and Diana finished the rest of the wake without any further words, and when it was over, London and her friends stood again under the No Smoking sign with London and Tate passing a cigarette.

"What did she say?" Reggie asked, referring to Diana's remarks. London shook her head. Reggie didn't need to hear those ugly words, and London didn't want to even say them out loud.

"Ms. Craft?"

London instinctively held the cigarette behind her back when she saw an elderly man approach.

"Don't worry, you can smoke your cigarette," he said. "I'm sure you've earned it. I won't tell."

"Thank you. Mr...."

"Kopp. Larry Kopp." He opened his suit jacket and pulled out a business card that read, "Larry Kopp—Attorney at Law," and below that, "Estate Planning and Wills." "I'm the attorney in charge of your parents' estate," he said. "Since your father is still living, most of your mother's assets stay with him, but I do need to meet with you. Your mother renewed her will a few years ago, and she added a clause pertaining to you that's a little...unorthodox."

London felt her throat tighten. "Unorthodox how?"

"I'd rather not get into it here," said Larry. "I don't know how long you're in town, but I'm available to meet tomorrow morning if you are. Stop by my office; the address is on the card." He rested his hand on London's arm. "I'm very sorry for your loss." His watery eyes looked kindly at her.

"Thank you. I'll see you in the morning."

He nodded and walked back inside the funeral home.

"What do you think that's about?" Thomas asked.

"I don't know. My mom was pretty traditional. If she did something unorthodox, it's probably not good."

"You don't know that," said Tate.

"I guess I'll find out tomorrow." Uneasiness crept into London's chest. She passed the cigarette back to Tate and held up her hand when he offered her the last drag before he stubbed it out.

The rest of the day was a blur. London felt as if she was watching herself at the funeral and then again at the cemetery. She couldn't seem to connect to what was happening, to the people around her, or to the finality of the services taking place. She opted to ride to the cemetery in Grant's enormous SUV with her friends rather than in the limo with her dad and sister.

After the final prayer, she dutifully took a rose from the top of the casket. The mourners began to mingle a bit, but she stood and watched the grave attendants begin lowering the casket into the ground. The cold numbness that seemed contained in her extremities earlier in the day now seeped into her core, making her chest feel chilled and her heart slow.

Car doors slammed, and she saw that people, including her dad and Diana, were leaving. She turned back and watched dirt cover her mother's casket. She wanted to cry. She wanted the holy heartbreak of tears and soul-wrenching sobs that leave the grief-stricken raw and vulnerable. But that cold numbness blocked everything.

Finally, she turned away from the grave and walked to the outstretched arms of her friends, who were waiting a few headstones away. They walked to Grant's Suburban, one of two cars left. The other, an older Nissan Maxima, was parked an inch or two from Grant's back bumper, and a woman inside watched them.

"I wonder who that is," Reggie said.

"Shit, not today," said Tate. The woman got out of her car, and London recognized Tate's mom. Tate took two steps backward.

"Hello, Tatum," his mom said. "I knew you'd be here."

"Marsha," said London, "this is not the time—"

Tate's mother held her hand up. "I won't be long." She walked to Tate, who was motionless, and stared into his eyes. She reached up slowly and touched the whiskers on Tate's cheek, her fingers barely grazing his face. Tears filled her eyes.

"Mom," Tate said, "It's okay. See? I'm still me." His hand gently covered his mother's smaller hand.

After a few moments, she pulled back and slapped that same cheek, hard. "Abomination!" she shrieked. "You're not my daughter!"

Reggie, Thomas, and Grant moved between Marsha and Tate while London went to Tate and hugged him fiercely.

"God is going to punish you for what you've done to yourself, Tatum," Marsha said, heavy tears rolling down her face. "You are dead, do you hear me? You're dead to me!"

"I hear you," Tate said, his voice shaking.

"Let's go," London said, guiding Tate to the Suburban and opening the door. As they pulled away, London looked back and saw Marsha was on her knees in the grass, her head bent. Her heart broke for her best friend. When she turned to look at him and saw the angry pink mark where Marsha slapped him, the tears she'd been wishing for all day filled her eyes. She took his trembling hand and held it all the way back to the hotel.

❖

"Here's to our mothers," London said, clinking her Guinness bottle against Tate's.

"Yeah, our mothers," Tate slurred. "Our motherfucking mothers."

Rather than attend the post-services gathering at her family's homestead, London hosted a gathering of her own at the hotel bar with the only people she cared to see. They sat in a semicircle around the fireplace in the back, and besides a few people sitting on barstools across the room, they were the only people in the place.

"Is that the first time you've seen your mom since you…" Thomas trailed off.

"Since I told her, congratulations, it's a boy? Yeah," said Tate. "She made it pretty clear she didn't ever want to see me again. I wonder what changed her mind."

"It's her loss," Reggie said. "Both of your mothers missed out on a lot. This is a problem with them, not with either of you."

"I know that," Tate said. "I do. It doesn't make what happened today any easier."

"No, it doesn't." London somehow felt worse for Tate than she did for herself. Yes, her mother was gone, but Tate's mom had gone out of her way to come to a funeral just to be hateful to him. Still numb about her mother's death, London had no problem feeling a searing thread of anger toward Marsha for what she'd put Tate through.

"I'm sorry, honey," Tate said to London. "As if you didn't have enough to deal with right now."

"Hey, don't do that," London said. "This isn't your fault. Nobody could have predicted what happened, even knowing how crazy your mom is. She outdid herself today."

"Yeah." Tate stared into the fire.

Grant pulled London aside. "I hate to do this, but it's getting late, and Thomas and I have to work in the morning. Will you two be okay tonight?"

"Of course," London said. "Thank you so much for everything. I'll walk you guys out."

Grant and Thomas got in the Suburban and waited with the engine running to give London and Reggie some privacy.

London pulled Reggie into a tight embrace. "Thank you for being here."

"You don't have to thank me." Reggie's voice was very close to her ear.

London pulled back to look in her eyes. "So I have to meet with my mother's lawyer in the morning before Tate and I hit the road. Will you be home when I get there?"

Reggie pulled back almost imperceptibly. "I can't, London. I'm going back to my parents' place for a while."

"I see. What is this, then? A breakup?" London took half a step back, breaking their embrace. The thought of going back to her house without Reggie was too much. She was sullen. No matter what kind of argument they had or what they'd disagreed about, London would never make Reggie go through something like losing a parent by herself.

Reggie held on to London's hips. "Don't do that."

"Don't do what?"

"Put your walls up. I'm not breaking up with you, not now. But I do need some space."

"Space to do what?"

"To think about how to move forward now that I know you're not going to marry me."

"Reggie, why does this have to change anything?"

Reggie dropped her hands to her sides and strode to the car door.

"See, that's the difference between you and me. You're asking why this has to change anything, and I'm wondering how it doesn't change everything." With that, she got in the Suburban and slammed the door.

London watched the Suburban pull away from the hotel. Grant and Thomas raised their hands to wave good-bye, but Reggie stared straight ahead. London's connection to Reggie that had seemed so strong earlier in the day now felt as tenuous as a few strands from a spiderweb. The loss of that connection hit her harder than anything she'd been through in the last several days. She clenched her hands into tight fists and unclenched them to match the rapid beating of her crumbling heart.

❖

Several beers later, London and Tate stumbled into their room. London went into the bathroom to change into her pajamas, and when she came out, Tate was in her bed.

"Hey!" She laughed when he patted the space beside him.

"Come on," Tate said. "Get in with me; it'll be like our slumber parties when we were kids."

"Okay. Scoot over." She turned off the lamp, got under the thick comforter beside Tate, and looked up at the ceiling in the darkness.

"Should we tell ghost stories or something?" Tate asked.

"Sure. Have you heard the one about the girl who was haunted by her homophobic mother?"

"Grace has better things to do than haunt you. I'm sure wherever she is right now, she's already busy redecorating and bossing people around."

"Her two favorite things." She thought carefully before asking the question that was on her mind. "Tate?"

"Yeah?"

"We're better off without them, aren't we?"

She couldn't quite see him in the shadows, but London felt Tate put his elbow on a pillow as he propped his head up. "We're better off without anyone who can't love the badasses we are, don't you think?"

"We are pretty amazing." She paused. "I'm sorry about your mom, about today. It never occurred to me that she'd show up."

"I know it didn't."

"Did you expect her to be there?"

"I prepared myself as much as possible. Marsha loves a public scene. Remember when she chaperoned our junior high dance and told off Billy Jenkins when he didn't want to dance with me?"

"God, I'd forgotten about that. We ate our lunches in the bathroom for weeks after that so you could avoid him in the cafeteria."

"I know. A worse friend would've let me sit in that stall by myself. The smells in there didn't exactly make our food that palatable."

"There's no way I would've let you go through that alone."

"You'll never be alone either, know why?"

"Why?" She was momentarily blinded by a bright light, and when she opened her eyes and squinted, she saw he'd turned on the flashlight on his cell phone and was shining it under his chin.

"Because I'm always watching you, little girl!" He made his voice deep and menacing. "Mwahahaha!"

"Shut up!" She hit him with a pillow and dissolved into giggles. He grabbed his pillow and popped her in the shoulder, and soon they were smacking each other as quickly as their arms would let them. Finally, out of breath but still laughing, they plopped their pillows down and rested their heads on them.

This was what family was supposed to be. She didn't have the unconditional love of her parents or sister, and she had no idea if she had a future with Reggie, but she was so grateful and relieved to have Tate. His presence filled all those fractured spaces in her heart, and she felt more relaxed than she had since before Reggie proposed, and she got the call about her mom.

Right before she fell asleep, she heard his sleepy voice murmur, "See? Just like when we were kids."

CHAPTER THREE

Tate and London sat in the car outside Larry Kopp's office. "You're sure you don't want me to go with you?" he asked.

"I'm sure. Besides, you have a mission, should you choose to accept it."

"Oh, I accept it." Tate laughed. "I dream about KC mocha chip cookies more than I'd care to admit." The KC Cookie Factory was a staple in Keys Crossing. They only sold their baked goods locally. There weren't many things London missed from her hometown, but KC cookies was one of them. "If I have to go to every market in town."

"Yeah, good thing there's only one." She stepped out of the Jeep and leaned in to wave good-bye. "I'll text you when I'm done here."

The Law Office of Larry Kopp was on the second floor of the brick office building. London gave her name to the receptionist, and before she could sit in one of the plush, burgundy-colored chairs in the waiting room, the woman told her Larry was ready to meet with her.

He stood and shook her hand, then sat behind his desk. London sat in a chair just like the one in the lobby and folded her hands in her lap.

"Thank you for meeting with me." He looked through a stack of manila folders on his desk. "Ah," he said, nodding when he found the one he was looking for. "Here we are.

"As I mentioned yesterday, when one spouse dies, the majority of their estate usually goes to the remaining spouse. That is the case with your mother...mostly. Two years ago, Grace asked if she could make an addendum to her will. Not much changed. The home your parents lived in had been in your mother's family for years, and your father is now the sole owner. The same with most of her other assets, except for a portion of money your mother allotted to you, provided you agree to follow the instructions."

"What instructions?"

Larry pulled out a sheaf of papers and handed them over. "I'll let you read for yourself."

The top paper was written on thick cream-colored stationery with the letters "GC" in gold script on the top right-hand corner. Grace's unmistakable, orderly handwriting in navy blue ink covered the page:

Dear London,

We've been estranged many years now. My expectation is that we will not reconcile before my death because we both have very strong feelings about what is the appropriate way to live one's life, and our views are diametrically opposed to the point of no accommodation.

I know you believe you were born a certain way. You think you were a radical from the beginning and that you have followed the life path that was destined for you based on the way your DNA was arranged. How short your memory can be, my daughter.

I found this school project a few days ago while I was going through some of your old things. It reminded me of the London I raised, the London I knew you were going to be. I know while I'm alive, you won't even consider what I'm asking of you, but I hope my death will be a catalyst to open your mind. And if that's not enough, maybe a bit of inheritance will motivate you. I know you're proud of your non-materialistic lifestyle, but everyone can benefit from some extra money.

I didn't raise you to be the person you've become. You're better than what you're doing. Please take this opportunity to live up to your full potential.

Sincerely,
Grace Craft

London set the letter down on Larry's desk with a trembling hand. "What's this all about, Mr. Kopp?"

"Larry," he said. "And I think it's better if you continue reading. Would you like me to get you some water?"

She nodded. "Yes, please."

"I'll be right back." He rested his hand on her shoulder as he walked past.

She sat with her eyes closed for a moment. After a few deep breaths, she looked down at the next piece of paper. It had the heading "Letters to the Future; Mrs. Watson, Fifth Grade." Under the heading were detailed instructions from London's fifth grade teacher saying that each child was to write a letter to themselves as an adult, discussing goals they would like to reach by a certain age, designated by the child writing the letter. The letters would then be sent home and hopefully saved for the child to read in the future. Maybe even on the birthday of the chosen age, the instructions suggested.

After reading Mrs. Watson's instructions twice, London placed them on Larry's desk. She looked up as he reentered with a glass of water. She thanked him, took a few gulps, and set that on the desk, as well.

The final document was a piece of mint green construction paper with her own messy ten-year-old handwriting in orange marker. She smiled. Her penmanship wasn't much better now.

Dear London (Age Forty),

Happy birthday from back in time! I hope you're having a good birthday. I hope someone made you a cake, and you got to eat it in bed for breakfast. Maybe that makes up for how old you are now?

My teacher says we're supposed to predict what life will be like at the age we choose, and we need to set at least five goals we want to achieve by the time we look at these letters again. I've been thinking a lot about what I want to accomplish by the time I turn forty, and I think I have a pretty good list now.

1. *Wear business suits every day.*
2. *Get a job in marketing.*
3. *Fall in love with a really awesome boy.*
4. *Get married.*
5. *Volunteer at least once a week to help people in need.*
6. *Have a dog named Chowder.*

I chose the age of forty because it gives me plenty of time to do all the things on my list, with some extra years in case of unexpected events like not being able to find a dog who answers to Chowder. I guess I'll see this letter again in thirty years.
    Sincerely,
    London (Age Ten)

London read the letter three times before setting it down, settling back in her chair, and closing her eyes. "I have absolutely no memory of this."

"That's not surprising," Larry said. "I can't remember much of my schoolwork. I'm quite a bit older than you, but I don't think that's unusual."

"No. I mean, I have no memory of wanting those things. Any of them. I'd say my mother was making it up, but that's definitely my handwriting."

"Maybe now is a good time to go over the conditions of your inheritance."

"All right."

He opened the folder and took out a sheet of paper. "As I said, your mother requested an addendum be added to her will. I'll read it to you: 'I, Grace Elizabeth Craft, being of sound mind and body, wish to give my daughter, London Victoria Craft, a sum in the total amount of one hundred thousand dollars upon my death. The funds will be transferred to my daughter on the condition that she completes the items in her own written letter (attached).

"'London will have one year from receipt of this notice to complete every item on the list. Upon completion of these items, one hundred thousand dollars will be transferred directly to London. If every item is not completed within the allotted one-year time frame, this addendum will be null and void, and London Craft will receive no inheritance. Signed, Grace Elizabeth Craft.'"

Larry peered over the tops of his bifocals. "That's it."

London realized her mouth was open and popped it closed. She shook her head, simultaneously trying to absorb what she'd just heard while also dealing with her disbelief.

"Is this...is this even legal?" she finally asked.

"I admit, it pushes some legal boundaries." Larry took his glasses off and cleaned them with the front of his sweater-vest. "And enforceability would be a challenge. However, if you went to court to challenge the validity of the will, the judge would most likely find that you're not entitled to anything. If we work through this privately, you'll—"

"Wait. You don't think I'm actually going to do this, do you?"

"Well—"

"Because I'm not doing it. I'm not becoming a completely different person to appease the dying wish of a crazy woman."

"You think your mother was crazy?"

London waved her hand over the papers in front of her. "Don't you?"

"No. I think your mother had no idea how to connect with you, as much as she wanted to. I think she waited to ask you to do things in death that she didn't dare to ask in life."

"If you really think Grace Elizabeth Craft was scared to ask me to change, you didn't know her at all. When I was a teenager figuring out who I was, she did nothing but demand that I change. She demanded that I be the daughter *she* wanted. The daughter who would grow up to have the fancy job, the immaculate home, and above all else, the perfect husband." London picked up the green construction paper. "She demanded that I be the woman who has a life like the one on this list and made it clear I wouldn't be a part of her family anymore if I was going to 'live that gay lifestyle.'" She felt her neck and face flush as they always did when she was really angry.

"I understand," Larry said. "And yet, it wasn't your mother who made that list, London. It was you."

She didn't speak. The anger continued to manifest, and she felt the heat spread to her chest. When she glanced down, she saw that her skin was very pink.

"Listen," he said. "You're under no obligation to do this. I, however, *am* under obligation to disclose all the information to you, and I've done that. What happens from here is completely up to you. I'll give you all the documents to take with you, to do what you'd like."

London accepted the file with all her papers. "Thanks a lot."

"You're welcome." Larry either didn't understand or chose to ignore her tone. "Good luck to you."

❖

London rapped on the solid wooden door at her parents' house. After waiting a few moments, she raised her fist to knock again when Diana opened the door.

Her eyes narrowed. "What are you doing here?"

"Good, I'm glad you're here." London sidestepped her twin and went inside the house. "I can talk to both of you." She strode toward the den, assuming, even after all these years, that it was still where her dad spent most of his time.

"I don't know if now is a good time," Diana said, trailing after her.

"That's not true; it's the perfect time." She stood in the doorway of the den. It was still the horrid forest green her father thought was distinguished but always made the room feel oppressive to her.

Her dad sat in one of two high-backed chairs arranged in front of the fireplace. He had a book in his hands but must have heard her coming because he was already studying her with a frown. "We weren't expecting you."

She laughed, and there was no humor in it. "You mean you weren't expecting your ostracized daughter who you cast out without a second thought almost twenty years ago? No. I'd imagine you weren't expecting me."

Diana moved across the room and sat in the empty chair beside their father. "Daddy, she just barged in without even waiting to see if you'd be able to talk to her and—"

He held up his hand. "That's all right, Diana." He reached to the small table beside him, picked up his pipe, and lit it. "What seems to be the reason for your visit?"

"It's amazing," London said. "You can sit there like the last two decades didn't even happen. Like I stop in a few times a week to talk about the weather and the neighbor's cat. You don't even acknowledge that I was forced out of this family."

"You did that to yourself," Diana said. "You could have chosen not to live the way you live."

"You mean being gay. You can say the word; it won't make you catch the gay virus. And while we're talking about choices, let me ask you, when did you choose to be straight?"

"That's enough," their dad said. "London, you obviously have a reason to be here. Would you mind telling us what that is?"

She trudged to where they sat and dropped the file on the table between them. "Did you know about this? Either of you?" She stood with her arms folded, watching them pass the contents of the file back and forth until they'd read the papers inside.

"I don't believe this," Diana said. "You run off to live a life of moral corruption, and you get rewarded with one hundred thousand dollars? Meanwhile, I stayed here, did all the right things, and what do I get? Nothing." She turned to their father, who must have been reading the addendum for the third time and appeared not to be listening. "Daddy! It's just not fair!"

"Well, that answers my question about whether you knew," London muttered. "Dad? I assume by that astonished look on your face that you didn't either?"

"I did not."

Diana sulked. "Must be nice to be the prodigal daughter."

"Nice?" London gathered the papers and shoved them into the folder. "You think it must be nice? Do you have any idea what it's been like for me being estranged from my family? Of course you don't." She trembled with hurt and anger. "My first birthday when I couldn't come home, I ate cake alone at a diner. When the holidays roll around and people talk about going home for Thanksgiving or Christmas, I have to admit that I don't have a home or a family anymore. And I wasn't here when my mother died." Her voice broke. "Trust me, nothing about this is nice."

She turned to leave. When she got to the door, she heard her father call her name. He was a few steps behind, his face grave.

"I won't come back unannounced if that's what you're worried about." She clutched the folder tightly with both hands.

"That isn't what I'm worried about," he said slowly. "London... your mother and I..."

"Yes?"

"Parents invest in their children. With money, yes, but also with a lot of effort. It's our job to instill morals and values in you. And we did that. We worked very hard. Surely you must understand how frustrating it is to put years of your life into a person who then goes against all the principles you've taught them. What were we to do? We couldn't very well just ignore your loss of moral compass."

"Wow. Yeah, it's a real shame your investment didn't bring the kind of return you expected."

"Come now, I'm just trying to explain—"

"Oh, you explained perfectly. My being gay was a deal breaker for the right to be your daughter. It doesn't matter that I'm a good person, a compassionate friend, a hard worker, a loyal girlfriend. It doesn't matter that I run a successful business or that I have two master's degrees. Who I love is a deal breaker, and nothing else about me matters enough for you to let me be in your family."

"If you'd just given yourself a chance to meet the right man—"

"I'm out of here," she said. "I could talk for days about why there was never going to be the right man, but you won't listen, and we'd end up right here again. With me standing in the foyer, one foot already out the door." Before he could say another word, she got outside and slammed the door behind her.

Tate sped down the highway in London's old Jeep. "Read them to me again," he said.

"I've already read them to you three times," London said.

"I know. Maybe the fourth time will be the one where it starts making sense."

"I doubt it." She closed the file with a sigh.

"I can't believe your mom is trying to pay the gay away. After she's dead, no less!"

"Oddly enough, I can believe it."

"That's because you got to read it a fourth time."

She didn't even have to look at him to hear the smirk in his voice. "Ha ha. Tater Tot made a joke."

"Call me that again, and you'll walk the rest of the way home. That name wasn't even funny when we were kids."

"Agree to disagree on that."

"Anyway," he said loudly, "why are you not surprised about all this?"

She shrugged. "It's high drama. It's bribery. It's got Grace written all over it."

"Literally."

"Yep."

He glanced at her. "What are you not saying?"

"I just don't know what to do with this." She smoothed the corner of the file with her hand.

"What do you mean? It's not like you're gonna go through with this insanity."

"Of course not. Do you remember this project? These letters? You were in Mrs. Watson's class; you would've had to do this too."

He shook his head. "I don't, but that doesn't mean anything. I can't remember any other schoolwork from her class either."

"Right." She took out the green construction paper again. "But you did know me; you knew me better than anyone. Diana was my twin, but you were my family. Do you remember me being the kind of person who wanted the things in this letter?"

He rested his hand on her knee. "I remember you being the kind of person who wanted to make her parents happy. At least when we were really young."

"That's true." Her heart broke for the ten-year-old girl who wanted so desperately to be accepted by a family that never really let her be a part of it. She'd spent so many years working to numb herself to the feelings she had about their rejection. Those feelings rushed to the surface when she remembered always trying so hard to be what they wanted. It made her realize how hurt she continued to be. "I guess that's all it was."

"You shouldn't have had to bend over backward to make them happy. You were a kid that any parent would be proud of. Still are."

"Thanks, Tate."

After several moments of silence, he said, "Hey, you wanna play a game? Get your mind off things?"

Despite herself, she smiled. "What game did you have in mind?"

"For Times Three?"

London couldn't remember which of them had invented the game with the funny play on words, but she had a feeling it had been Tate.

"Okay," she said. "Give me something."

Tate thought for a moment. "KC mocha chip cookies."

"That's easy. Forever." If Tate had named something she liked but didn't love, she would've said, "For now." If he named something she couldn't stand, she would say, "For never." She had forgotten all about the game and was happy he had jogged her memory.

They played For Times Three the rest of the way home, and London didn't think about her mother, father, sister, or the letters she'd read at the attorney's office for the remainder of the ride.

❖

London's apartment felt emptier than she expected. She'd brushed off Tate's offers to stay with her a few nights. "It'll be good for me to be by myself for a while," she told him.

The emptiness was punctuated by things gone missing. Reggie must have gotten more of her stuff when London was gone. The stack of books on the end of the coffee table, the scarf that had been hanging on a hook by the door since last February, and the blanket on the back of the couch, knitted by Reggie's gran, were all absent. Reggie wasn't just out, she was moved out.

London sat on the edge of the couch and opened the file to take yet another look at its contents. Unpacking her suitcase could wait until later. She picked up the construction paper and traced the orange letters with her fingers.

Wear business suits every day. She'd never owned a business suit. She wore ripped jeans and graphic T-shirts with the occasional skirt and fishnet stockings thrown in. And she never left home wearing anything on her feet besides combat boots.

Without knowing exactly what she was doing, London walked to the bedroom. The closet door stood open from where Reggie had taken more of her clothes out, but she hadn't taken all of them.

London pulled a white button-down shirt out and held it to her face, inhaling Reggie's scent. Sandalwood and patchouli and Reggie. Before tears could fill her eyes, London laid the shirt on the bed and turned back to the closet. A stylish gray suit Reggie had worn to speak at an equality rally hung near the back. London pulled it out and walked over to the full-length mirror on the adjacent wall. She held the suit in front of her. It was hard to get a clear image of how it would look.

Before she knew it, her clothes were in a pile at her feet, and she was slipping into the white shirt and gray suit. She looked back in the mirror.

Reggie's suits were all immaculately tailored to fit her. London was a little shorter and more than a little thicker, but it wasn't so far off that she looked terrible. She looked at her reflection and tipped her head to the side. Most of her tattoos were covered under the conservatively cut suit, but her blue hair and nose ring and eyebrow piercings seemed to stick out even more next to such a neutral canvas.

"What the hell are you doing? Have you lost your mind?"

London jumped and screeched. She whirled around to see Grant standing in the doorway to her bedroom, his mouth open in horror.

"What are you doing here?" she yelled. "You scared the shit out of me!"

"Me? You're the one dressing up as Corporate Barbie." He huffed. "Am I interrupting your identity crisis, sweetie?"

"Not exactly. Come with me." Taking Grant's hand, she led him to the couch and handed him the file. "Read."

He stared at her for a moment, nodded, sat, and began looking through the papers. London left to make coffee. When she returned from the kitchen with two full mugs, Grant had closed the file and gazed at her, shaking his head.

He took the mug she offered. "Is that what this business suit is about?"

"No. Yes."

"Well, which is it?"

She sipped her coffee and pondered for a few moments. "No, it's not about the money. Yes, it's about the letters, I suppose."

"Okay," he said. "Tell me?"

She leaned back into the thick cushions of her couch and used her free hand to squeeze the bridge of her nose. "I have no memory of being the girl who wanted the things on that list. Did I want them? Was I trying to just make my parents happy? When did I stop wanting those things and start wanting the life I have now?"

"If this is about your sexuality—"

"No, it's definitely not. I've known I was gay for a long time. I don't think I had the verbiage for it when I wrote that letter, but I knew something was different about me."

"What then?"

"It's everything else. Coming out was that proverbial last straw, the final blow that pushed my family from blatant disapproval to cutting me off completely. I didn't dress the way they did or want the kinds of careers they had. I never wanted what they wanted, and they barely kept their disdain in check. When I came out, they stopped trying to keep me in the family. That's when they decided I wasn't worth it anymore. We all have our coming out stories, you know? And mine is that I came out and was ostracized from my family. That's true, but it's also not that simple."

"I get all that." He rested a hand on her knee. "What I don't get is what you're trying to accomplish now. Were you just trying on Reggie's clothes, or is there more to it than that?"

"I don't know yet." She'd been on edge since she'd read the words on that construction paper. She had a dizzying pins and needles sensation in her head, the kind that usually indicated a part of her body was waking up after a brief sleep. It seemed as if her mind was trying to come into focus after having been settled in a hazy slumber. "A part of me feels like…if I can get back inside the mind of that ten-year-old who wrote the letter, I'll be able to make some sense of things."

"Your mom dying after a decades-long estrangement is never going to make sense."

"I know. But maybe if I can put together pieces of who I was then and who I am now, I'll get some closure."

"Listen, do your experiment if it makes you feel better. Get a corporate job, volunteer at the library. Hell, get a dog and name him Chowder. You suffered a terrible loss; you're trying to figure things out with Reggie. You've earned the right to do something crazy for a little while."

"But?"

"But implementing all these changes to try to figure out what went wrong with your family puts the responsibility and blame on you. You can try to get in touch with your inner child as much as you want, but that doesn't change the fact that your family failed you. Their job was to love you unconditionally; no matter what you wore or where you worked or who you loved, their job was to love you and to be there. They failed. *They* failed, London, not you."

"Thank you." She leaned over and rested her head on his shoulder. "I needed that."

"Any time. Now go change out of those clothes; it's time to go."

"Go where?"

"Drag Queen Bingo."

Her mouth dropped open. "I just got back. You don't really think I'm going out for bingo night, do you?"

He fidgeted with the sleeve of his shirt. "I know it's not the best time, and I wouldn't ask except…I need you there tonight. Please? If you're really not up for it, I'll understand, but if you can possibly be up for it, I'll be your best friend."

"Fine." She stood and headed toward her bedroom to change. "I'll go. Having you as a best friend is too hard an offer to turn down."

CHAPTER FOUR

As much as London hadn't felt like going out, she was glad to be at Cavan. She and Grant got there early, got their boards and drinks, and grabbed their favorite table in the back before all the festivities started.

She sipped her beer. "It's good to be home."

"Good to have you home," he said.

"*All right*, boys and girls," boomed Lotta Lays from the front of the bar. "It's about that time! Grab your wood and take a seat because it's time to play bingo. If you'll look to the front to see our prizes for this evening, my gorgeous assistant will pull them out. That's right, you pervalicious freaks, I said pull out!"

Marcus's husband Bill, dressed in a polo shirt and khakis, went on the stage with a basket filled with goodies for the night.

"Three people will win at bingo tonight," Lotta said. "They will get to choose from these fabulous prizes."

Bill pulled a black T-shirt out of the basket. The shirt had sparkling rhinestone letters across the front in a bold font.

"The prizes tonight all come from London Craft and our friends at Hell in a Handbasket," Lotta said, raising her glass to London. "The first prize is this gorgeous 'BadAss Bitch' T-shirt. Prize number two is a set of 'Fuck the Patriarchy' postcards."

Bill raised the shiny package of postcards above his head, then dropped it back in and held up the basket itself.

"Last but certainly not least is the basket, which gave the shop its name. This beautifully made basket in brown and black is classically designed. The handle reads, 'We're all going to hell…we're gonna need a bigger handbasket.'"

The crowd laughed and cheered.

"London Craft is here tonight at that table in the back." Lotta raised her glass again. "We're always lucky to have an artist like her in the Cavan family. Thank you for sponsoring bingo and donating these prizes tonight."

She raised her bottle back to Lotta and took a long swig of her beer.

"I didn't know all this was happening tonight," Grant said. "It was fortuitous timing for me to drag you out on the night your goods were the main event."

London laughed. "Lotta's bingo is the main event. I'm the opening act, at best."

"Still, it's amazing, what you've done with your business. I'm proud of you, you know that? I don't know if I've ever told you."

"I do know." She smiled. "Thank you." Grant nodded, and London looked at him carefully. "Do you want to tell me why you dragged me out? I'm happy to be here, but I know there's a reason besides the desperate need to lose at bingo."

"Hey, we might not lose."

"We always lose. Besides, now that I know they're using the stuff I donated, it's probably best if we don't even play. I don't want us to win merch from my own store."

"Good point." He fiddled with the switches on his bingo board.

"Grant?"

He raised his head to face her, tears in his eyes. "I cheated on Thomas."

"*What?*"

"Don't make me say it again." He hugged the bingo board to his chest and stared down at the table.

"Okay, I'm sorry." She pursed her lips and tried to think of an appropriate way to dig into this conversation. "When?"

"About a week before Reggie's birthday. I was going to try to find a way to pull you aside and talk to you about it that night, but…well, you know how things went down. I know you have so much going on right now, and you shouldn't have to deal with my problems too, but I just can't sit alone with this anymore. I can't."

"It's okay, you don't have to."

"Do you hate me?" He wiped his eyes with the back of his clenched fist.

"I could never hate you. Come on, let's go out to the patio and talk."

The chilly October air hit them the moment they stepped outside. London zipped up her black leather motorcycle jacket—she didn't own a motorcycle, but she rocked the clothes—and Grant put on his knit hat and gloves. If it was already this cold now, they were going to be in for a frigid Ohio winter.

When they were seated at a table in the tented corner of the patio, London took Grant's hands in hers. "Tell me what happened." A jagged sigh escaped his lips, and she squeezed his hands. They were almost twice the size of hers and fleshy, matching his round physique. "Come on. Talk to me."

"Thomas and I…we've been having problems. We both work long hours, you know. Lawyer hours. And we've been bickering a lot. It started out small, mainly about whose turn it was to do chores and stuff. We're both exhausted when we get home, and I think we both were hoping the other one would pick up the slack."

"That all seems typical. I'm pretty sure all couples have those kinds of fights."

"True. But we never resolve it, and things keep building. We fight and agree to work things out the next day when we're both calm and rested, but we never do. The next day comes, and we're busy and tired, and then we have another fight."

Grant paused and took a long drink from his beer. "One night, we made plans to have some quality time. I made him this beautiful candlelit dinner, and I waited. I waited over an hour and finally called his office. His secretary told me his boss had scheduled a last-minute dinner with clients. He didn't even text to let me know."

Grant looked over to the other end of the patio where a group of friends had stumbled outside, singing "Bodak Yellow" by Cardi B.

"What happened next?" London squeezed his hand.

"I went over to AWOL and got trashed. My friend Damon was bartending that night, and as soon as I finished with a drink, he'd set another one in front of me. I closed the bar, and Damon said he'd drive me home in my car and Lyft back to his place. He took me home, walked me up to the door, and before I went in…we kissed."

"And?"

He glared. "What do you mean, and? We kissed. Not a peck on the cheek, either, it was a long, make-out kind of kiss. It lasted a few minutes." He looked miserable. "Thomas was asleep right inside."

"I am going to kill Damon." She pulled out her phone and began looking through her contacts.

"What are you doing?"

"I'm looking for Damon's number."

"Oh God, no! I don't ever want to talk to him again, and I don't want you to, either."

"That asshole. He's always had the hots for you, and he knows you and Thomas are together. I bet he was thrilled to see you come in alone and upset so he could get you drunk and make a move."

"London, stop. I mean it."

The force of his voice made her set her phone down and look at him.

"I did this," he said. "Yes, I was drunk, and yes, Damon probably took advantage. But I had a bunch of choices that night, and I made all the wrong ones."

"Are you going to tell him?"

Grant put his head in his hands. "I don't know. I don't know what to do. What do you think?"

"I think you need to tell him."

He lifted his head, tears spilling onto his cheeks and down to his chin. "I could lose him."

"I know," she said softly.

"How can I tell him knowing I might lose him?"

"How can you move forward with him knowing you're keeping this kind of secret?"

"Fuck. You're right. I know you're right. I just don't know how to even have the conversation with him. He's going to be so hurt. He's the best man I've ever been with. Of all the shitheads I've dated who deserved to have their hearts broken, I go and cheat on the only one who doesn't deserve it. How big a fuckup can I be?"

"Listen to me. Yes, you made a mistake, and yes, your relationship might not survive it. I'm sorry about that, babe, I really am. But we're all fuckups in our own ways. You are a decent, compassionate human being, and you don't deserve to be judged solely on your mistakes. Nobody does. You screwed up, you'll learn from this, and you'll move on. Whatever happens, you know I'll be here."

"Yeah? You promise?"

London extended her last finger. "Pinkie promise."

❖

The next day, she sat on the floor in the back room at Hell in a Handbasket surrounded by fabrics, thread, paper stock, and paints. She was supposed to be working on her designs for spring, but she kept opening the file from Larry Kopp. She had added the folder to her bag that morning almost as an afterthought, thinking she wouldn't even get a chance to look at it. Two hours into her day, she'd barely looked at anything else.

She read the letter from her mother again. What had she hoped to accomplish with this scheme? Did she truly think that after all these years, London would turn straight and narrow and be the kind of daughter Grace wanted her to be, all for some money? It was a lot of money, and they hadn't known each other well for years. Still, hadn't her mother realized she would always choose happiness over wealth? Indeed, hadn't that been where most of their disconnect had occurred?

London set Grace's letter aside and picked up her own. Her eyes went directly to the middle portion, where she had made the list of things she planned to do before she was forty:

1. *Wear business suits every day.*
2. *Get a job in marketing.*
3. *Fall in love with a really awesome boy.*
4. *Get married.*
5. *Volunteer at least once a week to help people in need.*
6. *Have a dog named Chowder.*

If London had been asked to do this exercise even a few years later, it would have looked very different. She knew that. What bothered her was that she couldn't remember ever feeling this way or wanting these things, at least not all of them. Volunteer work and a dog with a weird name? That she would totally be down with even today. Hell, she already donated ten percent of her profits to Compass, an organization that worked with at-risk LGBTQ youth. Many of the kids associated with Compass had been put out by their families because they were gay.

And she loved animals, so having a dog certainly was never out of the question. In fact, she and Reggie had talked about adopting one from the shelter, but they lived in such a tiny place with no yard. Besides, they both worked long hours and had to travel occasionally for their jobs. A dog was something they decided could wait a few years until life settled down a bit, and they could give an animal the attention it deserved.

Still, both of those items were at least feasible. But those first four goals really maddened her. Who was that child? It was easy to say she'd been trying to conform to what her parents and their peers expected, and she was sure that was definitely a contributing factor. Had there been others? Had she truly ever wanted to put on a pinstriped suit and head off to the office every day? Had she ever envisioned putting on a white wedding dress and making vows of obedience and honor to someone, while "Pachelbel's Canon" played softly in the background? Those seemed like the kinds of things Diana really loved. How many times had her twin wanted to play wedding, trying to get London to put on a fluffy dress from their dress-up chest so they could pretend to have a double wedding? Diana had always been the perfect picture of the kind of daughter Grace and Frederick wanted.

And then there was the whole "falling in love with a really awesome boy" thing. She distinctly remembered feelings of embarrassment and bewildered gross-out that year when many of her friends started having crushes on boys. When her hormones finally caught up, it was never boys she was interested in. So what was up with the boy thing?

"Are you doing okay?"

London jumped and craned her neck to look behind her, pulling a muscle in the process. She hadn't heard Jasmine step into the back room.

"Sorry, I didn't mean to scare you."

"No, it's okay." Her skin flushed. "I'm fine, really." She massaged her neck. It was probably going to be sore for a few days.

"Tate is here. He said you weren't expecting him."

"I wasn't, but he can come on back." She'd barely gotten the words out when Tate popped his head in behind Jasmine.

"What's up, buttercup?" he asked.

"I'll leave you two alone," Jasmine said.

"Thanks, Jas." He walked over to a stool in the back corner, dusted it off with the arm of his jacket, and pulled it to where London sat on the floor.

"This is a surprise," she said. "You could've just texted me back." She'd texted that morning asking if he'd made any marketing connections in his career because she was considering looking into corporate jobs.

"I could've, but there would have been a higher chance you'd get mad at me if I didn't respond in person."

"I won't get mad if you think I'd suck at marketing," she said. "I know it's a long shot."

"Not at all. In fact, I've got a contact name for you."

"Really?" She stood, dusted off the back of her pants, and hugged him. "How could I be mad about that?"

"The method, my dear," he said. "My method might drive you to madness."

She pulled back. "What did you do?"

"Well, as much as I want to help you on this project you seem to need to pursue, I can't be of much assistance in the connections department. All my contacts are in IT. But I knew someone who would be a huge help."

She shook her head. "Tell me you didn't."

"I did, and she came through." He pulled a piece of paper out of his pocket and handed it to her. "Reggie reached out to one of her connections, and you have an interview with Joan Robinson, executive director at Compass."

"Tate, *no*," she said, and even to her own ears, she sounded whiney. "If I wanted her help, I would've contacted her."

"I know you guys are on the outs right now, babe. But Reg is the one who has the right connections, so just take this and go to your appointment." When she didn't take the paper, he leaned over and stuffed it in her pocket. "Stubborn."

He sat back down, avoiding her glare, and started scrolling through his phone. She went back to work, and they sat in silence for a while, her pretending to be mad, and him pretending to ignore her. The silence broke when he burst out laughing.

"Check this out." He handed his phone to her. "Remember this?"

She saw he was looking at his Facebook memories. Three years ago, he and Grant had taken a quiz to see what their baby would look like, as a joke, and the picture was the scariest-looking child any of them had ever seen.

"I'm so glad I never reproduced," he said. "I would've had *Rosemary's Baby*."

She laughed. "Not necessarily. Facebook quizzes don't predict the future as much as you might believe."

She scrolled down a little farther in his memories and saw that she and Reggie tagged him in the picture of what their much less frightening baby would look like. "Meet your godson," Reggie had said. London handed the phone back, and when he saw what she'd been looking at, he put his phone deep in his pocket.

"Sorry."

"There might not be a baby in my future anymore," she said. "Not if Reggie splits for good."

"Did you two really want to have kids?" He sounded surprised.

"Yes. We wanted to adopt, though, give a baby or a toddler a home who really needed one."

"You never told me."

She shrugged. "It was all just late-night conversations. I would've told you when we got serious about it."

Here was another loss she had to face, one she hadn't thought of until now. If Reggie was truly done with their relationship, she probably wouldn't have a child. The idea had been Reggie's, and something they'd been talking about the last year or so. She felt overwhelmed at the thought of having something else taken from her.

She turned back to her work, picking up different spools of thread and holding them up against a dark gray piece of fabric.

"Hey," he said, "when do you visit Ross again?"

"Tomorrow."

"Sounds like perfect timing. Tell him I said hi, okay?" He stood and headed to the door.

"You're out of here?"

"Better go before I cause more trouble," he said. "You coming over after you see him?"

"I always do."

He grinned. "My place, then. I'll have a horrible selection of snacks for you to choose from."

"I'd expect nothing less."

CHAPTER FIVE

L ondon walked up the cobblestone walkway toward the old brick house, careful to make sure the heels of her stilettos didn't get caught in the cracks between the ancient stones. German Village was an historic area just south of downtown that was perfectly preserved. Wearing anything with a heel in GV could be hazardous and should only have been done with extreme caution.

Inside, she walked into a classically decorated and understated room. Ross appeared in the doorway from the next room and smiled. "London!" His booming voice filled the entire space. "It's been a few weeks. I'm glad to see you."

"Hi, Ross," she said. "Sorry I had to cancel last week."

He waved a hand. "No, please don't worry about that, not with everything you had going on." He motioned to the room behind him. "Come on back."

She went into the room with the two couches facing each other, went to the couch she liked best—she let him sit on the leather sofa; she felt more comfortable on the older one with the soft, worn corduroy fabric—took off her coat, and sat.

He looked at her with the steady gaze that used to rattle her when she first met him. He rarely looked away, and that took some getting used to. She'd been coming to therapy for six years now, and most of the time, she didn't even notice it anymore. She felt a little exposed today.

"This is a different look for you," he said after a few moments.

She smoothed her pants a little. She'd gotten a jump on her Christmas shopping this morning and had somehow ended up in the women's section of a department store. She couldn't remember the last time she'd bought clothes that weren't from a thrift store or made by a fellow independent artist. She'd bought a few suits and was wearing one now.

"I'm trying something new." She felt so vulnerable without the comfort of her normal clothes in this place where she was always in her rawest state.

He folded his hands over his lap, a sign he wasn't going to ask another question because he wanted her to speak about whatever was on her mind.

"I emailed copies of some stuff from my mother's lawyer to you yesterday," she said.

"I got them."

"What do you think about them?"

Ross smiled. "What do *you* think about them? Based on your clothing, it looks like you've definitely had a strong reaction to those letters."

"You're my therapist," she said. "You know all about my relationship with my mother. It's probably seventy-five percent of what we talk about." She was accustomed to the tears that had pricked at her eyes the last several days, but these spilled onto her cheeks and fell on the lapel of her new suit. "What are we going to talk about now?" She buried her face in her hands and bent over, shaking with sobs. They started to wind down, and when she looked up, she saw Ross had gotten a box of tissues and stood over her. She took the box and started crying all over again.

Something about being in this office with him made her feel free to let go of all of her protection and barriers she'd built to keep from feeling things she didn't have time or energy or tools to feel. She'd refused to let herself cry since her mother died...except that wasn't quite accurate, was it? She had been unable to cry. Now, on this brown corduroy couch, she was an undammed river.

She wept unabashedly, knowing when she finished that Ross would be there, his hands in his lap, his expression compassionate and calm, waiting for her to be ready to speak without pushing her to say anything until she was ready. As if they had all the time in the world. A cynic would say that of course they had time; he made a steady profit with every pause she made, every unfinished story, every unresolved issue that would need to wait until her next session. This was true, but she didn't care. It had taken her years to get to a place where she could even go to therapy and then a few tries before she found one she felt comfortable with.

"Wanna know what my first thoughts were after I got the call that she died?"

"Yes, I do."

"I thought I wasn't going to get emotional about it." She laughed coarsely and wiped her nose. "I thought she'd been out of my life so long, and I'd mourned losing her so much already that there wasn't any sadness left to feel about her dying. Is that crazy?"

He leaned forward. "You know I don't care for that word. And no, I think it's neither crazy nor unusual that you would mourn the death of your mother, no matter how long it's been since the two of you last spoke."

"Even though I've already been grieving for years?"

"Yes. Your mother isn't just gone from you now; she's gone from the world. Any chance of reconciliation is gone. If that's not worth mourning, I don't know what is."

London considered that for a while. Ross waited.

"Do you think it's…" She paused before she said the word "crazy" again. "Do you think it's unreasonable for me to want to try to do some of the things I wrote in that letter?"

"That depends. You've always presented to me that you're a lesbian. Do I recommend that you marry a nice straight man? I'd be a pretty poor therapist if I did."

"No, not that," she said. "Not the boy part. This isn't about my sexuality; it's about rediscovering who I was then, how I felt, and why those feelings changed."

"Maybe." He nodded slowly. "I suspect it's also about something else."

"What do you mean?"

"I think the truth is in what you said when you first got here. What are you going to talk about now? We've spent years combing through every wisp of your relationship with your mother. Many of our sessions have begun and ended with conversations about her."

"So? Isn't that what therapy is for, dissecting mommy issues?"

"Sure it is; that's a lot of it. It's for whatever issues people want to tackle, and issues with parents are usually pretty high up there. My point is, this is a conversation you're not ready to stop having. And if you start trying to cross items off this list, like some postmortem scavenger hunt, you won't have to stop. As long as you're trying to achieve some level of happiness set out for you by your mom, you won't need to stop talking about her."

"Whoa." London wiped her eyes. "I guess this is why you make the big bucks, huh?"

Ross shrugged and tipped his head to the side.

"Does that mean you think I shouldn't do this?"

"I think you've already made up your mind to do it. And that's fine, as long as you take some precautions to keep yourself safe in the process."

"Like?"

"Well, we've already touched on one. Don't mess with your sexuality. It's not worth sacrificing who you are to become some beacon for heteronormativity."

"I won't. What else?"

"Don't jeopardize your business or your relationships to make these changes. If those things begin to suffer, that's a red flag you're taking things too far. And of course, I'll always encourage you to keep me aware of the changes you're making so we can talk about how it feels to try on different things."

"Okay. That makes sense." She began to relax a bit. His guidelines brought some structure to the chaos that had been her emotions. She knew she could explore the items on the letter without going against his rules, and it was a relief to feel like she could move forward.

"Oh, and one last thing."

"What?"

"If you get a dog, please consider naming it something besides Chowder. The poor thing will get bullied at the dog park with a name like that."

❖

"Oh my God, did he actually say 'postmortem scavenger hunt'?" Tate choked out his smoke mid-drag.

"Yeah." London giggled. "He did." They sat on the postage-stamp-sized patio outside his studio apartment. It made London a little claustrophobic every time she was there, but he loved it. He hated cleaning and the accumulation of unnecessary stuff. He basically had one room to clean and no space for collecting material possessions.

"Jesus. My therapist mostly just says shit like, 'and how did you feel about that?' and then takes some notes on his legal pad."

"I couldn't deal with that. If it didn't feel like I was just talking to one of my friends for an hour every week, I wouldn't be able to go. I hate doctors, and I'm glad he doesn't feel like one."

"I get that. Is he taking new patients?"

"I'll ask him."

"Good. This run-in with my own mom has had me pretty messed up."

"I'm so sorry."

"Please stop apologizing. You didn't invite her to your mother's funeral. You had nothing to do with it." He tapped some ashes into the ashtray on the table between them. "It's not like my mom ever needed a special occasion to let the cray-cray out."

"That's the truth."

"It's cold out here." He smudged out his cigarette. "I'm done; let's go inside."

They stepped in and hung their coats on the rack by the front door. London almost tripped over Tate's bike on her way to the couch.

"You want anything to drink?" He moved over to the kitchen side of the room. "I've got vodka and white wine."

"To drink together?"

"If you like."

"How about some water?"

"Water it is." He pulled two glasses from the open-faced cupboard.

London realized how long it had been since she'd seen him with a short-sleeved shirt. She walked to the makeshift kitchen island and stood across from him. "Let me see your arms."

He grinned and held both arms out for inspection.

She held on to his wrists and slowly rotated his arms to see what they looked like all the way around. "You're so hairy!"

"I know. You should see my armpits."

"Show me."

Laughing, he pulled up his shirt so she could get a good look.

"Wow! You have man pits."

"I know!"

They sat on his couch. London took a long sip of water and carefully placed the glass on a coaster. Tate's fastidious nature meant she'd never hear the end of it if some water stained his table. He took immaculate care of his few pieces of furniture.

"Are you going to get more hair?"

"I'm not sure yet. I've been on testosterone for almost a year now, and things seem like they're kind of leveling out."

"Coming out of that second puberty must be a relief."

"You have no idea." He grimaced. She'd been with him at doctor's appointments when he'd been warned that taking testosterone would put him into a state of puberty, but nothing could have prepared him for the embarrassment of being a man in his thirties with a voice that cracked and squeaked as it deepened or acne that sprouted up on his formerly clear face. "But I have a new set of issues now."

"What's wrong?"

He pulled his phone out of his pocket, opened an app, and showed it to her.

"You're on *Tinder*?" she screeched. "Now that you're done with puberty, you're moving on to be a twenty-one-year-old frat boy?"

He grabbed the phone back. "Hey, not everyone can have a meet-cute like you and Reggie. This is what people do now. Can you stop mocking? I know it's asking the impossible, but I need your help here."

"Okay, okay, you're right. I'm sorry." She held up her hands, palms out. "No more mocking."

Slowly, he slid the phone back across the couch cushion, his eyes never leaving hers. She picked it up again and saw a few really good pictures of him and read his bio, which captured how interesting and funny he was. She even laughed out loud a couple times.

She looked up at him after she finished. "It looks really good."

"Thank you."

"If you're not getting responses on this profile, I don't know what's wrong with Tinder women."

"Oh, I've gotten plenty of responses. I have dates set up with two different women next week."

She smirked. "Is that a football field you're standing on? Because you're obviously a player."

Tate furrowed his brows and frowned.

"Sorry. Unintentional mock." It took all of her effort to remove the sardonic smile from her face. "So, what's the problem? You need help picking outfits?"

"I need help deciding when and how to tell them that I'm trans."

She felt the last of her smile leave her face. "Oh. Oh, wow, I hadn't even thought of that."

"The thing is, I had it in my bio that I was a transgender man, and I got no hits except for a few women who were only interested in me as some sort of fetish. I took it off as more of a social experiment than anything else, but then the response was so drastically different. It's disheartening."

She nodded. "It must be."

"Don't get me wrong. I'm happier being a trans man and finally being comfortable in my identity and my body than I ever could have been trying to live as a woman. Even if I had to spend the rest of my life alone, it would still be worth it."

"I hardly think you'll be alone forever," she said. "We know tons of people just in this city who are trans and have successful relationships."

"I know." He sighed. "It's just weird, learning how to date all over again. I'm nervous, can you believe that? I'm nervous about dating. That hasn't happened since I was seventeen."

She grinned again. "When you went on that date with Randy Jacobs?"

"God, don't remind me." He laughed. "He showed up in a silk shirt and shorts with white socks pulled up to his knees. I can't believe I wasted time getting nervous for that."

"I would've been nervous once I saw him in that."

"Not me. I was just plain horrified. Longest night of my life." He shook his head. "Seriously, though…what should I do? It feels dishonest to start dating these women without full disclosure. At the same time, I want someone to get to know me for me. I want to be more than my gender identity; shit, I *am* more than that."

It hurt her heart to think of Tate struggling with being seen as a whole person. He was the best person she knew, and sometimes she couldn't believe they lived in a world where he had to worry about whether someone would love him the way he deserved to be loved.

"I know you are. And as much as I want to help, I don't think I can answer this for you. Just like I couldn't talk you out of going on that date with Randy Jacobs. Your voice may be as low as it's gonna go, but I don't think you're completely out of the puberty stage yet. It may take some trial and error to figure out when to tell the women you date, but you'll get there. When and how to do it is completely your call."

"I guess you're right." He sighed. "I'll figure it out."

"When is the first date?"

"Not till this Friday. Her name is Amanda; she's seriously gorgeous and really funny. We're going on a group date with some friends of hers."

"I like that; it keeps things low key."

He nodded. "That's what I thought too. I was happy when she suggested it. We're going hiking."

"That's a fun idea for a first date. Wanna meet for dinner afterward? You can give me the rundown on the date."

"Sure, on one condition."

"What?"

"Don't utter the name Randy Jacobs to me ever again."

She grinned. "No promises."

❖

"Ms. Craft?"

London looked up from her résumé to the receptionist who'd moved from behind his desk toward the door leading to the main part of the building. "Yes?"

"Ms. Robinson will see you now."

London stood on legs that felt as if they were made of chewing gum. She steadied herself and walked toward the open door. The receptionist pulled the door wider and walked her through a living room area with a pool table and down a hallway with a long galley kitchen on one side and an office on the other. Next, they passed two sleeping rooms with half a dozen cots with white sheets and dark gray comforters. She wanted to keep up with the receptionist's brisk walking pace, but she also wanted to take in the space around her.

"I'm Keith," the receptionist said, smiling. "We've spoken on the phone."

"Oh, of course. I knew I recognized your voice."

"Yes, everyone has to go through me to get to the top here."

"No truer words have ever been spoken," said a woman's deep, contralto voice. "London? It's wonderful to put a face with the name. I'm Joan Robinson." Her slate gray hair matched her eyes, and she had very pale, very smooth skin. She wore thick-rimmed bright turquoise glasses, the stems of which were attached to a delicate silver chain around her neck.

London wondered how old she was; her age could have hovered anywhere between forty and fifty-five. The imposing Joan Robinson stepped out of the room at the very end of the long hallway, took a few long strides toward them, and grasped London's hand firmly, shaking it.

"It's wonderful to meet you, as well." She tried to match the firmness of Joan's handshake. She wasn't easily intimidated, but one look at this woman, and she knew she was a force. London straightened her spine a little. She could do this.

"Can I get you any water or coffee?" Keith asked.

"Oh no, thank you, I'm fine." If he'd been a stranger or someone she met in a nonprofessional capacity, she'd be telling him how much she liked his handlebar mustache. Was that something she could say to a potential colleague in this kind of work environment? She had no idea. It wasn't exactly the corporate office for a bank or anything, but it was still galaxies away from anything she'd ever done.

"I'll leave you two to your meeting, then." He turned to Joan. "Buzz me if you need anything."

Joan ushered London into her sunny office and went behind her desk to sit, motioning to the two chairs facing her so London would do the same.

"I must say, I was pleasantly surprised to receive your email asking about opportunities with Compass," Joan said. "You're a bit of a local celebrity in the LGBT community, as I'm sure I don't need to tell you. I've followed your career with some interest. Tell me a little about what prompted you to reach out to me and what specific kinds of opportunities you're looking for."

London felt as if her stomach were making zigzags in her body, first jumping toward her throat, then to the bottom of her spine, and back again. She worked with well-known designers and celebrities, and she hadn't been this nervous in years. "Well, I've had a bit of an epiphany lately. I'm happy with my store, of course, and the national recognition and growth we've been getting has been pretty amazing. But I've been reevaluating goals…goals I set for myself a long time ago. At one time, I was interested in a career in marketing, and while marketing is certainly a part of my business, I'm looking to make it more of a focal point.

"Since you've followed my career, you know I built my shop up from nothing. I was quite literally a starving artist in the beginning, and now several celebrities have become fans of my work and include my pieces as party favors after awards shows. A lot of items from Hell in a Handbasket are included in the guest bags for people who appear on *Julian Spencer Live*, the late night talk show."

"Yes, I knew most of that," Joan said. "Very impressive."

"Thank you. Compass is a respected organization in the

community. You do such amazing work with these kids. I'd like to use my marketing skills to help reach as many people as possible. I have lots of ideas in terms of creative donor events and fundraising that I'm really excited about."

Joan looked at London thoughtfully, a small smile on her face, then turned to the notebook on her desk—a lined, paper notebook. London hadn't seen a computer anywhere in the room. Joan wrote a few notes with her black ballpoint pen, and when she was done, she took off her glasses, perched them atop her head, and said, "How about a tour? I know you saw some of the place when Keith brought you back, but I think an official tour is in order." Before London could answer, Joan had risen from her chair and was making her way to the front of her desk.

London tried to hide her surprise. "Oh yes, I'd love an official tour."

"The best way to take it, or the way I like to give it, is to come in as if you're one of the kids." They walked toward the front where London had come in, but instead of going back out to the lobby, they made a sharp right and ended up in a small room with a large bulletin board on one wall and a mammoth set of bookshelves filled with books on the other wall. Directly in front of them was a small red door leading outside.

"This is where our kids come into the building." She opened a door by the bookcase, revealing a room with a table and chairs. "When we have new youth coming in, they're often in crisis. This is a community center, but it's also a place for teens to come when they've been kicked out of their homes, usually after coming out to their parents or refusing some type of 'pray the gay away' intervention. We bring them in here to talk with them about their options. The preferred option is always to get the kids back with their families after some family counseling, but that's not always possible. We work with the county to get foster families who qualify to take in LGBT youth."

Back in the living room, she pointed at the pool table. "I've never been any good at pool, myself. The kids fight over who has to let me be on their team when I decide to play. We have game nights in here, both board games and video games; in fact, one of your donations bought our Xbox and a lot of games last year, so thank you for that. Over here where there's more space, we have our art classes. Painting, photo editing, writing, and anything else we can get the kids interested in."

They walked farther down the hallway and stood between the kitchen and the bedrooms. "The kitchen is fully functional. We have volunteers who make meals, and we offer dinner every night of the week and breakfast and lunch on the weekends." She looked at her watch. "We also have snacks available, and in about an hour when kids are off school, that kitchen will be packed with hungry teenagers."

She crossed into one of the rooms with cots. "Since getting kids home with their families or into foster care often takes more time than we'd like, they can stay here until we make suitable arrangements. We have enough space to comfortably house eight children, and right now we have five, although that number is constantly changing. These aren't the fanciest accommodations, of course, but you'd be surprised at what having a safe place to lay your head down can do for someone who needs it."

London, who'd been taking everything in, blurted the first thing that came to her mind. "What can I do? How can I help?"

Joan smiled. "First thing's first. You have a lot to offer, and I appreciate all of your experience and skills that could be put to good use. However, we do have a protocol in place, and as much as I'd like to help you work around that, that's not what we do here. In order to fly, you must first learn to walk, if you know what I mean."

"I...I'm not sure I do." She'd been in a whirlwind of confusion since Joan had initiated a tour rather than respond to her speech. Nothing about this day had gone as expected.

"Well, we certainly do need volunteers, and your expertise would be a wonderful addition," Joan said. "I'm certain our donors would be impressed to receive calls and marketing information with your name on it. But everyone who works at Compass must start at the bottom and work their way up. Everyone from the volunteers to the staff psychologist. You'll start in the kitchen. At least one meal a week, you will be one of the volunteers preparing the food that is served."

"But...I'm not what you would call a good cook."

"All skill levels are welcome, and you won't be alone. The others will help you. You'll do this for one month, and then you'll be evaluated to see if you're ready to move on. If so, you'll be assigned to your next area; if not, you'll stay in the kitchen for another month."

She pulled a business card out of a pocket in her jacket and handed it over. "I'm sure you're familiar with our website. Here on the back of my card is the information to access our volunteer portal. Log in, and you'll see what days we need kitchen volunteers in the coming weeks. Menus are planned a month in advance, so you'll also be able to view what meals are being served on any given day."

London stared at the card, not really seeing the information, and looked up to see Joan walking toward the door to the lobby.

"Dress code in the kitchen is casual," Joan said, not seeming to notice London jogging a little to catch up. "You'll definitely want to leave the business suits at home; you don't want to ruin that lovely fabric. Comfortable shoes are also a good idea. The dinner shift takes about three hours from start to finish. The kids clean up after the meal, but they need supervision, of course."

"But—"

Joan opened the door to the lobby, all but pushing London through. "I look forward to seeing you soon." She gripped London's hand in another firm handshake. "I'm one of the first to taste test the meals prepared by a new volunteer, so I'll make sure to be here when I see you've signed up. Thank you so much for taking the time to see me today." With that, the door closed, and Joan disappeared.

As London stood, gaping at the heavy door that had all but been slammed in her face, she realized that Keith was laughing.

"I see you've gotten the tour." He chortled. "Welcome to Compass!"

CHAPTER SIX

Orange, red, and gold leaves crunched under London's feet as she walked from her car toward the storybook Cape Cod home on Sumner Street. It was always pretty, a pale yellow house with white trim, but it was especially charming at this time of year. The great oak and maple trees surrounding it seemed to constantly be losing leaves, and they made a patchwork of color on the ground.

A brown and gold sign reading "Bless this House" adorned the door, and it wasn't until London knocked that she realized it had bells attached. The door opened, revealing a smiling woman with graying hair and the same luminous mahogany skin as her daughter.

"London! This is a nice surprise. I haven't seen you since our barbecue on Labor Day."

She was enveloped in an almost crushing hug, and she returned it, surprised at the pressure she felt in her chest. She absolutely adored this woman.

"Hi, Betty." She breathed in the familiar scent of sugar cookies and peppermint. No matter what she was doing or where she was, Betty Williams always smelled like sugar cookies and peppermint. "Is Reggie home?"

"Yes, she sure is. I'll get her for you. Come on in out of the cold." Betty took London's hand and guided her toward the kitchen. "Regina," she called, her voice echoing through the house. "Regina!"

"Mama? Are you okay?" Reggie stopped when she saw London in her parents' kitchen.

London exhaled a long breath when she saw Reggie. She'd been longing to see her so much, and now that they were face-to-face, London's heart swelled with love and hope.

"Oh, I'm fine," Betty said. "You just have a visitor is all."

"I see that."

London wished she could read Reggie's face, but even after all this time, Reggie was a master at keeping her expression blank. London had hoped that Reggie's referral to Compass might be an indication she was softening in her stance on their not speaking, but this unreadable face wasn't a good sign.

"Regina, don't you want to offer London something to drink?"

London hid a smile. She and Reggie would be staying together if Reggie's parents had anything to say about it. They'd been crazy about London from their first meeting, and the feeling was mutual.

"Would you like some of Mama's sweet tea?" Reggie opened the refrigerator. Betty and Herb had moved to Columbus when Reggie was just a baby. Originally from North Carolina, they always had sweet tea in the house. You couldn't get sweet tea like Betty's at any restaurant in the Midwest.

"I'd love some."

"You two enjoy," Betty said. "Feel free to stay for dinner, London. If you can't, make sure you come say hello to Herb before you go. He's in the sitting room watching football, heaven knows why. I'll be working on my cross-stitch in there beside him, and I'd love to show it to you."

"You know I wouldn't miss a chance to see it," London said, delighted at how Betty beamed at her.

"Good. Regina, give her some of those shortcakes I made, will you?" Betty squeezed London's shoulders. "I don't like how thin you're getting."

London laughed. "You're the only person in the world who calls me thin."

Betty smiled, kissed London on the cheek, and left to join her husband in the sitting room.

"Your mom looks good." She joined Reggie where she sat at the table. "She's feeling well?"

"Aside from some arthritis flare-ups, yeah, she's doing really well."

"I'm glad." London sipped her iced tea, and after a moment, Reggie did the same. "I guess you're wondering why I'm here."

"I am. You know you're always welcome, and of course, my parents love to see you. But we are taking time apart."

"I know. I won't take much of your time, I could just really use your advice on something."

"All right. Shoot."

"Well, I know Tate filled you in on the papers I got from my mother's lawyer. I appreciate the referral and just wanted to let you know Tate asked for it on his own."

"It's no problem."

"Okay. Well, long story short, and after conditional approval from Ross, I've decided to try checking off a few items on the list from the letter I wrote myself. Do you want to see the letter?"

Reggie shook her head. "Tate sent me the screenshots."

"He did?" She couldn't keep the astonishment off her face.

"He's worried about you. I am too."

"Well...well, okay, I guess I get that. Anyway, I met with Joan Robinson yesterday, from Compass. You know her pretty well, right?"

"Of course. She's one of the board members at Stonewall, and there's a lot of overlap between the two organizations."

London explained what had happened during her interview.

"Yeah." Reggie chuckled. "That sounds like Joan."

"So it's not just some brush-off because she doesn't want me working there? I thought maybe she was trying to drive me away with some hazing or something."

"Nope. That's just how she operates."

"I see."

"Are you gonna go for it?"

"I don't know. No. Maybe? Probably not."

Reggie didn't speak, letting London process her thoughts. She was still as confused as she'd been the day before at Compass. She'd gone in with a clear idea of what she wanted to accomplish and how her time with the organization would help her cross items off her list. Her meeting with Joan had mixed everything up.

"I don't know, Reg. This isn't how it was supposed to go. I'm supposed to dress in smart suits and sit in an office, or at least a cubicle, and bring in big donations. Even if I used this opportunity to cross the volunteer work off my list, that would be great. I could make art projects with the kids and make a difference that way. But cooking? Kitchen duty?"

"I'm sure those meals make a big difference to the kids."

"You're right, but...you know what I mean."

"I do. But according to that letter, you're also supposed to fall in love with a man, right?"

"Yes."

"And unless something has drastically changed, you're not doing that, right?"

"Right."

"So is there any reason you can't make adjustments to other parts of the list too? I can't tell you what to do here," Reggie said. "If you need to go on this pilgrimage to your past to reconcile something within yourself, I'd never tell you not to do that. But life doesn't go as planned. Sometimes you're thrown into what you need when you're seeking what you think you want."

"That's true," London said.

"Just think about it, okay? You don't have to decide what to do today. Process. Breathe. Then decide."

"I will. Thank you. I know you may not have been ready to see me yet, but I really appreciate you talking this out." Taking in Reggie's profile as she looked out the window, London had to admit that while she was grateful for Reggie's advice, this visit had been as much an excuse to see her as it was getting feedback about her meeting with Joan.

"You're welcome." Reggie took another drink of sweet tea. "I saw that getting married was on the list. Are you putting the same kind of thought into that item as you are into these career goals?"

"I…I'm not there yet. I'm honestly starting at the beginning as best I can and going from there. I've barely made it past number one on the list."

"I see."

"Please don't take this personally." London pushed back the desperate need to grab her hand. She wanted so badly to pull Reggie out of the distance she'd put between them.

Reggie shook her head. "I'm not."

"Reg—"

"London, I said I'm not. You told me once that I was the love of your life. Is that still true?"

"Of course it is!"

"Then you not being ready to think about marriage is one hundred percent not about me. Take this time, do your thing, become the damn CEO of JPMorgan Chase Bank, for Christ's sake. Do whatever you have to do to find the pieces you feel are missing, and once you put yourself together, come see me. Tell me if we are going to get married or if I've spent these years with you wasting my time loving someone who can't give me what I need."

Reggie's words tore into London like pieces of hot shrapnel. The pain of them would've brought her to her knees had she not been sitting.

"You don't mean that," London said. "You don't mean we won't be together if I can't marry you."

"You can marry me. If you won't, it will be the end for us."

Tears pricked London's eyes, but she blinked them back. "I can't believe you. After everything we've been through together, I can't believe you would throw us away because I won't sign a piece of paper."

"And I can't believe you won't sign a piece of paper to keep us together. Looks like we're both blindsided." Reggie squeezed her eyes shut and massaged her temples. "I can't do this. This is the exact reason we shouldn't be talking to each other yet. We need to get some space between our emotions and our decisions. Go visit with my parents. I'm going to take a walk."

As Reggie walked past, London reached to grab her hand. Reggie stopped and looked at her, and London couldn't bear the pain in her eyes. She was too aware of the emotions Reggie had been concealing with her carefully neutral mask. Knowing Reggie was in as much pain as she was made it worse. She ached so badly, for both of them.

"I love you, London. But I have to go." Reggie's hand cupped her chin for a moment, and before London could say anything else, Reggie walked out the front door, closing it behind her.

❖

London sat on her couch that night after changing into a T-shirt and her favorite flannel pajama pants and absorbed the quiet. She'd always enjoyed being alone, comfortable living in her own silence, so it felt odd that she was so lonely. It was seven o'clock, around the time she and Reggie would normally be sitting down to dinner. Reggie was a great cook and was always thrilled at how much London enjoyed eating the food she prepared.

London pulled up the Grubhub app on her phone, reconsidered, and tossed the phone onto the couch. She'd gotten takeout every night since coming back from Keys Crossing. Maybe there was something she could make for herself. As she'd told Joan Robinson, cooking wasn't her thing, but she could operate a microwave as well as the next person.

Toward the back of the pantry, behind some ramen noodle packets and ancient Pop-Tarts she ended up throwing away, was some movie theater butter popcorn. Awesome. While it popped away, she poured herself a large glass of Shiraz because of course, nothing classed up a meal like some red wine.

Back on the couch with a bowl of popcorn and wine, London spied Joan's business card poking out from a pocket on her new leather briefcase she'd spent way too much money on because it looked so polished and professional.

Careful not to spill her popcorn or wine, she pulled out the business card and laptop. Soon she was in the volunteer portal section of Compass's website. She clicked on the "Volunteer Today" link and was taken to a page explaining what Joan had already told her: every volunteer started in the kitchen and moved on from there. She clicked on the "Calendar" link and viewed meals being served for the next four weeks. Tomorrow was fried chicken, mashed potatoes and gravy, and green beans. London clicked on a day next week: meatloaf, broccoli, and potato pancakes. Could she help with that? She wasn't even sure what potato pancakes were.

"This is stupid," she muttered and was getting ready to close her laptop when she saw an email come through from the law offices of Larry Kopp.

She opened her account—CraftyLady@Hell.com—clicked on the email from Larry, and began to read:

Dear Ms. London Craft,

As you are aware, a sum of one hundred thousand dollars has been set up in a trust as a part of your inheritance from Mrs. Grace Craft, payable upon your satisfactory completion of the terms as described in the letter designated as entry A (copy attached) within one year of receipt of original notification.

This communication is to inform you that as of today, an additional sum has been added to this trust. Mr. Frederick Craft has contributed an additional fifty thousand dollars with a new total of one hundred and fifty thousand dollars to be paid to you upon satisfactory completion of these terms.

If you would like further clarification on this

communication, please reach out to our offices Monday–
Friday, 8:00 a.m.–5:00 p.m., EST, or simply reply to this
email at your convenience.
We look forward to hearing from you regarding this
matter.
Sincerely,
  Larry Kopp
  Attorney at Law

London had never truly experienced what it meant when people
said they were seeing red before. She assumed it had something to do
with bull fighting and red flags, and maybe it was, but in that moment,
her anger was so thick that it filled the room, and everything was a red
haze.

How dared he? How fucking dared he do this? Somehow it
seemed so much worse than the initial proposal of an inheritance from
her mother's estate. Maybe that was because her grief had made her
mother's offer seem softer and more benign. Most likely, that was it. It
had all felt like the last-ditch effort of a dying woman who didn't know
how to reconcile and made a final attempt—albeit a pretty offensive
one—to connect with her daughter one last time. But this? This felt
like a bribe.

The wine and popcorn churned and soured in her stomach. She
hit the reply button and wrote her response, her fingers stabbing at
the keyboard with every sharp, staccato push on the buttons. Before
proofreading it or otherwise giving a second thought, she sent this letter
back to Larry Kopp:

Dear Larry,
  Since you are in contact with my estranged father,
please give him my sincere congratulations. I thought there
was nothing my so-called "family" could do to insult me any
more than they already have. It's not often I admit I'm wrong,
but this time I was way off.
  Please assure my father that while I did not see this
offer coming, I have very strong ideas about what he can do
with it. If you need further clarification regarding this letter,
please feel free to kiss my ass forever.
  Sincerely,
  London Craft

"There." Tomorrow, she'd probably feel remorseful about burning a bridge she hadn't even known was still standing, but tonight she didn't care. "Fuck 'em."

The Compass website tab was still open when she closed her email. She clicked again on the calendar, closed her eyes, and clicked on a random day. This Thursday, the meal was going to be pulled pork sandwiches, corn, and salad. At the bottom of the screen, she clicked on the "Register Now!" link. She entered her information, and before she hit the submit button, she saw in small italic print, "Can you bring a friend?"

She hesitated and picked up her phone to call Grant. She'd like some moral support for this, and he was the best cook she knew. Well, the best cook after Reggie, but London knew she couldn't call her. Before she could press the call button, there was a knock at her door. She looked around the living room, but there was nobody to ask, "Expecting someone?"

Checking the peephole, she saw Grant and pulled the door open. "Hey! I was just getting ready to call you." Then she noticed his red eyes and puffy cheeks. "What's wrong?"

"I told Thomas. He kicked me out." Grant buried his head in his hands.

"God, I'm so sorry. Come on." She took him by the arm and guided him to the couch. They sat next to each other, her facing him and him staring directly ahead for several moments. Every once in a while, he'd use some part of his fist to push a tear from his face.

"Can I get you anything? I opened a bottle of wine."

Grant shook his head. After several more minutes of silence, he spoke. "I told him everything. I didn't even plan it. Me, the man with the plan. I wasn't going to tell him. I know how you felt about it, but I decided nothing good could come of it. It only happened once, I'd never be that stupid again, and it would only hurt him if he found out."

"Okay, so what changed your mind?"

He leaned forward and put his head in his hands. "I don't know." His voice was muffled, and his shoulders shook. London rubbed his back while he sobbed. "He says it's over. No second chances, no starting over. I know I fucked up, but don't you think, since it was just the one time and just a kiss, he could see if we could have a fresh start? Do what you and Reg are doing and take some time apart and start with a clean slate after a while?"

"I wish he could." She felt a twinge of guilt. She was the one who'd told him to tell Thomas the truth, and now he was devastated, and his relationship was destroyed. "I know you love him, and that's what you would like to see happen."

He lifted his head. "You don't think I deserve a second chance either?"

"That's not what I said. It's just not up to me. We knew there was a chance if you told him that things could go this way. Should you have a chance to prove yourself and rebuild your relationship? As far as I'm concerned, yes. I know you; you're not a cheater. This was a once in a lifetime slipup. It's not my choice to make. Hopefully, after Thomas has some time to process through the pain he's feeling, he'll be able to see things a different way."

"What if he doesn't?"

London bit her lower lip. She'd never seen her friend like this before, not in over ten years of friendship. She'd seen him cry once, at his grandmother's funeral. But of all the relationships and breakups they'd been through together, she'd never seen him upset like this over anyone. He was desperate, a word she'd never attributed to him. And as much as she wanted to give him the sliver of hope he so badly wanted, she couldn't build him up for what could be a terrible downfall.

"Then you'll have to find a way to respect that and move on."

He picked up her wine glass from the coffee table and took a long drink. "There's another reason I'm here."

"Yes, you can stay with me."

"Really?" His eyes, normally a deep hazel, were bright green after all of the crying.

"Of course. There's the…well, it's not exactly a bedroom, but it's semiprivate. It'll do until you figure out what your next move is." There was an alcove off the living room that was supposed to be a dining room, but London and Reggie had always sat on stools at the high counter that separated the kitchen from the living room. They'd put a bed and small dresser in the alcove and closed it off with Asian screens shortly after they moved in when Reggie's cousin had a summer internship in Columbus and had crashed at their place for a few months. It hadn't gotten much use since.

"I really appreciate this; you have no idea," said Grant.

"Yes I do. Besides, it'll be fun, slumber partying it up with you."

He smiled for the first time since he arrived. "Oh, yeah. I'll be a party animal. I even brought some board games."

CHAPTER SEVEN

E xplain to me again why we're doing this," Grant said.
"You want me to explain again that I hope I'll figure out why we're doing it after we get in there?"

They walked toward the red door that led into Compass Youth Center. There'd be no entering through the lobby tonight; kitchen volunteers used the same entrance as the kids. She was surprised how many kids there were once they got inside. Rooms that had been completely empty last time were now packed.

"They're so young," Grant whispered, nodding toward a couple boys who were playing video games. "That kid looks like he's only ten years old. I was expecting them all to be older teenagers."

"Me too."

They walked toward the kitchen and found an older woman in her sixties and a younger man in his thirties already taking food out for preparation. The woman noticed them first and nudged the man.

"Hey, Michael," she said, "fresh blood."

He turned and looked at them, seemingly unimpressed. "I don't know how much use they'll be, Doris. It doesn't look like either of them even brought a ladle."

London and Grant exchanged confused looks. "Uh," London stammered, "the volunteer website didn't say anything about—"

Doris and Michael burst out laughing. "You scared the poor things!" Doris had the deep voice and harsh wheezy laugh of a woman who'd been smoking since she could drive.

Michael laughed. "We're making pulled pork sandwiches. You don't even need a ladle."

"You owe me for this," Grant mumbled under his breath, and London elbowed him.

When the pair had finally stopped laughing, they came over to the kitchen's doorway and extended their hands to shake.

"I'm London, and this is Grant. We're the fresh blood, as you already know."

"Great to have you here," Michael said. "Thanks for letting us joke a little at your expense."

Doris grabbed two aprons from a hook near the door and handed them over. "Here you go. It's going to be pretty easy tonight. We've already started the pulled pork. The two of you will make the corn and salad as well as set up the plates and get them out to the kids. We've already set everything out that you're going to need."

"Sounds simple," Grant said.

"It is," Michael said. "Mostly."

"Want me to make the salad?" London asked Grant.

"No, salad involves a lot of chopping and shredding, which means the chances you'll lose a finger before the night is over are pretty high. With corn you can just dump a can into a saucepan and stir it every once in a while."

London opened her mouth to protest, then shrugged and nodded. Grant was bossy, but his reasoning was solid. She went to the largest can of corn she'd ever seen and set to opening it and getting it into the pan. After she'd gotten the entire can into the saucepan and turned the burner on, Michael came and stood next to her.

"So far, so good?" he asked.

"Yep."

"Great. The plates, glasses, and silverware are over there on the counter. Did you see the two tables in the living room?" She nodded. "Go ahead and start setting them if you don't mind. The kids help clean everything up after dinner, but right now is their free time. A lot of them are still finishing up homework."

"How many kids will be eating dinner?"

"Seven. Four who are living here right now and three who came for dinner and the activities we have going on afterward."

"Okay. I'll get started." She grabbed as many place settings as she could lift and started setting the table. When she went back into the kitchen she went over to Michael. "Hey. I thought you said there were seven kids eating dinner."

"There are."

"There are thirteen place settings."

"Yeah," Michael said, "we eat with the kids. The four of us, plus one of the counselors, and of course, Joan will be joining us."

"Joan is here?"

"She eats dinner with the kids three or four nights a week. More if she doesn't have a fund-raiser or networking event to attend."

London pondered that as she went to stir the corn before taking another set of plates to the tables. Joan had told her she would be here, but she thought it was a joke. How did she have time to be here all day during business hours, through dinner, and on to head up some of the evening activities? Sure, she had plenty of volunteers and a small full-time staff, but still. She couldn't have much of a life outside this place.

A violently loud siren pulled London from her deep thoughts, and she almost dropped a plate when she covered her ears. She looked toward the kitchen and saw dark gray smoke coming from the entry. She ran over and saw Doris taking the flaming saucepan of corn from the stovetop and into the sink with Michael behind her shoving a large lid on top of the pan to suffocate the fire. As soon the fire went out, Grant took off his apron and used it to fan the smoke detector on the ceiling, and finally, it stopped its heinous screaming.

For several moments, nobody spoke or even moved. Then Doris and Michael started howling with laughter, and after a second, Grant joined them. Soon, London heard raucous laughter behind her and turned around to find most of the kids crowding around the door to the kitchen, pointing and falling over themselves. And standing in the middle of them, her arms crossed and a smirk on her face, was Joan Robinson.

"I see we've got the only woman on earth who can burn a can of corn helping in the kitchen tonight," said Joan, and everyone except London roared with delight.

London stood in the kitchen, blushing and giggling. Of course it was funny, but why, *why* did it have to happen on her first night volunteering, and why when Joan was there?

The kids went back to what they were doing, and Joan stepped into the kitchen.

"I'm really sorry," London said. "Do you want me to pay to replace the corn?"

Joan waved her off and went to the cupboards to retrieve a new can of corn and a clean pan. She opened the can, dumped it in, and when she went to place it on the burner, she peered down.

"This is what your trouble was." She turned the knob on front of the stove. "You had it turned up to the highest level. You only need to have it about halfway."

"I thought it would get done faster," London said sheepishly.

"You don't spend a lot of time in the kitchen, do you?" Joan asked.

"Only when I'm fridge surfing."

A twinge of amusement passed across Joan's eyes so quickly that London thought she might have imagined it. "Come with me," Joan said. "I'll introduce you to some of the kids." She turned toward Grant, who was just finishing the salad. "Forgive me. I haven't introduced myself. I'm Joan Robinson, the director here." She reached out, and this time London was a bystander to one of those aggressive handshakes.

"I'm Grant Vogel, a friend of London's."

"Pleased to meet you. It's wonderful to have you here. I was going to take London to meet some of the kids. If you'll bring the salad out to the table, I'd love to introduce you as well. Doris, Michael, keep an eye on the corn, will you?"

The three of them walked out to the living area, and Grant set a bowl of salad on each table.

"Hey, everybody!" Joan called. "Come on over here so you can meet the new volunteers." Moments later, they were surrounded by a group of kids ranging in age from about ten to eighteen. Joan introduced each, and they all gave a little wave or smile when their name was called. "Everyone, these are our volunteers tonight. This is Grant, and this is—"

"The lady who burns corn!" said the youngest child, and they all giggled.

"Indeed, Quentin, you're right," said Joan, "but you may call her London."

"London Craft?" asked Lila, an older girl in a black leather jacket and black leggings with skulls on them.

"Yes," London said, surprised. "Do we know each other?"

"I've been to your store." Lila opened her jacket to reveal a T-shirt that said, "Smash the Patriarchy" with a pink fist in the background. "I love your stuff."

"Thank you," London said. "The shirt looks great on you."

Lila smiled. "Thanks."

Doris and Michael brought out the rest of the food, and Joan asked everyone to take their seats. "London, Doris, if you wouldn't mind, please take a seat here." Joan placed them at a table with Quentin, Lila, a wispy blond girl named Bernadette, and a smiling boy named Jacob. "Grant and Michael will sit with me at the other table."

Everyone stood behind their chairs, hands resting on the backs, and closed their eyes. London stole a look at Grant, who mouthed the words, "You owe me," before he closed his eyes as well. London expected Joan to say a prayer or something before they sat, but it was Quentin who spoke:

"I wish for love in a world that hates me. I wish for peace in a time of violence. Most of all, I wish for a home and a family." He was quiet for a moment, then said, "That's it." He pulled out his chair to sit, and everyone else followed.

Jacob picked up the salad bowl, put some on his plate, and passed the bowl to London.

"So, London," Lila said, scooping up some corn. "Do you think you'll be doing some art classes with us here?"

London spotted Joan looking in her direction. "I'm not sure. Who knows if I'll even be allowed to come back after almost burning the place down." The kids laughed.

"Do you want to come back, though?" Bernadette asked.

"I think so. I'd like to."

Quentin pointed at Lila. "You made that shirt?"

"Well, I designed it. I have a few other people who also work with me after I've created the designs, but there's a one in three chance I'm the one who made it."

"That's pretty cool," Quentin said.

"Thanks. So, how old are all of you?"

"Seventeen," Lila said.

"I'm fourteen," said Jacob, "but I turn fifteen next month."

"Fifteen," said Bernadette.

Quentin, who had taken a huge bite of pulled pork sandwich as London asked the question, was the last to answer. "Just turned twelve." He was older than she thought but not by much.

"I see," London said. "And do you all live here right now?"

"I don't." Jacob grinned. "I'm just here for the food."

London laughed. "You must have been really worried when that smoke alarm went off, then."

"Oh, I was," Jacob said. "Don't mess with my side dishes."

"The rest of you stay here, though?"

They all nodded.

"What's that like?" She glanced at Doris after asking the question, wondering if she was overstepping any boundaries, but Doris was busy piling pork on her bread.

"It's way better than being at home," Lila said, and the others nodded.

"Really? You all feel that way?"

"If I could go back home and have the same relationship with my family I had before I came out and still be myself, that would be better. But I can't." Bernadette spoke in a flat tone that London recognized all too well, and it made her heartsick for the girl. She was far too young to sound that hopeless.

"My parents kicked me out the minute they found out I'm trans," said Quentin. "There's no going home for me."

"I can understand that." London rested her hand on the boy's shoulder. "I can't go home either."

"Your parents don't want you because you're gay?" Quentin put down his pulled pork sandwich and looked at her intently.

"Well…my mother just died a few weeks ago. But no. They didn't want me anymore after they found out."

"How old were you when they found out?" asked Lila.

"I was twenty. I wasn't brave enough to come out when I still lived with them, like all of you."

"I'm not that brave either." Jacob looked down at his food. "Otherwise, I'd probably be living here too."

"I didn't know you hadn't told them," Lila said.

Jacob shrugged. "I know. I kind of feel like a sellout compared to the rest of you. Passing as straight until I'm out of the house and out of high school."

"You're not a sellout, Jacob," said Doris. "Everyone has a right to come out when the time is right for them."

"I wish I'd waited," Bernadette said. She'd pushed her food around on her plate a lot without really eating much.

Doris patted Bernadette's back. "I wish I'd come out sooner. All we can do is all we can do."

"So." Quentin's voice was loud. "You came out when you were twenty, and how old are you now?" His dark eyes had brightened, and London thought she saw a well of tears. She glanced uncertainly at Doris, who nodded.

"I'm thirty-nine."

"Thirty-nine," Quentin repeated. "After nineteen years, your parents still hate you." A tear tumbled down his face. "So all of that

'It Gets Better' stuff is total garbage." Before London could respond, Quentin pushed away from the table and ran out of the room. With a trembling hand, London set down her spoon.

Doris rose from the table. "I'll go talk to him."

"No, I'll go," said Joan. "The rest of you, please enjoy the remainder of your meal."

After a brief silence, Jacob asked, "How old were you when you came out, Doris?"

"Sixty."

"*Sixty!*" All the kids stared at one another with open mouths and wide eyes.

Doris smiled. "It's shocking these days, in this place, but I grew up on a farm in Alabama. I didn't even have a word to name who or what I was when I was a kid. That wasn't something people knew. I'd love to believe my hometown has changed a lot since then, but I doubt it. So, I did what everyone did and got married really young." She looked at Lila. "I wasn't much older than you when I married my husband."

"Oh, hell no," said Lila, and everyone laughed.

"I got lucky," said Doris. "My husband was an amazing man, and he was my best friend in the world. Years later, when we moved here and I finally met some people who were out and proud, I thought about coming out. But I loved him, and I knew I was the great love of his life. I was ready to stay with him forever, but the universe had other plans. He died when he was fifty-nine and I was fifty-eight."

"I'm sorry you lost him," London said.

"Thank you," Doris said with a small smile. She looked around the table. "Well, it looks like everyone has finished. Time for you guys to start gathering dishes and loading the dishwasher." With no further discussion, the kids stood and cleared the table. Michael and Grant joined them, and within minutes, the tables were once again blank.

"Should we help in the kitchen?" asked Grant.

"Nah, it's crowded enough in there already," said Michael. "If they need help, we'll know it. Do either of you want coffee?"

London deferred to Grant since she'd dragged him here against his will. He surprised her when he said, "Coffee would be nice."

"Come with us," said Doris.

When London realized where they were headed, she stopped walking, causing Grant to run into her hard enough that she almost tumbled to the floor.

"Joan's office?" she asked after they regained themselves.

Michael smiled. "That's where the coffee is. Don't worry, she's cool with it." London hadn't seen the large Keurig in the corner when she was here before. "Pick your K-cup." Michael held out a large tub filled with the coffee pods. Doris gave them some heavy mugs, and they took turns preparing their coffee. London blew on hers and walked to the wall with a dozen or so pictures featuring Joan either shaking hands or arm in arm with notable people. In one, she was accepting an award from the mayor of Columbus. Another showed her at Compass with a group of volunteers and staff. London peered closer at one photo. *Is that Ellen DeGeneres? Holy shit.*

"I see you've found my wall of infamy."

London turned to find Joan standing behind her. "Oh, uh, yes. It's impressive."

"It's something." Joan sat on the corner of her desk. "Tell me, how did you two like your first night? What were your first impressions?"

"The kids were so well-behaved," said Grant.

Joan nodded. "They have their moments, but yes, they're good kids, and they are grateful to be here."

"They're lucky to have this place," said Grant.

"How is Quentin?" London asked.

"He's not having an easy time. The way his parents removed him from his home was rather violent, which means they'd have to jump through substantial hoops in order for Child Protective Services to even allow him back with them. So far, they've been uninterested in making any necessary changes. I've been trying to work with his parents and educate them on the best ways to accept and support a transgender child, but I think they're a lost cause. It's frustrating for me, but for Quentin, it's devastating."

London nodded. "I can imagine."

"Think you'll be back?" Doris asked.

London laughed. "You want me to come back after almost burning the place down and sending a child running from the room in tears?"

"Yes," said Joan.

London paused, expecting her to go on, maybe tell her that everyone made mistakes on their first day, but she simply held London's gaze. "I'll come back next week," London said finally.

"I'll come with you," said Grant.

"Excellent," said Joan. "We'll look into installing a new sprinkler system before then."

❖

"Well, that was entertaining." Grant grabbed his coat off the hook in the small vestibule.

"A new sprinkler system," London muttered.

"It was funny. Lighten up."

"That woman bugs me."

They went out into the chilly air, and she zipped up her coat.

"Hey." He pulled on her elbow before she stepped into the parking lot. "Isn't that Quentin? The kid who got so upset?"

London looked back toward the building and saw him sitting on a bench on the sidewalk that led to the street. "I'm gonna go talk to him," she said.

"Yeah?"

"Yeah."

"I'll pull the car up. Take your time."

She walked to where the young boy sat and stood a few feet away. He said nothing, so she moved to the far edge of the bench and sat. "I'm sorry I upset you."

"It's not you." He kicked a few crisp leaves with the tip of his tennis shoe. "Sometimes I let myself believe I'll get to go back home."

"And that's not possible?" she asked gently.

He shook his head. "Not for me." He turned away from her, and his body began to tremble. She scooted closer and put her arm around him. She didn't know what the protocol was at Compass for dealing with upset kids, but she couldn't let him sit on that bench crying without holding him.

"I'm sorry," she said. "I wish things were different for you."

Quentin sniffed. "You're not going to tell me things will get better?"

She thought for a moment. "Well, I do think they'll get better for you in time. But I also know you have every right to feel hurt and upset about where you are in this moment. It's going to get better, Quentin, but it sucks right now."

"It really does." He wiped tears away with the cuff of his jacket.

The red door to Compass opened, and Joan burst out, coatless, looking around wildly. When she spied them on the bench, she ran to where they sat. "Quentin, thank God! I was so worried; we've been looking for you everywhere." Her steps slowed a little when she saw London. "You're still here?"

"I guess I should've let you know he was out here. It didn't occur to me you didn't know where he was."

"I'm sorry, Joan," Quentin said.

"We'll talk about it inside." She extended her hand, and he stood, taking her arm. "I'm just glad you're safe."

Quentin's shoulders slumped, and his head bent. He was clearly grieving, and who could blame him? She knew all too well about the damage of parental rejection and its long-lasting affects. He was just a little boy, though. What tools did he have to even begin to deal with any of this? The thought troubled her.

The pair walked toward the door. Quentin looked over his shoulder and waved. London waved back and sat on the bench until they stepped inside, the door closing behind them.

❖

"Did someone need some coffee?" Grant entered Hell in a Handbasket with a drink carrier filled with steaming cups.

"Bless you!" Jasmine rushed to him and kissed him on the cheek, taking the carrier. "Maybe this will convince the boss lady to finally take a break. Nothing else has worked; she's been at it all day."

London laughed. "I'm right here. Can I be included in this conversation?"

"Sure you can, princess," Grant said. "Drink your dark chocolate latte first, though."

London scowled but took the cup from him. "We'd be scrappin' if I didn't need this so badly." She inhaled the rich smell and took a sip. "Yum."

"See?" Grant said. "Isn't being a lady with coffee better than being a lady without coffee? Besides, you've been all work and no play for days."

"I have to send my spring design concepts to people who distribute pieces for me by the end of the month," London said. "Normally, I'd already have them done, but…"

"But your mother died," said Grant.

"And she always used to be so impeccable with her timing." London pretended not to see the look of concern between Jasmine and

Grant. "Anyway, if you've come to take me to lunch, I don't have time, so you may as well go back to work."

"Lunch? Sweetie, it's seven o'clock. Do you mean to tell me it's dinnertime, and you haven't eaten lunch?"

"I tried to tell her," said Jasmine. "Every time I interrupt her, she says she'll take a break in a minute. Now, a thousand minutes later, still no break."

London looked over and saw Jasmine had already put the closed sign on the door. "Okay, okay, you two. I'll shut down for the night. Do you guys wanna have dinner? I'm supposed to meet Tate at Tip Top at seven thirty; I'm sure he wouldn't mind if we made it a foursome."

"You sure?" Jasmine asked.

"Of course, he'd love it."

"So would I," said Jasmine.

"Me too," Grant said. "And I'm starving."

The dinner rush at Tip Top was just ending, with several tables clearing out when the three of them arrived.

"Let's ask for a table in the back," said London. "It gets drafty in the front when it's cold outside. I'll text Tate and let him know we're back here."

One of the servers led them past the bar to the back of the restaurant. Exposed brick walls gave it a cavernous feel the deeper one went into the place. The tall, bearded server took their drink orders as they sat at the high table with barstools.

"We're expecting one more," said Jasmine.

"He'll just want water." London pulled out her phone. She sent Tate a text: *Hey, punk, we're at a table in the back. Jas and Grant are with me.*

"So, aside from feeling rushed, how are the spring lines going?" Grant asked.

"Pretty well. I'm happy with what I've done so far. This will probably be the last year I'll be waiting until fall to finish the spring line."

"Really?" Jasmine asked. "But that's always been our time line."

"I know, but with the notoriety we've been getting, a lot of my pieces are going to be carried in some more shops in New York City and Los Angeles." It was great to have something to feel so excited about, especially with all the drama she'd had lately. There had been many moments in the last few weeks when she needed a distraction from her feelings, and her busy work schedule had been the perfect solution. She'd worked so hard in her career, building her brand up from nothing, and could now enjoy the payoff. "It's amazing, you know; this is what I've been working toward. What we've been working toward." She squeezed Jasmine's hand. "We did all this work to get Hell to be a bigger name, and now that it is, we're working with people who want to get their hands on designs a year in advance."

"A year?" Jasmine screeched. "That's insane!"

London shrugged. "It's business. And getting the designs done early will help us too, with us having to make and distribute more products."

"Products?" Grant was staring at her with sharp interest. "I've never heard you talk about your work using that word."

"I create art, yes, but in the end, the pieces I sell are products. There's nothing wrong with calling it what it is."

"I didn't say there was," Grant said. "Just pointing out that it's new for you."

The server arrived with their drinks. "Did you guys want to wait until your friend gets here to order?"

"Yes, please," said Grant. "I'm sorry; he should be here any minute."

"No problem," said the server. "Just grab me if you need anything before he arrives."

"Thanks." Jasmine looked at her watch. "He's not usually late."

London checked her phone. Almost seven forty-five and no text from Tate. She texted again: *Hey jerk, where are you? I hope you're not stuck looking for parking.* Trying to find a spot on Gay Street at this hour could be tricky. Grant had offered to drive them over, and they had lucked into a spot right out front.

"So," Jasmine said, "are you still trying to cross things off your bucket list?"

"Sort of. I started working my way up toward a marketing job. Kinda."

"Ugh," Grant said. "Did she ever. I only wish she'd had the decency to do it by herself."

"You loved it. You'll be telling that story for years."

"Oh, tell me the story," said Jasmine.

Grant regaled Jasmine with the whole scene: being dragged to this strange place, the comedic stylings of Doris and Michael, London's burning of the corn, poor little Quentin running away, and the eccentric woman that was Joan Robinson.

London laughed. "And at the end of it all, Grant said he wanted to go back, so it must not have been that terrible."

"True. I actually do feel like volunteering there can really make a difference."

"This isn't what you had in mind with your business suits and office work and big corner office, though, is it?" Jasmine asked.

"It's not, but I think it could be a step toward that. I feel like I'm building to something anyway. And besides, once this was put in my path, I felt like I needed to see it through."

"It definitely sounds like you two are doing some good work there," Jasmine said. "Are you going to have to tell this story again when Tate gets here? Maybe we should've waited."

"Where the hell *is* he, anyway?" Grant asked. "This isn't like him. It's almost eight o'clock."

"I hope he didn't blow us off for some hottie," London said.

"What hottie?" Grant demanded. "Tate has a hottie?"

"He had a first date with this girl from Tinder today. He went hiking with her and a few of her friends, and tonight we get the dirty details."

Jasmine smirked. "You think they ran into some bumpy terrain?"

"If they did, I wouldn't blame him for blowing us off," Grant said. "How long has it been since that poor guy got laid?"

"Since before he transitioned." London didn't feel bad telling them this bit of information. If Tate had been there, he would've told them himself. "I doubt they're bumping and grinding yet; he seems to want to take things slow right now while he's still getting used to the dating scene as a trans man."

At that moment, London's phone began to ring, and Tate's face filled the screen. "There he is." She hit the accept call button. "Hey, where are you?"

"Hello?" said an unfamiliar voice. "London Craft?"

She pulled the phone away from her ear and confirmed that it was Tate's number. "Yes?"

"This is Patricia Fielding, and I'm a nurse at Saint Ann's Hospital. I'm calling from Tate Morgan's phone. You should come to the hospital right away."

Chapter Eight

The mixture of disinfectant and sickness permeating London's nostrils always made her feel on the verge of throwing up, and this night was no different, although nervousness and sheer terror probably contributed to her upset stomach too.

She rushed to the ICU wing with Grant and Jasmine right behind her. After an eternity on the elevator and a chaotic maze of hallways, they finally arrived at the nurse's station. A nurse was hanging up the phone, and when London approached, words began tumbling out.

"Hi, I'm London, I got a call from Patricia Fielding from Tate Morgan's phone telling me to come right away."

"Yes, I'm Patricia." She turned to another nurse. "Bill, I'm going to be talking to these folks; can you cover the desk?"

She stepped out from behind the station, a small, grandmotherly-looking woman with short gray hair, plump cheeks, and bifocals. She took the glasses off as she got closer and tucked them into her breast pocket. "Step over here with me. There's an empty room where we can speak privately."

Panic swept through London as she followed. First, Patricia wouldn't give her details over the phone, now they had to go to a private room to speak.

Once inside the room, Patricia offered them some chairs, but London shook her head. "Please, just tell me what's happening."

"You were listed as Mr. Morgan's next of kin, is that correct?"

"Yes." Last year, when Tate had his top surgery to remove his breasts and then a hysterectomy, she'd been with him and was on all his paperwork as his emergency contact. Panic gave way to desperation. She needed to know what was happening. Where was Tate? What had happened to him?

Patricia was consulting a chart. "What's your relationship to him?"

"He's my brother," London said. "Now, will you tell me what's going on with Tate?" Grant squeezed her shoulders, and Jasmine took her hand.

Patricia looked up. "I'm afraid your brother has sustained some very serious injuries as a result of an assault."

London took in a sharp breath. "An assault?"

"He was brought to us in critical condition after some hikers discovered him on the side of a trail. He'd been badly beaten, and they called an ambulance. He was rushed into surgery to repair a collapsed lung and several rib fractures."

"Sweet Jesus," Jasmine said.

"He's out of surgery now," Patricia said. "He isn't awake yet. Unfortunately, he also sustained trauma to his head and isn't currently able to breathe on his own. He's in a coma, Ms. Craft."

London realized she'd been breathing shallowly. Her lungs pushed air out without her permission, as if the weight of this news forced it out and was crushing her. She felt flattened, one dimensional, as if she could neither breathe nor think nor feel because she had lost her depth.

"Who did this?" Grant asked. "Do you know anything?"

"We don't. One of the hikers rode back in the ambulance, and police interviewed her, but she found him after the fact and wasn't a witness to the crime itself. And Mr. Morgan is unable to speak on his own behalf, so…" Patricia trailed off.

London's head felt heavy, and her vision blurred as she tried to process all of this. Her knees began to buckle, and Grant grabbed her waist. Jasmine grabbed one of the chairs and put it behind her. She sat and put her head in her hands. The room spun as if she rode a terrible merry-go-round, and she had to grip both sides of the chair in order to be able to look at Patricia. "But he's going to be okay, right? He's in a coma, but he'll heal and wake up."

Patricia's mouth thinned. "The next several days will be critical, and we're doing everything we can. We will know more in the coming forty-eight hours as we monitor his brain activity."

"He's going to be okay," London said. "You don't know Tate; he's going to pull through this. There's no one in the world stronger than him." She didn't even want to let the thought that he wasn't going to be okay enter her mind. It seemed as if she could keep Tate safe and help him get better if she believed hard enough that he would overcome his injuries.

Patricia didn't speak, and London hated the look of sympathy. It was the kind of look one gave a child who desperately clung to the last shred of belief in Santa Claus even when she had proof that the man was just a myth. She didn't want Patricia's forlorn expression to permeate the shell of positive thought she was creating. Tate was going to be okay. He had to be.

"Can we see him?" she asked.

"Absolutely," Patricia said. "Follow me."

In the second from the last room on the right, they found him, although if London hadn't been told it was him, she wouldn't have recognized her best friend. Her illusions about getting him better by sheer force of will fell away. She paused in the doorway, not able to move closer to the broken person who was supposed to be Tate. Never had she been so at odds with herself. She wanted to rush to him and hold him as much as she wanted to run away. She took a few deep breaths and slowly walked to the bed.

The tissue around both his eyes was so swollen, he wouldn't have been able to open them even if he'd been awake. His bottom lip had stitches holding it together, and his entire face was covered in blue and purple bruises. London gently picked up one of his hands and saw that the knuckles were raw and swollen too. He'd put up a fight. Of course he had.

"Tate," London said, "I'm here. Grant and Jasmine are here too. We're going to get you through this, do you hear me? I know you do. We're going to get you through this. You'll wake up and get better. You can come stay with me to recover. Grant's already crashing at my place, and it's going to be the best slumber party ever. It'll be like old times when we were kids and never wanted to leave each other's houses. Remember all the times I came over to play with you, and we were having so much fun that when my parents came to pick me up, we'd pretend to be asleep so I could spend the night? It'll be just like that, except we can stay up all night if we want to, and instead of drinking chocolate milkshakes, we'll drink beer. Well, we can do milkshakes too. We'll do whatever you want, okay? Whatever helps you get well, that's what we'll do."

She didn't feel the tears streaming down her face until Jasmine, armed with a box of tissues, wiped them away. That act of kindness made her come completely undone, and she laid her head down on the bed beside Tate and sobbed in a way she hadn't since she was a kid. Anguished wails escaped her mouth, and she felt as if her entire body was being twisted from the inside out from the force of the tears pushing their way to the surface. Jasmine rubbed her back and pulled her hair away from her face. Every minute or so, she blotted London's cheeks with a clean tissue.

London began to get a grasp on her tears, but as they dried, her vision cleared, giving her a harsh view of Tate's injuries again, and she quaked with fresh sobs. Her sweet Tate. What kind of monster could have done this? Who could have so beaten those eyes that were always filled with compassion and adventure? Who bruised the lips that could never stop themselves from singing in the car? She couldn't understand what she was looking at. She couldn't recognize this poor creature in front of her, who was both Tate and not Tate.

After repeating this process several times, her tears finally began to wind down. She looked around the room. "Where's Grant?"

"He stepped out to make a few calls," Jasmine said. "He got Tate's phone from the nurse so he could notify people."

"He's not ready to deal with this yet."

Jasmine smoothed London's hair back and did another once-over with a tissue under her eyes. "No, he isn't. He's still here, sugar. He just needed to take a few minutes."

"Yeah." London, squeezed the bridge of her nose. "I get it."

They sat in silence, one on either side of Tate so they could each hold one of his hands. London wanted to keep talking to him, but she was so tired. She stroked his hand and would occasionally say, "I'm here. I'm here."

Patricia returned with an armful of blankets and pillows. "I brought you a few things." She crossed to the far side of the room and pulled back a curtain that London hadn't even noticed, revealing another bed. "Normally, we'd have you sleeping in the foldout couch," she said, pointing to the plastic sofa in the corner. "But since we don't have another patient in here, you can sleep in this bed." She looked at Jasmine. "Will you be staying the night as well?"

Jasmine looked at London, who shook her head. "Go home and get some sleep, Jas. I'll be fine here."

"Are you sure?"

"I'm sure. I'll call you if anything changes."

Jasmine leaned in to give her a tight hug. "I love you."

"I love you too." Tears began to surface again, but she squeezed her eyes shut and swallowed the thick sadness building up in her throat.

She needed to keep it together if she was going to get through this night on her own with Tate.

The sound of someone clearing his throat separated them from their embrace. Grant stood in the doorway, his eyes red rimmed and his hair disheveled. He took a tentative step into the room, not able to tear his eyes away from Tate. His lower jaw trembled, and a few tears tumbled down his cheeks.

"London, can I talk to you out in the hallway?"

"Okay." She leaned down, kissed Tate's hand, said, "I'll be right back," and followed Grant out to the hall.

"I've been pacing out here trying to get the nerve to come in." He raked a hand through his hair. "I want to. I know I need to, but, London..." His face crumpled, and he choked out a stifled sob.

London hugged him and stroked his hair. Caring for Grant, even for a moment, removed her from her own pain and worry. She could be strong for him, for Jasmine and Tate. She could think about their needs, their emotions, and their pain, and in doing so relieve the pressure of her own, if only momentarily. "Go home," she said. "Get some sleep and come back tomorrow."

"Are you sure you're going to be okay here?"

"I'll be fine. It's better that I'm the one here. I...I can't be away from him, and you can't be near him, at least not tonight. Go home and rest, eat a good breakfast in the morning, and come back and try again."

"I'm sorry," he said.

"I know."

"I'll get Jasmine home safe, and when I come back tomorrow I'll bring you clean clothes and shampoo and stuff."

"We're going to get through this, and Tate is gonna be okay."

Grant nodded. "Will you send Jasmine out?"

"I'm here." Jasmine walked over to them, and the three embraced each other, each supported by the other two.

"I'll see you guys tomorrow." She went back into the room with Tate. The clock said it was nearly midnight. Where had the last several hours gone, and how long had she been standing next to Tate, holding his hand? She clicked the buttons behind him so all the lights were off except for a dim one just above his head.

Patricia had made the bed, and after pushing the hospital curtain as close to the wall as she could so she had a full view of Tate, she crawled in the bed and pulled the blankets up to her chin. She lay on her right side, watching Tate and listening to the suction sound of the machine that breathed for him. She stared into the dim night at her best friend, thinking there was no way she'd be able to sleep tonight. Not long after that, she did.

❖

Just as London awoke the following morning, two strangers entered the room. One man and one woman, both in dark business suits with grave expressions. *Cops.*

"Ms. Craft?" the woman asked, and London nodded. "I'm Detective Harper, and this is Detective O'Connor. We're investigating the assault against your..." She pulled a small notebook from her pocket and paged through it. "Your brother, is it?"

"He's my best friend, and we grew up together. We're family." She made that last statement a little louder than she meant to.

"Understood," said Detective Harper. "What can you tell us about Mr. Morgan's whereabouts yesterday?"

"He was going on a Tinder date, a group thing." She saw their look of surprise. "Not like that, nothing salacious," she said hurriedly. "He was talking to a girl on Tinder, and she invited him to go hiking with some of her friends."

"Do you know the woman's name?"

"I don't remember, but...wait." She went to her purse and dug around in it. "Here it is." She pulled Tate's phone out. "He showed me her picture." London pulled up the app, staring at the circling dots as it opened. "There." She pointed at the messages between Tate and a woman named Amanda making plans to go hiking. "That's her."

"May I?" Detective O'Connor stepped forward and took the phone. He scribbled some notes, and when he was finished, passed it to Detective Harper, who did the same. When Harper returned the phone, O'Connor turned back to London. "Was there anything unusual about the date? Can you remember any other details?"

"Not about the date, no. He'd been talking to her for a week or so and had been flirting with a few other women from the site as well. She was the first one he went out with, though."

"But nothing stuck out about her or about their plans?"

London shook her head. "I've told you everything I know about it. But...are you the same officers who were here yesterday?"

"Yes, we are," Harper said.

"Did the doctors or nurses tell you that Tate is a trans man?"

"No." Harper looked surprised. "No, they didn't."

"He is, and this was his first time dating since he transitioned."

"Did this Amanda know he's transgender?" O'Connor asked.

"Not before he went on the date, at least, not as far as I knew. He planned to tell her; he was just trying to figure out when."

The detectives exchanged glances. "Thank you for letting us know," Harper said. "That does change things a little."

"It was a hate crime," London said. It was a statement, not a question. The words tasted foul coming out of her mouth. She'd been sure Tate had been a victim of a hate crime since she first learned he was hurt, but saying it out loud shocked her system. She clenched her trembling hands around Tate's phone.

"We don't know that yet," O'Connor said. His gravelly voice softened.

"I know it. I've known it since I got the call to come to the hospital."

"I'm very sorry this happened to your friend. To your brother," Harper said. "We're going to do everything we can to catch the people who did this."

"Yes," said O'Connor, "and you've been very helpful. May we take the phone?"

"Will it help you catch the bastards who did this?"

"It might."

London handed them the phone.

"Thank you," said Harper. "Write your phone number down here for me, and we'll be in touch."

After they left, London sat by Tate and used the remote to turn on the TV. "Let's see what we can find to watch. The only good thing about being sick is all the bad TV you get to see." She flipped past some morning news programs, past an infomercial for Rogaine, and past an evangelical pastor talking to his congregation about loose women. "They should really get Netflix in this place. Oh! *Golden Girls* reruns. Score."

London set the remote down and rested her hand beside Tate's, watching one of their favorite shows together. "I still say you're a Blanche, and I'm a Dorothy." She continued an argument they'd been having for years. "No question." She glanced at him and willed him to wake up and argue with her. Bickering had always been part of the foundation of their friendship, and she knew if he regained his ability to tell her she was wrong, everything would be okay. He remained silent and still. She'd been fighting overwhelming uneasiness since Grant and Jasmine left last night, and it pulsated through her now. She turned back to the TV and tried to focus on the women on the screen.

"London?" Grant said from behind her. "I brought visitors." She turned. Reggie, Thomas, Betty, and Herb all stood in the doorway.

London stood and Reggie half ran to her, folding her in a tight hug that felt as if everything was going to be okay. "I'm so glad you're here," London said.

"I couldn't stay away, once I heard." Reggie turned to Tate. "Oh, baby doll, what did they do to you?" She rested her palm over his heart. "How could someone do this?"

Grant and Thomas joined them at the end of the bed, and Reggie's parents stood on either side of London. "I hope it's okay that we're here," said Herb. "We just had to come."

London leaned her head on his shoulder. "It's a relief to have you here. You're like...you two are kind of like surrogate parents for all of us."

"That's a lovely thing to say," Betty said. "We couldn't love any of you more if you were our own babies. And we couldn't let you go through this alone."

London's voice shook. "Thank you. You don't know what that means."

After a few moments, Grant spoke. "I brought you some clothes and stuff from home. If you want to shower and change, we can hang out in here."

London looked down at Tate, stroking his hand as she had last night when she first got here.

"Go on now," Betty said. "We'll watch over him for you."

London washed the grime from the last few days away and got lost in the warm water pouring over her. She couldn't get the image of Tate's bruised and battered body out of her head, and hot tears began to mix with the soothing drops running down her face. She indulged herself for a few minutes before she scrubbed her face and body and twisted the nozzle off. When she was all clean and dressed, she stepped out of the bathroom. Reggie pulled her into the hallway.

"What do you need right now?" Reggie asked. "What can I do to help you?"

"Can I have another one of those hugs?"

Reggie wrapped her arms around London and buried her head in

London's still-damp hair. They stood like that for a long time. It was the first small sense of peace she'd had since this horrible nightmare began.

"Even with us spending time apart," London said, "you still rush to be with me every time things fall to pieces."

"I love you. That hasn't changed."

"I love you too."

An alarm sounded from Tate's room, and four people in scrubs rushed down the hall, clamoring through his doorway. London and Reggie followed, and although they couldn't see Tate for all the medical workers, they saw the very frightened faces of everyone else in the room.

Grant slowly backed away from the end of Tate's bed. "What's happening?"

"He's crashing," someone yelled.

"Okay, everybody, stand back," said a man in a white coat. "We need you all to get out so we can work on him the way we need to. Who the hell let this many people in here?"

They exited and stood anxiously in a semicircle around the doorway. Hours seemed to go by as they listened to the frantic chatter and movement behind the closed door. Thomas went to the alcove at the end of the hall and dragged two chairs back so Herb and Betty could sit. The rest of them stood motionless, except for Grant, who paced between Tate's room and the nurse's desk, back and forth.

Despite her hot shower, London was cold. It felt as if her blood was on ice, bringing freezing temperatures to all her extremities. She wondered if it was her body's way of trying to numb her to all the worry and fear. She rubbed her hands and put all her energy into focusing on the friction. Anything to keep her mind off what might be happening on the other side of that door.

Finally, the man in the white coat appeared before them. He rested his hand on London's shoulder when he spoke. "The trauma Mr. Morgan endured over the last two days caused unforeseeable damage. He just experienced a seizure as a result of that damage, which induced a stroke. We did everything we could, but I'm afraid we couldn't save him."

London lost the last shreds of control. She opened her mouth to scream and instead began keening, the mournful sounds coming out of her endlessly, with barely a second to take a breath before her grief song started again. Grant and Reggie reached out to her, but she backed away. She didn't want to be touched. She needed to undo this, needed it to not be real. She turned toward Tate's room, intending to rush in and take him in her arms and tell him he was the only family she had, and he couldn't leave her alone. Instead, she crumpled to the floor, legs tucked under her and bent at the waist, and wailed. She didn't cry; there were no tears. Just that terrible, uncontrollable sound. Finally, a nurse came and injected her with something, and everything wavered around her and faded to gray.

London dreamed of the time she and Grant had watched a show on Animal Planet in which a mother bird whose baby was taken by a predator began keening out of grief. The heartbreaking song went on for a few moments, and Grant had turned to London and said, "That's what sheer sadness sounds like."

She awakened to bright sunlight streaming across her face and tried to wipe the sleep and grogginess from her eyes. Something was missing or wrong. What was it? She blinked the last of the blurriness away and looked at a room that wasn't hers. White walls adorned with abstract pastel paintings surrounded her, and she was in a twin bed covered in a thin blanket.

"You're awake." Grant and Reggie appeared above her, their faces were twisted with concern.

"Did I dream it?"

"No, baby." Reggie stroked her hair. "You didn't dream it. He's gone."

"I want to go home."

"Okay," Grant said. "Let's get you home."

❖

Planning Tate's funeral was not easy, but it was simple. He'd been terrified when he'd had his surgeries to transition, half convinced he wouldn't survive, and made all the arrangements in the event of his death. London had to sign a few papers agreeing to go forward with the plans already in place, and that was that. She checked with Thomas, who'd taken on the wills and estates for everyone in the group, to make sure there was enough money to cover the funeral. He assured her there was plenty and that he'd get the bills paid.

A month earlier, she hadn't been a part of any planning for her mother's funeral, didn't know anything about the circumstances of her death until the last moment, and had basically been treated like a begrudging afterthought. Tears had been sparse and hard to come by, and it'd been extremely difficult for her to access any real feelings about it, with the exception of her therapy sessions.

Tate's death had been so very different. She was involved in every painstaking detail, and the urge to make sure his funeral honored him perfectly was so strong that she stayed up most nights checking and double checking his notes and the arrangements. She was either crying or near tears in all her waking moments and woke up sobbing on the rare occasions she actually slept.

The day before Tate's funeral, London woke up early and went to the alcove that was still serving as Grant's bedroom. She sat on the edge of his bed, and after a few moments, he opened his eyes and sat up.

"Are you okay?" he asked. "What time is it?"

"It's almost seven. Take a road trip with me."

"What? Honey, what are you—"

"We need to pay a visit to Tate's mother. We can be there and back long before dark if we leave soon."

"London…are you sure you want to do this?"

"I *need* to do this. I owe it to Tate, and he would do it for me." Nurse Patricia had attempted to reach Tate's parents when he arrived at the hospital but couldn't get through. London had tried as well, but their landline had been disconnected, and Tate didn't have any other phone numbers for them in his contacts. As much as she disliked Marsha's treatment of her son, London didn't feel she could send the woman an email telling her he'd died. Something so impersonal wouldn't do justice to Tate's memory. Everything else was set for his funeral. The last thing she had to do was help him connect with his parents one last time, and as much as she dreaded it, she was determined to give it everything she had.

Grant nodded. "Okay. Give me a few minutes to get dressed."

❖

London was painfully aware that the last time she made this journey, less than a month ago, she'd been with Tate. The closer they got to Keys Crossing and the familiar roads where she and Tate had first ridden their bikes and later learned to drive, the more she felt the loss of him. They passed the spot where she'd wiped out on her bike shortly after getting her training wheels taken off and Tate had taken off one of his socks to make a bandage for her. They passed the Dairy Bar ice cream stand—now closed for the fall and winter months—where they'd gathered all the change in their pockets to get one ice cream cone to share. Tate was gone. Tate was everywhere.

Grant pulled into the gravel driveway of the familiar colonial house of Tate's childhood. It looked the same, although the paint was a little chipped, and a few of the plants on the front porch were in bad shape, something that never would have happened when London and Tate were children. Tate's mother always kept immaculate care of the place. Or rather, she demanded that Tate's father keep immaculate care of it.

"You ready?" Grant had given up trying to make conversation shortly after they were out of Columbus and had turned on a political podcast to listen to while London was alone with her thoughts.

"As much as I can be."

They walked up to the house, and as they began to climb the steps to the porch, Tate's mother opened the inner door and peered at them through the screen. "What do you want?" she asked.

"I need to speak to you and your husband, Marsha," London said. "It's important."

She jutted her chin in the air. She was a fairly short woman, but it gave her the impression of looking down at everyone. "I had to put Tatum's father into a nursing home six months back. Early onset dementia."

London's first thought was that Tate didn't tell her, and she realized he must not have known. "I'm sorry to hear that."

"What do you want?"

"Can we come in? Please, this isn't the kind of thing we should talk about in the doorway."

"No." Mrs. Morgan paused and stepped out onto the porch. "You can tell me whatever you want to say right here."

When Tate had his surgeries, London had made fruitless calls, trying to get Mr. and Mrs. Morgan to come to Columbus and support him during his process. She remembered the last attempt she'd made.

"Tell my daughter she has broken my heart," Mrs. Morgan had said. "Tell her she can lose our phone number and forget our address because she won't set foot here again."

London took a deep breath and felt Grant's steadying hand on her back. She was nervous and shaky, but she needed to do this for Tate. "Mrs. Morgan, Tate died a few days ago. He was brutally beaten and left for dead on a hiking trail outside of Columbus. Some hikers found him, and he was taken to the hospital. They operated on him, but the damage was too bad." She swallowed hard. "He stayed in a coma until the next day when he had a seizure and a stroke."

Mrs. Morgan's olive skin had gone very white, but aside from that, she made no acknowledgment of London's words. She didn't move or look away or even blink.

London looked at Grant, her eyebrows furrowed, and Grant stepped out from behind her to speak. "Tate wanted to be cremated, so we had that done. His wake is tomorrow at two, and the funeral will be at four," he said in a soothing tone. "I can come get you tomorrow for the funeral if you like and drive you back after."

This surprised London, and she squeezed his arm as a way of saying thank you. She turned back to Mrs. Morgan. "I would've let you know sooner, but I couldn't reach you by phone."

Tate's mother remained perfectly still, pale and staring. London had never seen anyone in a hypnotic trance, but she imagined this is what it would look like.

"Mrs. Morgan? Marsha?" London took two steps, reaching out, and Mrs. Morgan seemed to come out of her trance. Her head snapped to focus on London, who stopped short of touching her. Mrs. Morgan turned and walked toward her front door, and when she pulled it open, Grant spoke.

"Mrs. Morgan, do you want me to pick you up tomorrow for your son's funeral?"

She turned back to them, not closing the screen door. "I don't have a son. And my daughter died last year. I'll never see her again because when I leave this world, I'm going home to my father, and my daughter is rotting in hell."

In that moment, something broke inside London. She felt too full all of a sudden. For years, she and Tate had lamented all the things they'd like to say to their mothers to somehow make them understand who their children were and how little they wanted from them. A little bit of acceptance and understanding, along with some unconditional love, was all either of them really yearned for. Now London's mother and Tate were both gone, and London was overcome with words they'd never get to say and fractures that would never heal.

"How dare you!" London gasped, not even realizing she was going to speak until the words burst from her lips. "You didn't deserve Tate. You never did."

"Come on, London." Grant pulled her by the arm. "Don't do this."

Even as she let Grant guide her off the porch, she couldn't stop her rage. "You aren't worth one speck of Tate's ashes! Not one goddamn speck!"

Mrs. Morgan stepped inside the house and closed the screen but did not leave the doorway or close the inner door that would've blocked London's voice. Grant had both hands on London's shoulders, pushing her to the car, and just before she got in, she yelled, "This was your last chance to be a mother, do you hear me? Your last chance to be any kind of a mother to him, and you have to live with that."

She got in the car, and before she could say another word, Grant shut the door and crossed to the driver's side, started the engine, and whipped out of the driveway. London caught one last glimpse of Tate's mother, still standing at the screen door, watching them go.

CHAPTER NINE

The sky was bright blue on the day of Tate's funeral, and the air was cool and crisp. Tate had requested a service outside, weather permitting, and while people needed to have their jackets on to be comfortable, most didn't need to have them zipped up.

They were at Schiller Park, in the center of German Village, one of Tate's favorite places. An amphitheater took up the southeast corner of the large park. During the summer, one of the local community theaters put on Shakespeare productions; this past summer, it'd been a month of *Macbeth*, a month of *Hamlet*, and a month of *Midsummer Night's Dream*, which was the one London had dragged Tate and Reggie to see twice. The amphitheater was also a popular place for weddings, but since it was the end of October and Ohio's weather was so unpredictable, nothing was on the schedule for this late autumn day.

The wake was informal, mostly people milling about and exchanging Tate stories. "Remember how he rode his bike everywhere, even in the winter?" And, "Were you there the time he put everyone's name on the list to do karaoke?" And, "He had the best taste in music. Any time I wanted to step up my playlist, he was the one I'd ask for new bands. I never would have discovered Chop Shop if it hadn't been for him."

London smiled as she threaded through the crowd, listening to the memories of the people who loved him. Every person here had been touched by his presence, and she felt as if his energy was moving through all of them.

People began taking seats as the funeral began, and Tate was in every detail. They faced a smiling, poster-sized photo with the Columbus skyline behind him. London sat in the front row along with Reggie,

Grant, Thomas, and Jasmine. Reggie's parents had opted to sit directly behind them, and when the first synthesized strains of Tate's favorite 80s song, "Forever Young" by Alphaville (*not* that garbage from the same name by Rod Stewart, Tate had been fond of saying) came on, Herb and Betty leaned forward and squeezed London's shoulders.

After the song faded away, there was nothing for several moments besides the sounds of people sniffling. London gathered herself up and moved to the front to speak. She stood beside the poster and gazed at it, then turned to the mourners. Her shoulders were tense with the pressure she'd put on herself to make this the perfect day for Tate and the anxiety that she might not be able to pull it off. When she began to speak, though, the words tumbled out naturally if not gracefully. She'd been waiting days to say everything she'd been storing up about her best friend.

"Tate and I grew up together. We met when we were five on the first day of kindergarten. When I thought about speaking today, I wanted to think of stories that really captured who he was, and he was a funny, compassionate, original person. There are so many stories to choose from.

"Like the time when we were eight, I got chicken pox and had to miss the field trip to Amish country, and I was devastated. Tate rode his bike to my house that night, put a black bonnet on his head, pulled out three apples from his backpack, and juggled them…well, tried to juggle them. He got hit in the face with an apple more than once. At the end, he reached into his backpack and pulled out a jar of apple butter and said, 'Ta-da! That's how they make it!'" She paused as the audience chuckled.

"A few days later, Tate didn't come to school, and when I called him that night, he said he'd be out for a few days with the chicken pox. He knew he'd catch it, and it didn't occur to him to not come and try to make me feel better."

She paused to wipe a few tears away. Reggie handed her some tissues, and when she regained her composure, she continued.

"That kind of selflessness didn't end when he got older. I remember only a few years ago, Tate was…" Her eyes overflowed. She gazed out at the people who had loved Tate and shook her head. "I'm sorry, this is just…it's so surreal to talk about him in the past tense. Isn't it? He isn't a *was*. How can that be?

"I want so badly to honor him with you today, to honor his

memory…except that I just can't wrap my head around the fact that he's a memory now. I can't understand that the memory of him is all I have left. Can any of you?"

London looked from face to face and saw people shaking their heads, many crying along with her. She was moving far from her prepared speech, but she couldn't stop herself. She was speaking from the heart, rather than from notes she made, and it felt so much better and authentic.

"It's just not fair that there's no tomorrow with Tate, that he and I won't spend Thanksgiving together eating fried chicken because he doesn't like turkey. It's not right that we won't take our awkward Christmas photos together so we can send holiday cards to all of you." Through her tears, she smiled when the crowd laughed.

"He should be here. That amazing human being should be here. Tate is an is, not a was. Tate is all about now, the present, this moment. Nobody was better at living in the moment than him. I don't know how long it's going to take to understand that he's part of the past now."

She had to pause, burying her face in one of her tissues and letting herself weep. Reggie went to stand beside her, wrapping an arm around her and holding on tight. London struggled to regain her composure and slow the tears that never seemed to fully go away. Finally, she was able to talk again.

"People think funerals are the end, that we've come to say good-bye. I'm not ready to say good-bye to Tate yet. I don't think that's reasonable. My entire life has been so closely intertwined with his. To say that I now have to let go is to oversimplify what he means to me, as if saying good-bye was as easy as snipping a tag off a new shirt.

"Our lives are woven together. It's going to take time to figure out what parts I'll have to untangle myself from so I can let him go and which parts will continue on, sewn together with everything I do from now on. I don't know if anyone else feels like that, but if you do…" Tears threatened to overtake her again, but she fought them away, stood straighter, and pushed her shoulders back. "If you do, give yourself permission to take that time.

"Tate taught me more about family than anyone I'm related to by blood. One of the things he was better at than almost anyone was taking time. Taking time to enjoy the day, taking time to feel what you're feeling, taking time to live in the moment you're in because that's all you truly have.

"Those are things I struggle with, and I know I'll never be as good at them as he is. Was. But I'm going to try. I think it may be the only way I can find my way through this world that no longer has him in it."

She began to walk back to her seat, and Reggie wrapped her in a tight hug. Reggie's parents, Grant, Thomas, and Jasmine came forward and formed a cocoon around her. She saw others begin to join them. She felt more and more pressure and warmth from the crowd surrounding her. Although she could only see a few rows of people, she knew everyone at the service had left their seats to support and hold each other. And somehow, despite the wrongness of Tate being so viciously taken from this world, there was a rightness to this. A gathering in which his loved ones helped each other stand is exactly what Tate would have wanted.

❖

A few days after Tate's funeral, London returned to Hell in a Handbasket despite Jasmine's protests. "Diego will help me mind the shop. Stay home!"

"I would, but I'm even further behind on the spring designs."

"So work on them at your house." Jasmine wrung her hands as she watched London take her place on the floor in the back room at Hell amidst the mess of fabric, paint, and cardstock. "You don't need to be here today."

"Jasmine, I can't stay at home anymore," London said. "I need to come in here with my creativity and close the door on everything else."

"Okay, I understand. I just worry about you, sugar."

"I know." London tried to smile. "I need to try to be okay for a little while. Not happy or normal but just okay for a couple hours."

"Tell me if you need anything?"

"I will."

Several hours later, as she was just finishing the designs for a set of LGBT-themed playing cards, there was a knock to the door leading from the shop to the back room, and Jasmine popped her head in.

"There are two detectives here asking for you." Jasmine looked at the jumble of London's creative mediums which were taking up even more space than usual. "Do you want me to send them back?"

"Are there any customers up front?"

"A few, yeah."

London raised her hands. "Sure, send them back, I guess."

"Ms. Craft." Detective Harper entered the room and stopped short when she saw the mess. O'Connor walked into her, bumping her a little farther in. They carefully stepped as close to London as they could without stepping on sequins or silk. "Sorry to bother you at work."

"It's okay." London stood and followed a narrow path, hopping from blank spot to blank spot on the floor until she reached them. "What's up?"

"We followed up on the lead you gave us," O'Connor said. "The woman from Tinder is Amanda Alexander."

"You talked to her?"

"We did," he said. "In fact, we did more than that. We arrested her."

"And two of her friends," Harper added. "Tate joined them for a hike, and it seems they all felt things were going well. They were having a good time, drinking water and a little beer. It had been several hours, and Amanda and Tate were hitting it off. Amanda's friends, Karl and Dave, got hungry, so they stopped at a picnic table to eat. Amanda wanted to see a waterfall less than a mile away, so she and Tate hiked over there."

"While they were looking at the waterfall," O'Connor continued, "Amanda started to feel romantic. She leaned in and kissed Tate. Tate then informed her of his…" He trailed off and glanced at his partner.

"Of his transgender status," Harper finished. "Amanda grew angry and ran to the picnic area to tell her friends. By the time Tate arrived, Karl and Dave had consumed a lot more beer and were ready to fight whether Tate wanted to or not."

"He wouldn't have wanted to," London said quietly.

"Yes," O'Connor said. "Mr. Morgan's wounds were defensive in nature. You can guess what happened, Ms. Craft. They beat him extensively and left him there."

London nodded, waiting for the tears she was sure were coming. Her eyes stayed dry and instead, that familiar cold numbness fell over her. "What now?"

"That's up to the prosecutor," O'Connor said. "They've all confessed. There will probably be a trial unless one or more of them work out a plea."

"I see."

"We'll leave the prosecutor's card with you." Harper handed her a business card. "He'll be able to tell you more about what happens from here."

London stuck the card in her back pocket without looking at it. "I appreciate the update."

Harper reached out to shake her hand. "We're very sorry for your loss, Ms. Craft."

"Thank you." She tried to think of something more to say but couldn't. After a brief silence, the detectives showed themselves out.

❖

"We don't have to do this tonight," Grant said. He was driving them to Compass for their second volunteer week. "We can stay home in our pajamas and watch TV and drink mimosas."

"I want to go." London paused. "Shit, Grant, I didn't even ask if you want to. I could've come by myself. I'm sorry."

"What do you have to be sorry about?"

"You lost him too."

In the dark, he nodded slightly. "I know."

"Everyone has been so busy taking care of me, making sure I'm okay. You all are grieving too. What's good for me right now is to stay busy. That might not be what's good for you."

"I'm glad to be going tonight. Don't worry."

Michael and Doris had obviously been informed of Tate's death. London didn't know how they knew, but she could see it on their faces as soon as she and Grant got there. "Hey, guys," Michael said, "how are you hanging in there?"

It was so different from the practical joke greeting of their first night that London was mildly uncomfortable.

"We're okay," Grant said. "How are you?"

Doris gathered them, one in each arm, into a tight hug. "We were so sorry to hear what happened. So sorry for your loss."

"Thank you," London said.

"Excuse me," said a voice behind them. "Are we in the right place?" Two rotund, goateed men who could have been brothers stood uncertainly in the doorway.

"Kitchen duty?" Doris asked.

"That's right," said the one with the bib overalls.

"Yep," Michael said. "Come on in. Doris and I will be walking you through your training tonight."

London and Grant exchanged a look before Grant spoke up. "Excuse me, Michael, what about—"

"It seems we have too many cooks in the kitchen." Joan appeared, and London marveled at her ability to show up with no warning. "London, Grant, you'll be coming with me tonight. Why don't you go ahead to my office while I get our new volunteers settled?"

"Okay." Grant nudged London out of the kitchen.

"What the hell is going on?" She followed him down the hallway and glanced behind to make sure Joan wasn't there. "I confirmed us to volunteer on the website today."

"I don't know. Why are you so freaked about it?"

"That woman is unsettling to me."

"You're intimidated?"

"Kinda." She caught a glimpse of his smirk. "Don't judge me."

"I'm not judging, just surprised. I can't remember the last time you were intimidated by anyone."

They sat in the plush chairs opposite Joan's desk. London made another quick glance over her shoulder, and when she saw that the hallway was still empty, she said, "She reminds me of my mother a little." Admitting that helped her put her finger on why Joan made her so uncomfortable. The relief at being able to understand why she was so uneasy any time she was in her presence was so palpable, London felt herself nodding in agreement with her own statement. "Not even in a bad way, necessarily, just…the way she commands a room. The way she expects people to do what she says without asking or even checking to see if they will. It's not a negative thing, it's just—"

"A little haunting?"

"I was going to say triggering, but sure, haunting works too. I need to get over myself, don't I?"

"Sure." Grant smiled and squeezed her hand. "But getting over ourselves takes time."

"Sorry to have kept you waiting." Joan entered the office and closed the door behind her. She sat behind her desk, folded her hands in front of her, and smiled. "How are you?"

"Well," London said, "I'm a little confused. We thought we signed up for kitchen duty tonight. Was there a scheduling mix-up?"

"No, not at all. I thought in the wake of what you've been through, it wouldn't be a bad idea to schedule some other volunteers as a backup."

"How do you know about what we've been through?"

"Regina let me know what happened. I am so, so very sorry to hear what happened. I understand he was like a brother to you both."

"He was," Grant said. "Thank you." London gave a half-smile but didn't speak. She didn't trust herself to talk about Tate without breaking down yet, and she didn't want to be that vulnerable in front of Joan.

"I wondered if you two might be willing to talk to the kids about what happened. Not tonight, of course, but soon."

London's mouth dropped open. "You want us to talk to a bunch of gay and trans kids about our trans friend who got murdered? What would be the benefit of that besides scaring the shit out of them?"

If Joan was offended, it didn't appear in her face or the tone of her voice. "It's very important that we teach them to be vigilant as they start to maneuver through life as queer people. We give them Compass as a safe place, but we also need to help them understand that many places aren't safe."

"With all due respect," Grant said, "a lot of these kids have been kicked out of their homes because they're queer. They probably know that it can be an unkind world out there."

"Certainly," Joan said. "However, it's important to remind them they need to continue to make smart choices in order to be able to protect themselves, as well as—"

"That implies that it was Tate's fault he died," London said. She heard her voice shaking with barely contained anger.

For the first time, Joan's seemingly unshakable self-assurance wavered, and she shook her head rapidly. "I'm sorry, I didn't mean—"

"You meant Tate wasn't smart enough to keep from getting murdered." Her voice continued to rise. She was absolutely seething, and her words poured out like water from a pot that had boiled over. "That he should have known better than do something so irresponsible as go on a date." She stood. "You won't be using my best friend's death as a cautionary tale of what happens to stupid trans people who don't have the sense to keep themselves safe. Not with my help."

She turned and strode out of the room, and Grant followed closely behind her. "Fuck that," she said.

"Shh," Grant said.

"I don't care if she hears me."

"I know, but you care about the kids hearing. Don't you?"

She pressed her lips together and nodded. The group of kids and volunteers were circled around their tables, standing behind the chairs with their heads bowed when Grant and London passed through the living area. Bernadette was speaking this time, and London heard her say, "I wish I'd either been born into a different family or born a different way," as they slipped past the group and out the front door.

❖

London dreaded her visit with Ross so much the next day that she left the house late and drove five miles under the speed limit to get there. She knew this session would rip her open over grief for Tate. She had messaged Ross the previous evening after getting home from Compass and told him she couldn't make today's appointment. In under five minutes, Ross responded that if she didn't come, his normal cancellation fee would be quadrupled, and she would owe him two hundred dollars. She almost texted back telling him it was well worth the price but instead flung her phone down and sighed.

Grant, who'd been sitting next to her assembling a game of Jenga for them to play, had said, "What's wrong, sweetie? You mad because Ross won't take your bullshit?"

"I'm going to bed." She'd stalked to her bedroom.

"It's eight o'clock," he'd called just before she slammed the door.

She hadn't felt any more motivated today, but she'd dragged herself out of bed, swatting shampoo and soap around while she showered and being as loud as possible in the kitchen when she made her coffee. It wasn't until she was walking out the door that she realized Grant had already left for work.

She trudged into the Impressions Therapy Center's building and saw that Ross's door was still closed, which meant he wouldn't even know she'd arrived five minutes late. She picked up a magazine and started to read an article about the positive powers of daily mantras.

"London?" She hadn't heard him open the door. "Ready to come in?"

She seated herself on the comfy corduroy couch, slipping her feet out of her slip-ons and drawing her socked feet up to sit, legs wrapped around each other. Ross, who'd commented on her last several outfits, said nothing about her sweatpants and long-sleeved T-shirt with the words "Fuck Off" scrawled across the front in curly, hot pink letters.

She looked at Ross, and he gazed back, his face neutral and his hands resting in his lap. She wanted him to ask her something. Anything. She wanted him to start this process, to begin the discussion that would lead to her ability to make sense of the reality that Tate was gone, to help her figure out how to work out the business of living a life without the only family she'd had left.

And now she knew why she'd dreaded today. Out there, she could throw herself into work and volunteering and staying busy because busy was what she was using to fill the blank space left by Tate's absence. But here in this room, she had to sit with her grief. She had to look at that blank space head-on and know that it wouldn't just go away.

"I really hate you sometimes," London said, and with those five words, the tears came. "I don't think I can do this." She pushed her words out through the tears, and her voice had that jerking quality that comes from crying really hard, like an engine that tries to turn over but can't quite get going. She took a moment to close her eyes and get her breathing together, but it only amplified her pain, as if shutting her vision down brought her emotions to the surface. "I think I need to quit therapy for a while. Just for a month or two."

Ross handed her a box of tissues and waited for her tears to subside to that weird hiccup-y breathing aftermath. "I'm very, very sorry you lost Tate. I know how much you loved him and what he meant to you. Any death of someone that close is tragic. But he was violently ripped away from you, and that's a quite unbearable kind of loss. It's left you with the equivalent of many open wounds, emotionally, and open wounds are a tricky thing. When left untreated, they fester and get infected, and soon that infection spreads, making the entire body septic and much harder to heal. When treated appropriately, they scab over and scar, and the body regenerates healthy tissue. That's what you need to do now, and I can help you."

"This is where we are again? The open wounds talk?"

When she'd first come to Ross, years ago, every session for several months had ended with her saying she wasn't going to come back. He'd be scheduling her next appointment, having moved from the couch over to his computer at the desk in the corner, and when he'd ask about her availability, she'd say, "It's probably better not to schedule another appointment. Therapy isn't for me, and I don't think I'll be back next week."

Ross would tell her to go ahead and schedule it so he could get her on the books, and as long as she gave him twenty-four hours' notice, she could always cancel. And of course, she did come back, arriving at her assigned time as if they'd never had that discussion. Ross would thank her for keeping her appointment, and he frequently made the open wounds analogy in those days. It had been years since he'd given her that talk.

He nodded and smiled. "It seemed appropriate."

She twisted a tissue. "I don't know how to live without him. And I don't say that to mean I'm suicidal in any way because I'm not. I mean, I literally can't comprehend my life without him in it. It doesn't make sense not having him here."

"I think that's natural."

"Is it? Why don't we ever hear about that?"

"It's a problem. In our country, there's a lot of pressure to move on with life after someone has died. We're not given much in the way of continuing to honor our loved ones or the tools needed to make adjustments in our lives after a loss. I see it all the time, people who lost a partner or sibling or parent years before they started therapy, and they are basically stagnant in their healing because they simply didn't have the tools to help themselves or even the language to ask for help."

"I can't imagine ever healing from this," she said. "I'll always miss him, always wish he was here."

"You will always miss him, and it's normal to wish he was here. Healing isn't the same as not missing someone."

"What is it, then?" Tears pricked her eyes but didn't spill over this time. She was beginning to wish for the numbness to swallow her up again. This pain was unbearable and unrelenting. How long could she go on feeling so completely shattered?

"It's learning to live with the pain. And not only live with it but grow from it. The biggest problem I see when people experience loss or trauma is that they think healing means they go back to who they were before it happened. That couldn't be further from the truth. Trauma requires change in order to heal, without exception. You're not going to be the person you were before you lost Tate. If you think about it, that's an absurd idea. Of course you won't. And the sooner you're able to understand that, the easier your healing will be."

She absorbed this for several moments. "That makes sense."

"Good. We'll keep working on that." He stood. "Let's make your appointment for next week."

She looked at the clock on the wall and saw that their time was indeed up. Good grief, how long had she been crying?

"Okay."

"Same day, same time work for you?"

"Yeah, if I decide to come back."

He handed her the card with her appointment written on it. "Oh, you'll be back."

CHAPTER TEN

That night, Grant and London sat in their pajamas in front of the television watching old *Family Feud* reruns from the 1980s. London was on the floor in front of Grant, who had a huge bowl of blue hair dye resting on an old towel on the couch beside him and a big bowl of popcorn on the other side.

"Don't get the bowls mixed up," London said.

Grant's gloved fingers worked the dye into her hair and massaged her scalp. This had become a biweekly ritual for them. Fantasy hair colors had to be maintained quite often, and before Grant moved in, London had always done it herself. Even when Reggie lived here, it had been a solitary task, done when Reggie was at work or at a meeting. But Grant enjoyed putting his naturally OCD personality to good use by meticulously covering each strand with blue.

"Ugh." London watched Richard Dawson, who'd hosted *Family Feud* in those days, kiss each female contestant on the lips before receiving their answer to the question. "Save me from misogyny dressed in a leisure suit."

"What's funny is the women seemed to love it." Grant shook his head. "I don't get it."

"Me neither, thank goodness." London reached back and grabbed a handful of popcorn. "How does my hair look back there?"

"You're almost done. I'm just doing one last coat all over, and we can set the timer." He added the final layer and took off his gloves. "Like a salon surgeon." He popped the second glove off with a loud snap. "And you're my medical masterpiece."

"I'm honored." She tapped the alarm button on her phone and set the timer for forty-five minutes.

A knock at the door startled them both.

"Did you invite someone over?" he asked.

"Yeah, because I always throw a party when I'm looking this marvelous. Can you see who it is?"

"I'm going, I'm going." He looked out the peephole and turned a frowning face to her.

"Who is it? Jehovah's Witnesses?"

"It's Reggie."

"Seriously?" She scrambled from the floor to stand up. "Great, and me never looking better."

"Should I let her in?"

She rushed to the mirror on the opposite side of the living room only to confirm that she did indeed look as awful as she thought.

There was another knock, more forceful this time.

"London," Grant said in a stage whisper, "what do you want me to do?"

"Ugh. I'm going to go try to deal with this. Let her in, and I'll be right back."

London closed herself in the bathroom just as she heard Grant open the door.

She opened a drawer and saw cotton balls, dental floss, and bobby pins. Not only was that not helpful; she couldn't remember the last time she'd even used bobby pins. The second drawer contained all her hair coloring supplies: gloves, brushes, boxes of dye. She found what she was looking for toward the back of the drawer: a shower cap. She unwrapped it and put it on her head, tucking the edges underneath her hair as much as possible. Next, she found a raggedy old towel that was well on its way to being cut up to use as dusting cloth and wrapped it, bandana-style, around her head.

There. This wasn't exactly the look she would have planned when she saw Reggie again, but it was better than she'd appeared a few minutes before. She drew her shoulders back, making sure to hold her head high, and stepped out of the bathroom.

Grant and Reggie sat on the couch, speaking in hushed voices.

"Why do I get the impression you're talking about me?" London asked.

They turned to her. London thought she saw a flash of affection on Reggie's face before her trademark neutral expression returned. Or maybe that was just wishful thinking.

Grant stood and cleared his throat. "I'm going to run to the store. You want anything?"

London paused to look at Grant's awkward stance, hands in his pockets and mouth drawn, then looked at Reggie and saw she was intensely staring into her lap. "I think you'd better get me some wine."

He nodded, grabbed his coat from the rack near the front door, and left.

She took Grant's still warm spot, turned so she was facing Reggie, and drew her legs up to sit cross-legged, much like she had earlier in the day with Ross. She felt both wary and excited about being so close to Reggie. Something had to be wrong for her to break her stance on them being alone, and even so, London couldn't make the fluttering in her stomach calm down.

"So, what's up?" she asked after moments of silence.

"A couple things," Reggie said.

"Like?"

Reggie pressed her lips together and didn't speak for another moment.

"Come on, Reggie, spill it. You didn't text or call. You just stopped by with no warning. Not that I'm complaining, because damn if it isn't good to see your gorgeous face. But I want to hear what's so important you couldn't pick up the phone."

"Okay, you're right. First, I'll tell you the reason I originally wanted to talk to you today, back when I thought I was just going to give you a call. I spoke to Joan this morning."

"Oh?"

"Yes. She told me what happened last night. I really think you ought to reconsider her proposition."

"I see." The jittery feeling in London's stomach bottomed out and was replaced with heavy anger. All her efforts to have a relaxing evening and decompress after her devastating therapy session were thwarted, and she wanted to distance herself from the discussion that was bringing all that tension back to the surface.

Reggie must have sensed her internally piling some bricks to build a wall between herself and this conversation because she put her hand on London's thigh. Not so high that it felt sexual but high enough that it felt very intimate. London stared.

"Don't pull away. Just hear me out before you make your decision."

Not tearing her eyes away from Reggie's intense gaze, London nodded. "Okay."

"For one thing, this is the kind of volunteer work you could cross off that list of yours, isn't it? You wanted to interact with the youth, make a difference. This is a chance for you to make a real impact on them. You can tell them what they'll be facing out there. Living in Columbus, we feel like we're in this safe little bubble most of the time. They need someone to teach them that even though we're fortunate to live in a place where our community is largely accepted, there are still dangers out there. All of us could stand to be reminded of that, couldn't we?"

London didn't say anything. Rhetorically, she could see Reggie's point, but she felt like there had to be a better way to have a safety conversation with the kids. Preferably one that didn't involve keeping Tate's violent death at the forefront of her mind. The thought of detailing Tate's death made her feel as if she'd be poking a stick into a wound that was still nowhere near healing. It was too soon to add more fractures to her shattered heart.

"And I honestly think it would do you a world of good to be able to honor Tate in that way. To be able to share who he was to you with people who didn't know him and to use his life and death as a way to help kids learn how to deal with being queer in a heteronormative world."

London closed her eyes and massaged her temples with her fingertips.

"Say something," Reggie said.

"I'll think about it. Even if you're right—and I'm not saying you are—I'm not sure I'd even be ready to have that kind of conversation right now."

"That's fair. You thinking about it is all I ask. And you're stronger than you think. I think this would be really good for you, and you'd be really great at it."

"I'll take that into consideration." London smiled despite herself. God, Reggie looked good. Those huge brown eyes had always done something to her; they were practically hypnotic.

"Good." Reggie reached into her jacket pocket and pulled out a piece of paper that had been folded twice. "Unfortunately, that was the easy conversation."

"You call that easy?"

"It's all relative. I got this letter when I checked my email today. I printed out a copy to show you." Reggie handed the paper to London, who unfolded it and groaned when she saw it was from the Law Offices of Larry Kopp.

Dear Ms. Williams,

    As you may know, London Craft has been offered a sum of money if she begins adhering to a life befitting her name and bloodline. This will, of course, mean she must part ways with you.

    I understand it may not be easy for you to separate any bonds you've built with her. Therefore, I'm going to present an opportunity to you, as well. I'd like to offer you twenty-five thousand dollars to discontinue all contact with Ms. Craft. I believe this will provide a significant motivation toward Ms. Craft's completion of the task at hand. You have ten days from the receipt of this letter in which to respond.

    Thank you for your attention to this matter.

    Sincerely,

    Frederick Craft

    Sent via Larry Kopp, Attorney at Law

"Are they fucking *kidding* with this?" London shook her head, read the letter a second time, then flung it toward the coffee table. It didn't make it, fluttering to the floor beside Reggie's feet. She felt like gathering every piece of paper from the offices of Larry Kopp and setting them on fire. Creating a blaze to match her anger seemed fitting. "This is…this is bribery! How can they do this, and through a lawyer?"

"I don't know," Reggie said. "Have you talked to *your* lawyer about all of this yet?"

"No, I haven't." In truth, it hadn't even occurred to her. She had no intention of taking their money, so what would be the point in getting another lawyer involved?

"I think you should. I don't think your father has any concept of how successful you've become. He thinks he can continue to send these letters, essentially harassing you and the people who love you, because he doesn't know you have any recourse. A scary letter from another attorney could go a long way. Besides, right now this is just an annoyance. A pretty major one, obviously—someone needs to teach your family about healthy boundaries—but nothing so crazy that you feel unsafe. Not yet. But we don't want it to get to that point, and it wouldn't hurt to let them know you're not a sitting duck."

"I don't think he'd actually do anything to hurt me." Unless ignoring her for decades counted. She pushed that thought from her mind.

"You're probably right," said Reggie. "Still, a paper trail showing an official response from another lawyer surely wouldn't hurt."

"Okay. I'll call Thomas tomorrow."

"Good."

London was livid, absolutely furious at her father. Yet something Reggie said had made her heart jump with happiness. "So my father is harassing the people who love me. Can I assume that still means you?"

Reggie placed her hand on London's thigh, and maybe London imagined it, but she thought it rested a little higher this time. "You know I love you. That's never changed. I don't think it ever will."

London lifted her hand and lightly stroked Reggie's cheek. "I love you too." Her voice was hoarse. "You know that, don't you?"

"Mostly," Reggie murmured. "Mostly, I do." She leaned in, her hand moving unquestionably higher on London's leg, her mouth brushing London's cheek, her neck, and moving toward London's lips.

The loud opening chords of the chorus of "Turn Down for What" blasted at them, making them both jump and causing Reggie to jerk back to the far end of the couch. It took London a second to come out of her haze, and when she did, she picked up her cell phone from the coffee table and shut off the alarm. It was time to rinse her hair.

"I should go." Reggie grabbed the letter from the floor and handed it to London as she stood. "I figured you'd want this copy to give to Thomas. Tell him he can contact me if he has any questions."

"Are you sure you need to leave? Grant will be back soon, and we can open a bottle of wine and—"

"I'm sure. As much as I'd like to stay, I think I need to go."

"If that's what you want." She didn't do a good job concealing her disappointment. She wanted Reggie to stay, and she definitely wanted to see what might happen if they had time to get their mouths together. She longed to kiss Reggie, ached for her touch. It took a few moments to remove herself from those thoughts. She stood and walked Reggie toward the door. Once there, Reggie opened the door, closed it, and turned.

"What is it?" London asked.

"I've been doing a lot of thinking about marriage and whether it's something I really need."

London inhaled sharply. "And?"

"And I don't know the answer yet." Reggie raised her hand and slid the tips of her fingers down London's cheek, a gesture that made goose bumps rise on the back of London's neck. "But I'll let you know as soon as I do." She leaned forward and brushed her lips against London's for a brief moment before turning to leave. London stood for several seconds, touching her fingers to her mouth.

❖

Grant returned twenty minutes later with snacks and wine, which had given London just enough time to wash and towel-dry her now bluer hair. She grabbed one of his bags, and they went to the kitchen. She had to smile when he went directly for the bottle opener before getting anything out of the bags.

"You're a great friend," she said.

He handed her a glass filled to an obscene level with dark red wine. "Same to you." He tapped her glass with his own and took a drink. "How did things go with Reg?"

"Well, I assume she told you about the letter, and that's what those spy movie voices were all about."

"I can't believe the gall of your family."

"Sadly, I can."

"What are you going to do?"

"Well, Reggie suggested going to my attorney, and I can't believe I never even thought of that."

"Oh." Grant set his glass down with a loud clank. "Are you going to try to set up a meeting?"

"I figure I'll call tomorrow to see what steps I should take." He nodded, and a light went off in her mind. "Shit, Grant. Thomas. I didn't even think about that. I'm turning into as much of a self-serving asshole as my dad and sister."

"You just have a lot going on. I get it." Grant was responsible for connecting London to Thomas's law firm; in fact, that was how Grant and Thomas met. Grant helped London research different legal firms to find the best one to help represent her with her business dealings once he realized she'd been winging it and hadn't bothered to find representation.

"You're getting too big and important to keep using *Legal Forms for Dummies* as your only source of expertise," he'd said, obviously flustered with her. "You've been lucky so far, but that can't last forever."

"It's not luck. I'm meticulous with those forms."

"I'm sure you are, but you're not a lawyer."

"Lawyers," she'd scoffed.

"Hey!"

"I don't mean you. You're not that kind. If you're so concerned, why don't you be my attorney?"

"Because as you said, I'm not that kind. I deal with adoptions and foster care, guardian ad litem work. I could do it for you in a pinch, but you're not in a pinch, and you should stop acting like you are."

Two days later, they'd had a meeting with Mr. Stein and his much younger associate, Thomas Wagner. For Thomas and Grant, the rest had been history.

"Have you talked to Thomas?" She leaned on the kitchen counter and dipped a pretzel in some hummus.

"Not since Tate's funeral, and he left before I could talk to him alone."

"Do you want me to set up a meeting, and you can tag along?"

He laughed. "Would you do that?"

"Sure. What are friends for?"

Grant paused. "No. Don't try to set up a meeting. If he asks for one, great, and I'll come with you. But don't ask if he doesn't offer; just see what he suggests when you call."

"Okay. May I ask why?"

"I'm leaving things in the hands of fate."

She snorted. "Really? Fate hasn't been very good to us lately."

"I know. Which means it's about time for a change of heart."

❖

London hadn't looked at the green construction paper, or even thought about it, in weeks. Now that Reggie had received this infuriating communication from Larry Kopp, it brought the list back to the front of London's mind. After a few glasses of wine with Grant, she said good night and closed herself in her room.

She opened the top drawer of her nightstand, grabbed the file, and pulled out the construction paper. As always, she stared, fascinated, at the list of items she'd felt, at ten years old, were destined to make her life complete.

She traced her fingers over number four, the one she had been glossing over since she'd first discovered the letter. Falling in love with a boy was out of the question, and maybe it was for that reason it didn't bother her much. She and Tate had both dated boys when they were kids because that was what you did. In the time and place where she and Tate grew up, little girls dated little boys. She felt pretty confident that was how number three had ended up on the list.

"Get married," she said softly. Was that on the list for the same reason falling in love with a boy was? Because it was just what people did? "Maybe," she said to herself. "Maybe not."

Being with Reggie tonight had caused a great ache in her. London wanted to tell her to come back home, to stop this foolishness because they belonged together. She hadn't said any of those things because she knew that Reggie was doing her best to at least try to find a way to move forward together right now. She was thinking about whether she really needed marriage, and if Reggie could think about that, surely London could do some thinking of her own.

Could she get married? It was a great question, a question that had been pushed further to the back of her mind with every new blow she'd been dealt. But she knew Reggie wouldn't wait forever, even as patient as she was.

She thought about the For Times Three game she and Tate used to play. If she were to play that game now and someone yelled Reggie's name to her, she'd respond with, "Forever," no question. She knew she wanted to spend the rest of her life with Reggie, so what was the big deal? Why was it so damn hard to say yes to promising forever to the only person she'd ever wanted to be with until death they did part?

"Because I'm the girl who wanted to quit therapy every week," she answered herself out loud. She lay down and buried her face in her down comforter. It was true. Even when something was good for her… and sometimes especially when it was, she always needed an escape route. Even when she knew she needed to go back, she couldn't commit long-term.

Ross's normal policy had been to schedule one month of appointments in advance, getting four dates at a time on the books for each patient. London had forgotten that part until this moment. She'd become so panicked when she was new to therapy, and he tried to schedule four appointments, that Ross said, "Okay! That's okay. Why don't we just do one week at a time for you? When you get to the point where you feel comfortable scheduling further out, we'll do that."

That had been five years ago. Had he simply given up on her ability to commit to long-term therapy? He'd never asked again.

With a weary soul and no real answers, she eventually fell asleep in that position, curled up on top of her comforter, her hand resting on the letter.

CHAPTER ELEVEN

L ondon woke the next morning feeling stiff and cold from sleeping in an odd position on top of her covers. Shivering, she fumbled around until she found her bathrobe, stumbled into the kitchen, and found Grant sitting at the counter eating Frosted Mini-Wheats.

"How can you eat that stuff?" she asked. "It's like somebody poured some sugar on twigs and formed them into little patties. It's like eating a frosted bird's nest."

"Good morning to you too. There's coffee."

"Thanks." She grabbed the biggest mug she could find, poured herself a cup, and sat on the stool beside him. "You're up and ready early." She noted that he was showered and dressed at a time when he normally would've been just waking up.

"I woke up ready to greet the day."

She sipped her coffee. When she got about halfway, she said, "Oh, right. I'm calling Thomas today. That's what you're ready to greet."

He grinned. "Touché."

"I guess I better call, then. Just let me finish my coffee."

Several minutes later, she retrieved her phone from her nightstand where it charged and found Thomas's work number in her contacts. She hit the call button, and Grant reached over to put the phone on speaker. She was surprised when Thomas answered.

"Thomas! It's London. I can't believe you're at work already; it's barely after seven a.m."

"There's not much rest for those who've been put on partnership track."

London glanced at Grant, and he looked as surprised as she was. "Wow, partner! Congratulations."

"Don't congratulate me yet. I'm deep in the proving myself worthy part of it right now, with no end in sight."

"I'm sure you'll make partner. You're a great lawyer."

"Thanks. Spread that around, will ya? Anyway, enough about me. Are you calling me in an official capacity this morning?"

"I am, actually." She filled him in on what was happening as quickly as she could.

When she finished, Thomas whistled. "I knew your family was a piece of work, but this is beyond my expectations."

"I know. They're charming. What do you think I should do?"

"The first thing I want you to do is send me copies of everything. Do you have access to a scanner?"

"At Hell, yeah."

"Great. Scan everything and email it all to me. And forward anything you've received by email."

"Okay," she said. "I can do that today."

"Excellent. Once I receive it all and look everything over, I'll write a letter. Basically a cease and desist, calling them out on harassment and telling them we'll be contacting authorities if they don't cut it out. It will all be very terrifying."

"Sounds good." She'd been taking notes, but when she looked up and saw Grant's sad smile, she dropped her pen and rubbed his back. To Thomas, she said, "Where do we go from there?" She hoped he'd suggest a meeting to formulate a plan of action for Grant's sake.

"We just wait. If all goes the way I hope, we won't have to do anything else. If they respond, we may have to file something in court. But we won't know unless you receive anything else from them."

"I appreciate this, Thomas. Truly."

"That's why I'm here," he said. "You take care now, and call me if you have any other questions."

"Thank you. Bye."

"Good-bye."

London hit the end button and turned to Grant's sullen face.

"He knows I'm staying with you," he said. "He didn't say one word about me, like he didn't even know my name."

"Looks like fate hasn't changed her ways."

"That bitch. I'm done with her."

❖

London scanned the documents and sent them off to Thomas as soon as she got to Hell that morning. She also sent a quick email to Reggie letting her know about her conversation with him and telling her he might be in touch. He hadn't said that, but she liked having a reason to reach out to Reg.

Then she went over her designs for spring again. She'd be sending them out today, and while it was later than she'd hoped or expected, she was glad to be finishing up with them, and happy with how they turned out.

She had enjoyed throwing herself into her work to keep her mind and heart occupied. What she did was so creatively fulfilling, it felt healing to her. She'd checked in with Ross on using her career as a coping tool to keep her preoccupied, and thankfully, he agreed it was fine as long as she continued to do emotional work in her downtime.

It had been a productive morning, and London popped her head into the shop. Jasmine was chatting with some customers near the front of the store, and Diego was behind the cash register.

"Diego!"

He turned and gave her a smile that seemed to take up his entire face. "How are you?"

"I'm hanging in there. How are *you*? Driving the girls crazy, I hear."

He laughed. "You can't believe everything that comes out of the mouths of mothers. Especially mine."

"Your mother is one of the few I trust completely." She couldn't help smiling. Diego had the same peaceful quality Jasmine had, the ability to put people at ease, the same easy smile. She couldn't believe it'd been so long since she'd seen him.

"I was really sorry to hear about Tate," he said. "I wanted to be at the funeral, but with midterms and everything..." He shook his head. "I should have been there."

"It's okay. Really." She wondered if she'd ever stop having the sharp twinge of pain in her heart when anyone talked about Tate. Would it ever stop feeling like a fresh loss any time she heard his name?

Jasmine said good-bye to the customers and joined them at the register. "You see how big and handsome he's growing up?" She played with the dark scruff on his chin.

Diego laughed. "Ma, come on! Hey, would you ladies like me to go pick up something for lunch?"

"Actually," London said, "why don't you two go? I can hold things down around here while you're gone."

"I don't know." Jasmine frowned. "I should stay. Diego can run out, and we can have a picnic in the back or something."

"Jas, I am perfectly capable of running the store for an hour or so while you're gone. You do remember it was just me here for over a year before I could afford to hire anyone full-time."

"Yes, but that was a long time ago, and it was before—"

"Stop it, I'm fine. Go on, now. Grab me a club sandwich from wherever you go or the closest thing they have to it." She practically shooed them out of the store.

As much as she loved Jasmine and appreciated everything she did, London was weary of being treated as if she was made of eggshells. Yes, she'd been through a lot, and yes, she was still struggling with the pain and shock of losing Tate, but it didn't mean she wasn't capable of running the business she'd spent years building.

When they were gone, she stood in the middle of the room, surveying this odd kind of heaven she'd created and named Hell. She ran her hand over a faux fur pillow that said "It's always a good time to question authority." Who would have thought that these strange things she'd started out making for herself and wearing around town while she worked as a server or receptionist at a tattoo parlor would turn out to be both a deeply satisfying and surprisingly lucrative living? She was glad she'd sent Jasmine and Diego out. It had been quite some time since she'd been here alone. She reveled in the pride she always felt when she let herself take a moment to be still in this place.

Her solitude was interrupted by the tinkle of bells signaling that a customer was coming into the shop.

"Welcome to Hell!" she said and saw that it was not a punk or goth or hipster, her normal client base. It was a pretty woman around her age wearing yoga pants and a jean jacket with blond hair pulled up into a high ponytail. She stood in the doorway as if unable to move farther into the room. "Can I help you with something?"

This seemed to jolt the customer, and she stepped toward a display of graphic T-shirts. "I'm just looking. I've been meaning to check out your store for a long time and just never made it in before."

"Glad you were able to stop by. Let me know if you have any questions."

London leaned against the counter in front of the cash register and regarded the woman. She seemed nervous, continuously looking over her shoulder. While London wasn't exactly a stranger to shoplifters, it definitely wasn't the norm around here, especially in the middle of the day in an otherwise empty shop. The customer glanced over her shoulder again, saw London watching her, and moved to a different display of magnets and postcards.

There was something familiar about her, but London couldn't place her. She moved to a pile of sweaters toward the middle of Hell so she could keep an eye on the stranger regardless of where she was and began to refold the already perfectly folded sweaters. *Jasmine would have a fit if she could see me ruining her display.*

"Those T-shirts you looked at when you first came in are on clearance," London said, and the woman jumped. "Sorry, I didn't mean to scare you."

"It's okay. I'm just a little jittery sometimes."

London moved closer. "I'm sorry, do I know you? You look familiar, but I can't place how we know each other."

The customer shook her head rapidly. "Oh, no. No, we've never met."

"Are you sure? I swear I know your face."

"I'm sure." She began backing toward the entrance. "Thank you; you have lovely things, but I'm on my lunch hour. I need to get back to work." She turned and made a sprint to the door, letting it close behind her with a thump and another tinkle of bells. London walked to the door and stepped out just in time to see her running and almost bumping into an elderly gentleman, then turning sharply down a side street in the distance.

❖

"Shoplifter." Diego nabbed one of the chips from London's takeout box. "Definitely a shoplifter."

"That's what I thought at first too," said London, "but I don't think so. She didn't even seem that interested in the merch. It was almost like she was here to…"

"To what?" Jasmine prompted.

"To see me." The thought gave her chills.

Diego grinned. "Someone with a crush on you?"

"That's not what I meant."

"It could happen," Diego said. "Why do you think I started helping out in here for free when I was fifteen?"

"*What?*" London and Jasmine screeched together.

"It's true." He sighed. "The day I found out you were a lesbian was the saddest of my life." He clasped his hands over his heart. "My dream woman would never return my love, even when I got old enough to make things legal."

London blushed fiercely and laughed until she saw the appalled look on Jasmine's face. "Anyway, can you guys keep an eye out for her? I need to know if she comes back."

"Of course, sugar." Jasmine was still looking at Diego with disapproval.

"Your security cameras still work?" he asked.

"Yeah."

"I can go to the time Shoplifter Susie was here and take a screenshot to print out. I don't know how good the photo will be, but it's better than nothing."

Jasmine's eyes widened with pride for her only child once again. "You know how to do that?"

"Sure."

"It's those tuition dollars being put to good use," London said.

"Nah, I had that summer job at White Castle. When Ma found out how often we got robbed, she made me quit, but not before I learned how to grab a screenshot from some security tape."

❖

That evening, Grant and London sat down for a dinner of various cheeses, olives, fruit, and pita bread. And wine, of course; they couldn't forget the wine. It was London's night to make dinner, and she joked that this was her specialty.

"Oh." Grant set down the piece of pita he'd used to scoop up some feta cheese and sliced kalamata olives. "I forgot, this came for you today." He reached to the stack of mail on the counter.

London set down her wine glass and took the envelope with neat, printed words. "Oh my," she whispered.

"You know what it is?"

"It's my invitation to Thanksgiving dinner from Reggie's mom." She tore it open and found the gold card with autumn leaves decorating the edges that she'd received every year since she and Reggie had been together; this year, it was addressed to only her. The same neat handwriting appeared on the center of the card.

London,

I hope you know that you are and always will be a part of this family. It won't be the same without Tate this year, we all know that. Still, we hope you will come and share the day with your family and let us love and care for you.

I'd like to find a way to celebrate Tate as we give thanks for the time we had with him. If you have any ideas, please let me know. We will see you soon.

Love,

Betty

London squeezed her eyes shut when she felt the burning sensation of tears. She hadn't begun to think about how to get through the holidays without Tate. The prospect sent fresh waves of grief over her.

"What is it?" Grant asked, and she handed the letter to him. He read it, then hugged her. When her tears subsided, he asked, "Are you going to go?"

"I don't know." She dabbed her eyes with a napkin. "I guess it depends on Reggie. I hadn't even thought about Thanksgiving yet this year."

"Yeah, that's not surprising. Do you think Reggie knows Betty reached out to you?"

"Maybe. I'm not sure. But I can only go if Reggie's okay with it."

"Well, if she's not, you can always come have a Thanksgiving on the farm with me." He said "on the farm" with a country twang.

"That's right. I forgot you go home for the holidays. I'm gonna miss your mug around here."

"Aw, shucks, Ma. I'll be back before you can say 'let the pigs out.'"

❖

After dinner, London took a long bath and went to her room. She lay on her bed, looking at the card from Betty Williams. After several minutes and without giving herself a chance to think twice about it, she picked up her phone, chose the number she wanted, and pushed send.

"Hello?" Reggie's voice was thick.

"Oh God, I'm sorry, were you asleep?"

"Yes."

London pulled her phone back from her ear to check the time. "It's eight thirty."

"Yes," Reggie repeated. "I'm sick." As if to punctuate this, she sneezed.

"Oh, I'm sorry." She was absolutely mortified. "I'll let you go back to sleep."

"No, go ahead and tell me why you called. Did you get another letter from your father?"

"Oh. Uh, no, nothing that serious."

"Well, that's good." Reggie blew her nose. "So, what's up?"

"I got the invite to Thanksgiving today. You know, from your mom." She rolled her eyes and wondered if she could be more awkward. "I just wanted to make sure it's okay with you that I come before I say yes or no."

"London," Reggie said, and in her sick voice, it sounded like "Luddid," and London pressed her lips together so a giggle wouldn't escape. "Of course it's okay. Mom and I sent that invitation together. I'm surprised you even have to ask."

"Well, last time I was there, you weren't so happy to see me."

"Last time you were here, you didn't give me any warning. This is different. It's Thanksgiving, and you're family; of course I want you there."

"Okay." London hugged herself, thrilled that Reggie still considered her family, and that she'd get to keep this tradition. She hadn't known how much it meant to her until she got the invitation. "I'll come."

"Good."

"I really will let you go back to sleep now."

"Thank you. Oh, and London?"

"Yeah?"

"I'd buy some cold medicine if I were you."

London frowned. "Why is that?"

"Because last night, our faces were very close together, and tonight, I sound like this."

❖

As if she'd been a real-life fortune teller, Reggie's prediction came true. London woke the next morning with a scratchy throat and stuffy nose.

"Dammit, Reggie!" she said, after a seven-sneeze jag. She dragged herself out of bed and went to the medicine cabinet in the bathroom. Allergy medicine, Band-Aids, Neosporin, vitamins (when had she last taken those?), Tylenol, Tums. No cold or flu medicine at all.

Coughing, she went into the kitchen to make some tea.

Grant stuck his head out of his alcove. "You sound awful."

"I sound how I feel. Sorry to wake you. I'm just going to make some tea before I get into the shower."

"Choosing tea over coffee? Now I know you're really sick."

"Because the sneezing and coughing left so much room for doubt."

He raised an eyebrow.

"Okay, and the grouch factor."

"You're not going to work today, are you?" He joined her in the kitchen.

"It's just a cold. I'll live."

"Ugh. At least let me make some tea for you." He reached into the cupboard and pulled down some choices. "Peppermint, Darjeeling, or chamomile?"

"Peppermint, please." She sat on the couch, her head throbbing. She pulled her phone from the pocket of her robe and found Jasmine in her contacts.

"Hello, sugar!"

London was always shocked at how perky Jasmine was in the morning. "Hey, Jas."

"You sound terrible."

"So I've been told." Grant brought her a steaming cup of tea, and she mouthed a grateful "thank you." "Listen, Jas, I'm all out of cold medicine, so I'm going to stop on the way in to work. I just wanted to give you a heads-up I'm going to be late, but I'll be there as soon as I can."

"No."

London paused. "No?"

"No, I don't think so. You're not coming to work today."

"I'm really okay; it's just a cold, and—"

"I don't want to hear it." Her perkiness was gone, and only no-nonsense Jasmine was on the phone now. "You'll only come in here, wear yourself out when you should be resting, and get a bunch of germs all over everything in the process."

When Grant came back to the couch with his own cup of tea, he asked, "What's going on?"

"I'm not allowed to go into my own store today."

"Who's that?" Jasmine asked. "Who are you talking to?"

"Grant."

"Let me talk to him."

She handed Grant the phone. "She asked to talk to you."

She sipped her tea while they spoke. His face went from questioning concern to sheepish amusement. Several minutes went by with him saying the occasional, "Yes, ma'am." Finally, he hung up and handed the phone back.

"What was that all about?" she asked.

"I've been instructed to get you cold medicine and make sure you get the proper amount of rest and vitamin C." He grinned.

"Seriously?"

"Yep."

"For the love of baby Jesus, I'm a grown woman."

"Tell that to Jasmine. And please, please let me be there when you do."

She sighed. "Well, if you have time before work to grab some meds for me, I actually would appreciate it. If not, I can go. And you definitely don't need to babysit me all day."

"I'd love to babysit you, but I can't. I have some meetings today that I can't miss. But I'll get you some meds and just have to trust you to look after your own self today."

❖

"Jeez, did you rob CVS?"

Grant had dumped the plastic drugstore bag onto the blanket covering London's legs. DayQuil, NyQuil, cough drops, Sudafed, vitamin C tablets, a thermometer, two additional varieties of tea, and a little ChapStick-shaped device that said to press to your nostril and inhale to relieve sinus pressure, lay atop the blanket.

"I don't want to give Jasmine any reason to hunt me down for not taking good enough care of you. I'm already nervous she'll find out I'm not staying home today." His eyes darted around the room as if he was scared someone was listening.

London laughed as he walked toward the front door, and her laugh turned into a coughing jag.

"Cough drops," Grant ordered. "And one of the Quils. Day or Ny, I don't care, but start taking one of them."

"I will." Her voice was raspy. "Thank you for all of this."

"You're welcome. I'll get home as soon as I finish these meetings, okay? Rest as much as you can. Love you."

"Love you too."

Since the goal today was resting, London decided she'd take some NyQuil and save the daytime formula for tomorrow, when hopefully, Jasmine would release her to return to work. She took a dose, popped a cough drop in her mouth, and leaned back on the pillows Grant had placed behind her before leaving for the drugstore. She turned on the TV, flipped through the choices offered by Netflix, and stopped on *Charmed*, one of her old favorites. Less than halfway through the first episode, she dozed off.

She awoke several hours later with her television asking her if she was still watching. She checked her phone and saw that not only was it nearly three o'clock, but she had received an email from diego.santiago@theosu.com. Curious, largely because she hadn't given her email address to Diego, she opened it.

> *London,*
>
> *I got the screenshot from the security camera today. Ma says you're home sick, and I shouldn't bother you, but I thought you'd want to have a copy of it. Plus, she doesn't understand that an email is different from a phone call; you can open it and read it whenever you want, lol.*
>
> *Anyhow, I did a few screen captures. One is of her full body, and one is as clear a face shot as I could get. It's fuzzy (remind me to talk to you about better cameras now that you're making Hollywood money), but you can make out her features a little bit.*
>
> *Hope you feel better soon.*
> *Diego*

London pulled out her laptop to open the attachments so she could get a better look. The full body picture showed the trim woman she remembered glancing over her shoulder. She looked at it only for a moment before closing that picture and opening up the one showing the woman's face.

Once again, she looked familiar. But how did she know her? It certainly wasn't from Cavan or Compass or any of Reggie's Stonewall functions. The image was blurry, as Diego said, but it was clearer than expected. Using the mouse, she traced the woman's features: small, almond-shaped eyes, fine nose, and thin lips.

"How do I know you?" she asked aloud and promptly went into a coughing fit. When it ended, she realized more than enough time had elapsed for her to take another dose of NyQuil. She did so and once again leaned back on her glorious pile of pillows. She fell asleep looking at the stranger's face.

Twenty minutes later, she snapped awake and sat bolt upright. She ran her fingers across her mouse screen to wake her computer from its slumber. The woman stared at her, and London knew who she was.

"Holy shit."

Grant got home just as Detectives Harper and O'Connor were leaving and rushed to where London sat on the couch. "Are you okay? What's going on?"

London turned her computer to show Grant the grainy photos. "I figured out who the mystery shopper is. It's Amanda Alexander, the woman Tate went on a date with."

Grant gasped. "The one who…"

"Stood by while her buddies beat Tate to death. Yes."

Grant dropped down into a seated position with a loud thud. "I thought she was in jail."

London shrugged. "Apparently, she posted bail. She's not allowed to contact anyone connected to Tate's case, though. The detectives are taking the photos to the prosecutor to show she violated the terms of her release; they think they'll be able to get her locked up until the trial."

Grant put his hand on her leg, and even through the thick blanket, she could feel how cold he was from being outside in the brisk November chill. "Are you okay?" he asked gently.

"What the hell was that woman doing in my shop?" she asked. He rubbed her leg and said nothing. "I didn't even know she was out of jail until today." She was shaken. She didn't think Amanda Alexander posed a threat to her, but she realized today how vulnerable she was.

"The detectives should've told you," Grant said.

"They tried." When he seemed confused and surprised, she stared at the blanket. "I haven't been answering their calls."

"But, why—"

"I don't know!" She realized how loud she was and lowered

her voice. "I don't know." But she did. It was the same reason she'd changed the subject when Diego started talking about Tate's funeral. She could talk about Tate as the living, vivacious person he used to be, but talking about his death made her feel cold in a way that seemed to promise she'd never be warm again.

Grant was silent for a moment, still rubbing her leg. His voice was soothing when he spoke. "I haven't read a single news article about Tate's murder. Not online and not in the *Columbus Dispatch.*"

"You haven't?" She was surprised. Grant was a news junkie; he consumed his news like she consumed coffee. He read world, national, and local news in three languages and from more sources than she previously knew existed.

"Nope."

"Why not?"

He shrugged. "I just can't right now."

She was relieved to know he felt the same way she did, and her heart filled with love for her friend. She didn't know what she would've done the last couple months if he hadn't been living here. She rested her head on his and stayed like that until a coughing fit made her sit upright.

"Want me to make you some chicken noodle soup?" he asked.

"Are there crackers?"

He smiled. "I think you're on the mend already."

CHAPTER TWELVE

"Do I look okay?" London asked for the dozenth time. It was Thanksgiving morning, and she was getting ready go to the Williams family gathering.

"You look great." Grant didn't look away from the mirror while he straightened his tie.

"You didn't even look at me!"

He sighed. "Do you look different from the last time you asked?"

"Point taken." She sidled up beside him. "Give me some mirror?" He stepped over a bit so they could both see their reflections. London unclipped her barrettes and refastened them in exactly the same places. Grant finished with his tie, and they turned to look at each other.

"Perfect," they said in unison.

She tried unsuccessfully to stop wondering if Reggie would notice the extra time she'd put into trying to look nice. The focus of today was going to be family and honoring Tate, and yet she couldn't help wanting Reggie to be happy to see her.

They put on their coats and walked outside together. Before they parted ways, Grant said, "Now, are you sure you don't need me to come back tonight? Because I can make this a day trip if I have to."

"Don't be silly. You'd be spending six hours in the car, round trip, and I'll be fine tonight."

"Okay. I just know how much you love dealing with Joan by yourself."

She laughed. "Don't worry, I can handle Joan." She'd received a mass email to all of Compass's volunteers, asking for people to help with Thanksgiving dinner. It was a tough time to get enough volunteers between people wanting to be with their families and the number of people it took to put out a holiday meal. London hadn't returned to Compass or spoken to Joan since she'd stormed out weeks before, but she was touched by the thought of those kids being unwelcome at home for Thanksgiving. She remembered all the years it had just been her and Tate for holiday meals.

She'd written a personal response to Joan, telling her if she was welcome back, she'd like to come help. Reggie's family ate at noon, so she'd have plenty of time afterward to help prep and serve a meal. Joan responded that they'd be happy to have her volunteer.

Grant and London hugged each other.

"Happy Thanksgiving, babe," he said.

"Happy Thanksgiving. I'll see you tomorrow night?"

"Tomorrow night, we'll have a post-holiday slumber party."

London pulled into the Williams's driveway a little after eleven o'clock. She parked behind Reggie's bright blue Toyota FJ and smiled. The SUV was spotless, as usual. Even in the winter, when everyone else's car was caked with salt and dirty snow, Reggie kept her vehicle almost impossibly clean.

London knocked on the door, and when Reggie opened it, all the air left London's lungs. "You cut your hair!" she said and mentally kicked herself. *Way to state the obvious.* "You look gorgeous."

Reggie had worn her hair in shoulder-length braids for as long as London had known her, and based on pictures she'd seen, it had been the same style for much longer than that. The sides were now shaved in a perfect fade, and the top was a few inches long and spiked up in a glorious cascade.

"Thank you." Reggie smiled and pulled London inside. Reggie looked behind her, then leaned in and kissed London on the lips, lingering a little before pulling away. "Happy Thanksgiving."

"Happy Thanksgiving." London flushed with surprised pleasure. She had to make herself take a half step back. The allure of Reggie's lips was powerful, and she wanted more, but this wasn't the time. "I thought you didn't believe in kissing me right now. Not that I'm complaining, trust me, but..."

Reggie shrugged, and her eyes shone. "It's Thanksgiving, we had mimosas at breakfast, and you're standing there looking all beautiful."

London laughed. "And that's the combination it takes for you to drop your principles?"

"I just want to be happy today." The smile left Reggie's mouth but stayed in her eyes. "Okay?"

London nodded. "Okay. Let's be happy."

Reggie took her coat and put it in the hall closet.

"Regina?" Betty called from the kitchen. "Is that London?"

"Yes, Mama."

"Well, bring her in here."

Reggie grabbed London's hand, and they walked into the kitchen together. Betty, busy at the stove, turned to them and smiled. "Now, that's what I like to see," She turned toward the living room. "Herb!"

"What?"

"London's here. Come say hello."

"I'm watching the game."

"The game hasn't started yet."

"I'm watching the pregame."

Betty looked to the heavens. "Lord, give me strength with this man and his football today."

London laughed. "How about I go in and say hi? Here, before I do, I brought your favorite wine." She handed Betty the bottle of Beaujolais.

"Oh my, how thoughtful you always are, dear." Betty picked up the bottle, inspected the label, and smiled. "You didn't have to go to the trouble."

London waved her hand. "It's the least I can do."

"Oh, hey," Reggie said, "did you bring the—"

"Yeah, it's in the trunk of my car."

"I'll get it. Keys?"

"In my coat pocket."

Reggie kissed her on the cheek. "Be right back."

London watched her go. She felt a palpable shift in the energy between them. Nothing in Reggie's body language or actions indicated she wanted them to remain apart. The distance of the last few months seemed to have dissipated. London wanted to pull Reggie outside so they could talk about it, so she could confirm this wasn't in her head, but it would have to wait until after Betty's Thanksgiving dinner.

"You go on and sit with Herb for a spell," said Betty. "Regina and I can keep working on the meal."

London raised her eyebrows. "Is this your way of telling me not to help you cook?"

"It sure is." Betty put her hands on her hips. "What are you gonna do about it?"

"Not a thing."

"Good. Now, go on. Reggie's aunt and uncle will be here soon, and we should be ready to sit down and eat shortly after."

London walked into the living room where Herb sat in his recliner, facing the television, which was on mute. London bit her lip to keep from giggling when she saw what was on it. Herb was watching the Macy's Thanksgiving Day Parade. She stepped a little farther into the room, and one of the old wooden floorboards squeaked. Herb jumped, fumbled with the remote, and started mumbling about commercial breaks. When he looked behind him and saw London standing there, he grinned and patted the seat of the recliner beside him, and London took it.

Herb leaned over and said, "I never miss this damn parade."

"Really?" Now she was grinning.

Herb bobbed his head up and down. He pointed his thumb toward the kitchen. "They're always too busy with the bird to notice, thank God. Otherwise, I'd have no dignity left."

"Your secret's safe with me as long as you let me watch it with you."

"Deal!" He stuck his hand out, and she shook it.

They sat for a while and watched the parade, mostly on mute. When a marching band came on, Herb turned the volume up to level two. She remembered that he'd played the trumpet in the Army band, so it wasn't a surprise. At this quiet level, though, she could barely hear, and she wasn't sure how Herb could hear at all.

"I turn up the volume on my hearing aid," he proclaimed when she asked him about it.

"I didn't even know you could do that."

"Oh, yes." He bobbed his head again. "You can hear a conversation in another room with it turned up high enough." He winked.

"Oh, yeah?"

"Mm-hmm. Or a conversation in the foyer just outside the room."

"Oh." She wasn't sure how to respond, or if to respond, so she kept her eyes on the majorettes on the TV.

"My daughter loves you very much." He put the marching band on mute.

"I know. I love her too."

"She's set on marrying you."

Here it comes. Here comes the part where he tells me to stop being a fool, get my act together, and make an honest woman out of his daughter. She couldn't bear to hear it from Herb. She was open to considering marriage, which was a first, but the thought of getting a lecture about getting her act together so she could stop breaking his daughter's heart filled her with forty kinds of anxiety.

"You've never been the marrying kind, though, have you?"

Her eyes left the television and went to Herb's understanding face. "No, I haven't."

"I wonder why my daughter would be so bent on marrying someone when she knew all along that marriage was never a part of that someone's plans." He scratched his beard in an almost caricature-like motion.

"Have you ever asked her why?"

He stopped scratching. "Have you?"

She blushed. "Not in so many words."

"Well. Maybe you should. In so many words."

Before she could say anything else, a knock at the front door interrupted them. She had to giggle when Herb jumped and fumbled with the remote again.

Moments later, Betty called from the kitchen. "Herb! Althea and Gordon are here."

"Damn," he whispered. "And I haven't even gotten to see Santa yet."

London stood and put her hand on his shoulder. "I'll cover for you."

He smiled up at her. "My daughter is very lucky."

❖

London almost cried when she saw the table. Betty always set a beautiful table, but this year was special. London had a tablecloth made with photos from previous Thanksgivings, and they all had Tate in them. She'd asked Reggie and Betty to send her pictures from years before, and they had delivered. His smiling face was everywhere. She ran her hands over a clear layer of plastic.

"So it won't get dirty," Betty said.

London shifted her plate to the side so she could see the picture from last year in which Tate had one hand inside the uncooked turkey, and the other hand was giving a thumbs-up. At Reggie's place setting beside her was a photo from…was it three? No, four years ago, in which Reggie and Tate had each taken a leg and were sitting on London's lap, giving her a kiss on the cheek.

As if that wasn't enough, to the left was an empty chair and a full place setting. A single piece of fried chicken—Tate's preference over turkey—on the plate.

"It didn't seem right not making his chicken," Betty said. "I couldn't help myself."

"Are you okay?" Reggie put her hand on the back of London's neck.

She wiped a few tears away. "My emotions are tricky these days."

"Understandable," said Aunt Althea. She sat on the other side of Tate's chair. "What a sweet boy he was."

"Let's have a toast." Betty raised her glass. "To Tate. We loved you then; we love you now. We'll always miss you and keep you alive in the ways we can."

London brushed more tears from her eyes and fought the sobs that threatened to escape. She wanted to honor Tate without it leading to a breakdown every time.

They clinked their glasses, and everyone took a drink.

Uncle Gordon led them in prayer, Herb carved the turkey, and dishes were passed around the table.

"London, what are your plans for the rest of the day?" Betty cut a piece of turkey and swirled it in the lake of gravy on her plate. "I know you and Tate always used to cut a Christmas tree after we ate. You're welcome to stay here as long as you like, you know."

"Cut down a tree this early in the year?" Uncle Gordon asked. "Seems like it would be dead before Christmas."

"Oh, it was," London said. "We'd cut down another one around December fifteenth or so."

"I didn't even know any places were open on Thanksgiving to cut down a tree," said Aunt Althea.

"We…" London scrambled for a moment. "We know a family who has a farm." She glanced at Reggie, who hid a smile by shoving sweet potatoes into her mouth.

Knowing a family who owned a farm was technically true. They'd hopped into London's old Jeep and driven the few hours to her family's estate where there were clusters of lovely blue spruces on the edge of the property. It was so far out on the acreage that London knew they'd never miss the trees, and she got an awful sort of pleasure from doing it.

It was a bittersweet memory. This was one of the best, most deliciously wicked traditions she and Tate cooked up, and she was glad for all the years they'd stolen a tree from her parents. The realization that there was one more thing she and Tate would never get to do together again made a fresh wound on her spirit.

Every year on the drive there, Tate would have a very short, very intense panic attack.

"How do I let you talk me into these things?" he'd ask.

"Because it's fun."

"But if we get caught—"

"We're not going to get caught," she'd say.

"But *if* we do, would your parents call the cops?" Tate's knuckles would go white as he gripped the steering wheel.

"We're not gonna get caught. Nobody ever goes out there. You know how high the grass is. It's so distant from the house that even the guy they hire to mow doesn't go that far."

"Okay, but on the off chance we did get caught?"

"I'd tell them I was finally taking my part of the trust fund."

But they'd never gotten caught in the four years since London had gotten the brilliant idea to start cutting down one tree every Thanksgiving. Once the first died, Tate, Reggie and London would go to a legitimate Christmas tree farm and cut down their second tree.

"So you'll be spending the day with us?" Herb asked.

"Well, as wonderful as that sounds," she said, "I'll be volunteering tonight. Compass."

"Really?" Reggie asked.

"Yeah. I'm sorry, I should have mentioned it to you."

"No, it's okay. I just didn't know you'd be going back there."

She shrugged. "They were short-staffed for Thanksgiving and needed help cooking and serving."

"You think they'd mind an extra set of hands?"

London flushed with giddy surprise. "You want to come?"

"If that's okay with you."

"It's more than okay!" She couldn't suppress the thought that had been running through her mind since she arrived at the Williams's house today: her Reggie was back. She tried to fight the giddiness because the last thing she needed was to build herself up for more heartbreak and disappointment, but she couldn't help it. All signs were pointing to reconciliation, and she was thrilled.

"It's a date," Reggie said.

They stared at each other, smiling like idiots. When Uncle Gordon cleared his throat, they turned back to their plates and shoveled food into their happy faces.

❖

There were five more kids that night than had been there previously. There would be no room for volunteers to sit.

"Praise David Hasselhoff, you're here!" Michael pulled London into a viselike hug. "I was afraid I'd be the only person in that kitchen tonight."

"What? Where's Doris?"

"She's with her kids and grandkids. When she asked me if I thought it would be okay for her to go, I said, sure, no sweat; I'll be able to wrangle the volunteers by myself. Except nobody has shown up. None of the regulars. None of the irregulars, except you, and your friend…"

"Reggie." She reached out to shake Michael's only to receive a bear hug instead. When she recovered, she said, "What do you need us to do?"

"Fortunately, Doris was here to help me prep most of the dishes last night, and the turkey has been cooking all day." He walked them toward the kitchen. "I need one of you to get the dishes and silverware organized and serve up plates when it's time and the other one to help me make sure nothing burns." Michael stopped and frowned, then turned his attention to Reggie. "How are you at not burning things?"

"Really good," Reggie said.

"Great. You'll be the woman helping me take things out of the oven and off burners at the right times."

"Looks like I'm on dish duty," London said. "Which is fine with me."

They set to work, Michael and Reggie basting the turkey, stirring and taste-testing the side dishes, and putting hot bowls and saucers onto oven pads; London set the tables, got the sides into their serving dishes, and filled glasses with water and juice. Finally, they carried out the turkey together, to the applause of the kids. London was touched by the smiling faces. When she spent her first Thanksgiving without her parents and sister, she hadn't been nearly this brave or gracious. These kids were amazing. Joan stood near one of the tables, clapping along and smiling. For a change, London didn't mind the fact that she'd come out of nowhere and smiled back.

The kids each took a spot behind a chair, bowing their heads. This time, it wasn't one of them but Joan who spoke. "I'm grateful tonight for all of you. The volunteers who made this meal possible and each of you kids, who amaze me every day with your strength, your honesty, and your bravery. Thank you for being real and true to who you are, even in the face of adversity. You are deeply loved and appreciated."

"Let's eat!" Quentin said after several moments of silence. The other kids laughed, sat, and started passing food. Michael went over and carved the turkey.

"London, Reggie," Joan said. "May I have a word?"

"Uh, sure."

They followed her down the long familiar hallway, and London felt as if she were going to the principal's office. She tried to shake it off. It had been such a pleasant day, and she'd made the decision to give Joan the benefit of the doubt.

Joan closed the door behind them in her office, the first time she'd done so since London's initial interview. London stared at Reggie with a "we're in trouble" look, and Reggie swatted her arm and sat in one of the chairs facing Joan's desk. London took the other chair.

"Thank you both for coming tonight," Joan said. "London, I know we've had our challenges, but I appreciate you coming back and helping on such a critical day."

"No problem."

"And, Regina, please tell your parents I appreciate them sharing you with us so you could be a part of it, as well."

"I will."

"Now," Joan said, drawing her shoulders back, "I'm sure you're wondering why you're in my office."

"No more than any other time," London muttered. Reggie rested the tip of her shoe on top of London's, and London closed her mouth. She was still tender from their last interaction, but she pinched her lips to keep her sarcasm under wraps. Joan seemed to have left the tension from their last meeting in the past, and London had to at least try to do the same.

"As you saw out there, we are completely full tonight. To get right to the point, we are beyond max capacity, which is not a huge deal for a dinner, but it is a very, very big deal in terms of sleeping arrangements. We simply don't have enough beds for all the children here right now, and that's not just a less than ideal situation; it is absolutely dire. While we obviously can't turn a child away, we also can't be overcrowded. If word got out, it could affect our licensing, and that could mean no housing at all for any child in need.

"We already have an emergency family in place for one child. We just need one more." She sat back in her chair and stared at Reggie and London.

"Wait a minute," London said, "you're not suggesting what I think you're suggesting."

"I believe I am. There are no other options at the moment."

"But…but don't foster families need to be trained? Parenting classes and stuff?"

"Ideally, yes, but as I said, this is a crisis. And you wouldn't be a foster family per se; you'd simply be providing temporary housing on a very short-term basis."

"But we aren't even trained in CPR," London sputtered. "How can we possibly be responsible for a kid?"

"Actually," Reggie said, "I'm CPR certified."

London gaped at Reggie. "Seriously?"

"We sponsor youth events at Stonewall. We all took the class."

"Good," Joan said. "There are, of course, a few forms to fill out: release forms, an agreement to take the child for up to six months if needed—"

"Six *months*?" Reggie seemed uncomfortable for the first time since this conversation started. "I thought we were talking about a few nights."

"Most likely, it won't be six months, but it could be a month or two," Joan said. "Things are tough during this time of year. Kids get into the holiday spirit, all the glad tidings and good cheer, and they start to think their parents will be more accepting. So they come out and end up on the street just before Christmas. We make it a six-month contract, just to be sure we don't take a child out of a home to put them back into it a week later."

London took a deep breath. "Okay. I understand all this, and I definitely don't want any of these kids to have to spend Christmas on the streets. And Reggie and I, we do want to help. But…you're sure there's nobody more qualified and who knows these kids better? What about Michael? Or you?" She felt quite certain there had to be a more qualified candidate. In this moment, it seemed almost anyone was more qualified than she was. What did she know about kids?

Joan looked baffled for the first time. "I thought you knew about my living arrangements. Certainly, Regina does."

Reggie nodded.

"What are your living arrangements?"

"Why, I live here. So does Michael. We have our own living quarters, each adjoining one of the sleep rooms we provide for the children."

"What?"

"A bunch of preteens and teenagers in a room together all night? The only way to keep them out of trouble is to have someone right there within hearing distance."

"But you?"

Joan smiled. "When Compass opened, there was no one else to do it. And now...it's my place in the world." She stood. "Listen, I know this is a lot to ask. I'll go check on the kids and give you two time to discuss. You can give me your answer when I come back."

London took this in. She knew Joan must not have much of a life outside this place, but she hadn't realized the extent of her commitment to her vision and to these kids.

"London?" Reggie asked. "I'm willing to do this, if you are. Together."

This pulled London out of her thoughts. "Together? You'll come home?"

Reggie nodded.

London's heart swam in what seemed like an ocean of emotions. This was what she'd wanted for months, for Reggie to come home. On the other hand, this wasn't the right way, was it? She felt as if she might get carried away in her desire to be back with Reggie, but before she did, she wanted to grab onto something and think clearly. "But this would be the only reason?"

"Does that matter?"

"To me it does."

Reggie sighed. "Okay, maybe it's the only reason I'm coming home *tonight*. But I want to help one of these kids, and I think you do too. I can't take them back to my parents' house, and I don't think you're prepared to take care of a kid on your own. It would be temporary, and even if you aren't crazy about the reason why I'm coming back, it will still give us a chance to have a trial run of sorts."

"A trial run, huh? A trial run to see if the relationship that worked beautifully for over six years is still going to work?"

Reggie's mouth tightened. "Do you want to do this or not?"

"I do, but I'm scared of getting my heart broken." London thought of all she'd suffered in the last few months and all she'd lost. She'd reached her limit of the heartbreak she could sustain for a long time. She loved Reggie and wanted her back, but not if it meant they would be back to a separation in a few months because they hadn't worked things out.

"I'm scared of the same thing. Look, I've been thinking a lot about our situation. My pride and my heart were really hurt after I proposed, and I needed some distance and time. I've been working my way back to you and to us. If you agree to this, then yes, we'll be back together, but it's only an acceleration of what would have happened eventually, as far as I'm concerned."

London stared a long time. "Yes."

"Really?"

"Yes, let's do it."

"Oh, that's wonderful!" Joan stood behind them, her hands clasped.

"How do you do that?" London asked, and this time she paid no attention to the tip of Reggie's shoe on her foot.

Joan looked puzzled. "Do what?"

"Come out of nowhere like a ninja."

"A ninja." Joan chortled. "My, that's a first." She moved to the credenza to London's left and pulled out a sheaf of papers. "Here we are."

London realized her question wasn't going to be answered.

"Michael will be here in a few minutes to assist us." Joan pulled a pen from her inner coat pocket. "He's a notary public and can make these papers official until we're able to get them filed at court. The two of you will have to agree to take a class for temporary custody within forty-eight hours, but it's an online class that only takes a few hours."

"That's all the time it takes to get certified to take a kid home?" Reggie asked.

"In a pinch, yes," Joan said. "Upon my recommendation, which I am obviously giving."

"What's the child's name?" London asked.

"Quentin."

"Quentin! But he's been here for a while. I thought we'd be taking one of the newer kids."

"We try to place the younger children with less experienced caretakers," Joan said. "It seems counterintuitive, but older kids bring older kid problems, so we like to place them with more seasoned families. And you'll love Quentin; he's a doll." She saw London's panicked face. "What's the matter?"

"Quentin and I have a history, remember?" Her voice sounded shrill in her own ears, a reflection of her anxiety. Joan was asking her take home the boy she'd sent running from the room in tears. Her nervousness was turning into full-fledged panic.

"I do. And I wouldn't be sending him home with you if I wasn't absolutely certain that history isn't going to affect your relationship. He was having a hard day when the incident happened, and he's truly a sweetheart." Joan smiled, and London noticed for the first time how maternal she looked when she talked about the kids. "I'm not supposed to play favorites, you understand, but Quentin? It's hard not to love him a little harder than the others."

Michael appeared, and they went through all the paperwork. London was astonished at how quickly it all went once they made the decision. Could it really be this easy to take someone else's child home? Apparently, it was.

Joan and Michael stood with Reggie, and London followed suit. "Now that we've gotten all that done, why don't we go talk to Quentin?"

"Does he know about these arrangements?" Reggie asked.

"I told him it wasn't certain," Joan said, "but, yes, he has an idea. I wanted to prepare him, either way."

"Okay." London grabbed Reggie's hand and tried to sound more confident than she felt. "Let's go."

"Here we are," London said when they arrived home.

Joan had been right; things had gone smoothly when they told Quentin. It had taken only minutes for him to gather his few possessions and say good-bye and Happy Thanksgiving to his friends. He had the most difficult time saying good-bye to Joan.

"We'll see each other again soon." She got teary eyed as she hugged him. "And I wouldn't let you go if I didn't know you'd be in good hands."

"I know," he said.

Now Quentin stood in the living room, surveying everything. "It's nice. Where will I sleep?"

"Shit," London said. "Shoot, I mean. Shoot." Quentin grinned. "Sorry, I'll tone down the potty mouth."

"I don't mind, Nothing I haven't heard before."

"Right, of course. You're twelve, not five. Reg, would you mind showing Quentin around? I need to step out and make a call real quick."

"Sure. Everything okay?"

"Grant," London mouthed.

"Shit," Reggie said.

Quentin looked up from the book he'd grabbed from the coffee table. "Is this just something you guys do at night? Curse for a little bit? Because I have earbuds; I can listen to some music while you get it all out."

Reggie laughed. "I like you, kid. Come on, I'll give you the grand tour."

London stepped onto the tiny slab of concrete that the condo association called a patio and called Grant.

"London?" He was breathless. "Are you okay?"

"Yeah, I'm fine," she said in a low voice.

"Really? Because you sound like a Bond girl on a secret mission a few scenes before she gets killed and dumped into a pool."

"I'd love to banter about double-oh-seven, but I only have a few minutes and a long story to tell you, so could you please let me talk?"

"Okay, go."

"Thank you." As quickly as she could, London told Grant the entire story, leaving out the part where both she and Reggie had completely forgotten Grant was staying with her. When she finished, she said, "What are we gonna do? Would you be willing to crash on the couch for a while? Quentin needs his own bed, according to the contract. We're pushing it a little with him staying in the alcove, but it's okay as long as he has his own bed to sleep in."

Grant said nothing.

"Oh, sweetie, I am so, so sorry." She felt terrible. "If this hadn't been a completely desperate situation, I would never have—"

"No, it's really okay. The truth is…well, the truth is, Thomas moved out of our apartment a few days ago. That place is mine, you know."

"I'd forgotten."

"Yeah. Well, he's out. Out of the apartment, out of the relationship, out of my life."

"Why didn't you tell me?"

"I wasn't ready for it to be real yet. Apparently, I'm in the denial stage of my grieving. Besides, you and I have so much fun together, and I didn't worry about you as much when I was there."

"You don't need to worry about me at all."

"That's not how we work, and you know it," Grant said.

"True story." They'd saved each other the last few months. She was grateful that he had been there with her, and she didn't know if she'd ever be able to find the words to tell him how very much he'd helped her stay earthbound when she felt in danger of floating away.

"This is just the prompting I need to get back to real life. I had painters come after Thomas moved out, so it'll have a fresh smell that doesn't remind me of him. It's time."

"Are you sure? Because regardless of everything else that's going on, my couch is still free."

"I'm sure," he said. "It'll be a clean start for everyone. I'll swing by and grab my stuff when I get back into town tomorrow night."

"Tomorrow night is our slumber party."

"You still wanna have it?"

"Sure. Reggie wants to take Quentin to meet her family tomorrow. I'd like him to meet mine too."

London could hear the smile in Grant's voice when he said, "I'd love that."

CHAPTER THIRTEEN

I'll just be gone for a few hours." Reggie pulled her jacket on over her T-shirt. "I promised I'd check up on a few things this morning, but I'll leave as soon as I can, and I'll take Quentin over to visit my family afterward so you can get some work done too."

"Okay." London hugged a pillow as she sat on the bed, legs tucked under her, looking at the time on her phone. Eight o'clock. She hadn't been prepared to be with Quentin alone so soon. It was hard to admit that she was afraid of being alone with a little boy all morning, but her shaky hands and palpitating heart confirmed it.

"You'll be fine," Reggie said. "Just give him some breakfast, hang out for a little bit, and I'll be home soon."

"What if he hates me?"

"He doesn't."

"What if he gets hurt?"

"Give him a Band-Aid."

"What if I poison him with my cooking?"

At this, Reggie paused. "Maybe take him out for breakfast."

London threw the pillow. "Get out of here!"

"I'm going. I love you."

"I love you too."

A few minutes after Reggie left, London pulled on her robe and went out into the living area. It was quiet, and she assumed Quentin was still sleeping. She went to the kitchen and began making coffee as quietly as possible. She heard movement from the living room and turned around. A very sleepy-looking Quentin was coming into the kitchen.

"Good morning," she said.

"Morning." He crawled onto one of the stools, crossed his arms on the counter, and rested his head on top of them, facedown.

A kid after my own heart. "Are you hungry?"

Quentin nodded without picking up his head.

"Me too. And since, as you probably remember, I'm the girl who burned the can of corn, I thought maybe I'd take you out for breakfast."

This brought Quentin's head halfway up, and he opened one eye. "Really?"

"Really. Anywhere you want to go."

Head fully off the counter, Quentin nodded. "Okay!"

"Cool. You know where the bathroom is; towels are in the closet by the tub. Go ahead and shower. I took one last night before bed. As soon as you're ready, we'll go."

Twenty minutes later, they locked the door and started the walk to London's car. "So, where am I taking you to eat?"

"Can we go to Tee Jaye's?"

London laughed. "I love that place. Are you sure? We can go someplace fancier or hipper if you want."

"I'm sure." Quentin nodded emphatically. "Tee Jaye's has my favorite pancakes."

"Mine too." London unlocked the car, and they got in. "Tee Jaye's, here we come."

❖

To say that Tee Jaye's wasn't fancy or hip was a vast exercise in understatement. The local chain offered restaurants that looked as if they'd traveled back in time to a rural area in the 1950s. From the hostess wearing a gingham dress and saying, "Howdy, folks," when they walked in to the old-timey furnishings and ancient menus with food like grits and mush—probably the only place in Columbus you could find them—it was like doing the time warp…but not *The Rocky Horror Picture Show* variety.

There was only one other table occupied when they took one of the deep, comfortable booths. London ordered coffee, and Quentin asked for orange juice.

"So," London said, "what sounds good? Do you always get pancakes, or do you switch things up sometimes?"

"I always get the pancakes. Sometimes I'll get eggs too, if I'm really hungry. Or I used to." He fidgeted with the corner of the menu. "I haven't been here in a long time."

"How long has it been?"

"My parents kicked me out in October, so not since last summer."

"I see. I'm really sorry."

Quentin shrugged. He didn't seem to want to talk about it, and she sure wasn't going to make him.

"Get whatever you want," she said. "I'm famished. I might even get the Barnyard Buster."

Quentin giggled. "That's the biggest meal on the menu."

"I know. I love to eat."

"Me too. I'm always hungry."

She was amazed at how this kid could chow down. She was less than halfway done by the time he finished. "Do you want anything else?"

He shook his head and smiled. "No thanks, I'm full."

"Okay. I was thinking maybe we could go over to Target and get you a winter coat." She'd noticed he only had a hoodie and shivered in the forty-degree weather. Winter wasn't even here yet, and that hoodie wasn't going to get him through it. He probably needed a lot more than just a coat, but she wanted to ease into things. She knew all too well that every item he had to replace would be a reminder of the parents who cast him out. It hit her again how very young he was to be going through this. She'd been in college when her family ostracized her, and there had been moments the pain was so great, she felt she wouldn't survive it. She didn't want Quentin to have any doubt that he would survive.

"Really?"

"Yep. It's not going to be warm again for a long time."

He was quiet for a moment. "You don't have to do that, you know."

"Buy you a coat?"

"Yeah."

"I know I don't have to, but I'd like it if you let me get you one."

"Why?"

"Well, um…" She frowned. "I mean, because it's cold. Please?"

"Okay," he said.

"Good."

Seeing the overflowing Target parking lot, she remembered it was Black Friday.

"We can do this some other time." Quentin looked anxious. His eyes darted around the parking lot, and he fidgeted with the zipper on his hoodie.

She glanced at him. "Not a fan of crowds?"

He hesitated. "I'm worried we'll run into my parents. They shop at this Target and are always here on Black Friday."

"Say no more." She navigated back toward the exit. "We'll get you a new coat tomorrow, okay?"

"Sure."

"I wanted to give you a heads-up," she said, "in terms of the rest of today. When Reg gets home this afternoon, she's going to take you to her parents' house; she really wants you to meet them. I think you'll like them. They're basically the nicest people ever. And tonight, one of my closest friends, Grant, will be coming over for a slumber party. He came with me to Compass, remember? It'll be chill, just eating junk food and watching movies. As long as all this is cool with you?"

"Reggie's parents. They know she's gay?"

"Yep."

"And they know you're together?"

"They're great with it, actually. They've been great about it since she came out."

He looked out his window. "That's nice."

"The holidays make it even harder, don't they?" When he didn't answer, she continued. "I remember my first Christmas after I came out. I was twenty and in college, and I'd come out to my family on Thanksgiving."

"Why did you do it then?" He still looked out the window, but he at least sounded interested.

"Actually, I guess I didn't technically come out so much as I accidentally outed myself," she said. "I'd been dating this girl I met in my English lit class, and I snuck off after we ate dinner to call her. This was back when everyone had a landline. My mother picked up another receiver in the house to make a call of her own and heard me talking to my girlfriend."

Now he did turn. "What were you saying?"

She blushed. "Let's just say, there was no way I could spin it to seem like we were just friends. She told my father, and within fifteen minutes of hanging up the phone, they kicked me out, and I ended up driving back to school. By the time Christmas came, I wasn't seeing that girl anymore. My roommate invited me to spend Christmas with her, but…"

"But what?"

"I was pretty gun shy about family stuff for a long time." That was an understatement, but she didn't want to go into too much detail. Family had been a dirty word for her until she'd begun to figure out that family wasn't necessarily linked to blood or biology. It had taken a lot of years to redefine what it meant to her, and it hadn't come easily. "I didn't want to be with her family or anybody else's. So I stayed in the dorms and studied and watched horror movies and went to clubs and did pretty much everything I could to pretend it wasn't Christmas."

"Did you ever see your family again?"

"I tried a few times. I called my parents on their anniversary and sent my twin sister a gift for our birthday. I wrote a lot of letters."

"What happened?"

She was a little sorry she'd started this conversation. That had been one of the most painful, isolating times in her life. Aside from the bond she'd had with Tate, she'd been lost in the world. As far as she'd come, she still didn't love rehashing how hurt and alone she'd felt. "They hung up on me. Diana sent my present back. And if anyone read my letters, they never responded. After the first year, I stopped trying to contact them."

"I'm sorry," he said.

She rested her hand on his arm. "I'm sorry too."

He shivered, and London cranked up the heat as high as it would go. She was sweltering, but she couldn't stand to see him tremble. She was rewarded with a grateful smile, and by the time they got home, he said he was all warmed up.

❖

"Pass the popcorn," Grant said. "I'm starving." He sat cross-legged on the floor under some blankets.

"I made a fruit and veggie plate, and you haven't touched it," Reggie scolded. "But you can complain about being hungry?"

"Okay, slumber party night is not made for fruits and veggies." He turned to London. "You gotta back me up on this."

"The man is right," she said. "Junk food only on slumber party nights. Pizza, popcorn, brownies. The staples."

Reggie shook her head. "You're both setting a terrible example." She wrapped an arm around Quentin, who sat between them on the couch. "You'll eat my cucumber slices, won't you, Q?"

He grinned sheepishly. "I'd rather have another slice of pizza."

Reggie laughed. "Heathens, all of you!"

They'd given Quentin full command of the remote for the night. So far, they'd watched two *Jackass* movies and were now starting *Cujo*. Reggie was wrapped in an enormous blanket made for a king-size bed.

"I can't believe I let you guys talk me into this movie." Her voice was muffled. All London could see was her eyes. "London, I hope you'll enjoy sleeping with the lights on tonight because I won't be staying in a dark room."

"I'll protect you from the imaginary movie dog," she said. "Don't worry."

"Someday," Reggie said, "when we get a dog, it sure as hell won't be a Saint Bernard. Not after this."

"You guys are gonna get a dog?" Quentin asked.

"We'd like to," London said. "Just not here. We'd rather be in a bigger place, somewhere with a yard."

"That's cool," he said. "I love dogs."

"Have you ever had one?" Grant asked.

Quentin shook his head. "My mom and sister are allergic."

There was an awkward silence, then London asked, "Hey, what do you think of the name Chowder for a dog?"

He considered it. "Sounds kind of weird."

She nodded. "Yeah, you're probably right."

"But," he said, "on the right dog, it could work."

"A weird dog?"

"Right."

Cujo lunged at the barely-closed-in-time car door in the movie, and Reggie jumped off the couch.

"Sorry, guys." She untangled herself from her gigantic blanket. "I tried, but I can't do this movie. If anyone needs me, I'll be in the bedroom watching *Marley & Me*."

Grant tossed some popcorn in his mouth. "You'd rather watch that sad dog movie than this angry dog movie?"

"Any day of the week." She kissed London on the cheek. "See you when you come to bed."

By the time *Cujo* was over, Grant was sprawled out on the floor, snoring.

"Should we wake him up and tell him to get on the couch?" Quentin asked.

London shook her head. "Grant sleeps like the dead; there's no point in even trying to wake him. In fact…" She went to the corner of the living room where she kept her art supplies and pulled out some markers. "Wanna decorate his face with me? Make this a real slumber party?"

He gave her an astonished smile. "Are you serious?"

She grinned and uncapped the red marker, handing the other colors to Quentin. "Yep." They drew hearts, shamrocks, and stars on his face and giggled when they were done. "He looks like a bowl of Lucky Charms."

"Is he gonna be mad?"

"Nah. Well, maybe for a half a second, but I'll take the heat. And I made sure we used markers that will wash right off." She held up one to show him the stain-free disclaimer. She stood, stretched her legs, and yawned. "I'm about ready to call it a night. Do you need anything before I go to bed?"

He shook his head. "I don't think so." He paused. "Thank you for today."

"You don't have to thank me."

"I know, but…you didn't have to do all this. You or Reggie. I didn't expect all this."

His gratitude at the simple efforts they made to feed him and introduce him to their friends and family broke London's heart. He was such a sweet kid, and she couldn't fathom any parents who wouldn't feel over the moon to have him.

She hugged him. "You deserve all this. All of it."

She was surprised to see Reggie was still awake when she went into the bedroom. "Are they asleep?" Reggie asked.

"Grant is, and I think Q will be pretty soon. Still watching your sad movie?"

"Just finished it. I was waiting up for you."

"Really?" London crawled into bed beside her. "How sweet. Any particular reason?" She kissed Reggie's neck and slipped her hand inside her T-shirt, running her fingers up Reggie's spine.

"Mmm," Reggie murmured. She kissed London deeply, their tongues intertwining, leaving them both breathless. London moved to take Reggie's T-shirt off, but Reggie held up a hand. "Wait. I had a different reason for waiting up."

London paused with her hand on Reggie's waist, and her mouth skimming over Reggie's collarbone. "What is it?"

Reggie scooted back a little. "I wanted to run something past you." She gently cupped London's chin, moving her face away so they were looking into each other's eyes.

"Okay, but this better be good, considering what you're interrupting."

"I think it is. I want to go steal a Christmas tree from your parents' property with you."

"*What?*"

Reggie nodded. "I've been thinking about it a lot. Even if this is the last year you do it, I think we should. I always wanted to go with you guys."

"You did?" She was genuinely surprised. She and Tate had always discussed their plans openly; she couldn't imagine why Reggie never spoke up. "Why didn't you ever tell me? We would've loved it if you came with us."

"I should've just asked. You and Tate were in your own world half the time. I spent way too long hoping for invitations into that world instead of jumping in and making myself at home there."

"I'm sorry." She felt terrible. She wondered how many other times Reggie had wanted to participate in one of their schemes and waited for them to ask her to join. It had never occurred to her that she and Tate had made anyone feel left out. "I'm sorry if I ever made you feel like you didn't belong."

Reggie shook her head. "It's okay. You two were a force. I don't know if you ever realized it. The people around you, sometimes all we could do was watch and just be glad to be nearby. I don't know how to explain it. It was magic, the way you interacted with each other. I never wanted to do anything to mess up the magic."

"You wouldn't have. There was enough magic to go around."

"I know that now. Anyway, what do you think? Given what your father has been doing, it would be fun to do a little thieving, a little middle finger in the form of a tree stump. And I think Tate would have approved."

"Yes, that's true." It was an enticing idea. Tate would have been giddy at the thought of sticking it to her father after the way he'd behaved recently. She could practically hear him giggling, and the joy and pain twisted her heart like a wrung-out washcloth. "There's just one thing."

"What?"

"Quentin. I don't think we should be involving him in misdemeanor trespassing and felony theft."

"Neither do I. But he's in school for seven hours a day. That gives us just enough time to get there, do the dirty work, and get back to surprise him with a freshly cut Christmas tree."

"When did you become such an evil genius?"

Reggie smiled. "I learned it all from you."

"Okay, I'm in. Monday?"

"Monday it is. Now, where were we?" She kissed London, nibbling on her bottom lip. "Here? Were we about here?"

London tugged Reggie's shirt over her head and pulled on her hips until Reggie was straddling her. "We were on our way here."

Chapter Fourteen

Y ou're sure you're good?" London peered up at the mammoth-looking school. "You don't need us to walk you in or anything?"

Quentin shook his head. "I'm twelve years old. And I come here every day."

"He'll be fine," Reggie said.

"Okay. Well, we'll meet you here at the end of the day."

"Got it." He hopped out of the car and zipped up his new coat. "See ya!" He ran off without looking back and joined a few kids walking in.

"Hey." Reggie rested her hand on London's. "You okay?"

"Yeah." London blushed and laughed. "I wasn't prepared for worrying about him like this."

Quentin walked through the large doors, and it looked as if the imposing structure swallowed him up. She knew it was silly to be so nervous, but she'd become protective of him in the few days he'd been with them.

"It's just school," Reggie said. "Kids do this every day."

"I know, but it's my first day doing it with him."

"Aww." Reggie spoke in a baby-talk voice she knew London hated. "We gotta wet the baby bird fwy away."

"You're a nightmare." She swatted Reggie's hand away and put the car in gear. She navigated carefully through the parking lot, and when they stopped at the red light, she turned to Reggie. "You're sure you wanna do this? Because once we get onto I-71, there's no changing our minds. When we hit the road, we hit the road."

"I'm sure," Reggie said. "I've been waiting years to do this with you."

Rush hour was crazy, and it took longer than they expected to get out of the city. Reggie performed the traditional Shotgun DJ duties and put on a Lenny Kravitz mix. They sang together to "Are You Gonna Go My Way," "Always on the Run," and "American Woman." Reggie even pulled the lever to drop her seat down, kicked her leg in the air, and played air guitar. London had forgotten how much fun it was to road trip with her.

Finally, and only a little behind schedule, they saw the signs for Keys Crossing. London's family lived on the opposite end of town on the outskirts. As they drove through town, Reggie turned down the radio.

"So, what's the plan?"

"Pretty simple," London said. "The property goes five acres back with the far edge of the acreage aligned with an old dirt service road that farmers used to use. Maybe they still do. We'll use that old dirt road, stop when we find a good tree, cut it down, pile it on your FJ, and be on our way back to civilization."

"And you're never worried about getting caught when you do this?"

"Having second thoughts?"

"Not at all, just like to know what I'm getting myself into."

"That's fair. I don't really worry about getting caught. Like I said, it's on an old dirt road. Nobody in my family would deign to drive their Mercedes back there. I didn't even know that road existed until I was in high school and one of my friends took it as a shortcut to get to my house."

"Okay." Reggie pulled a saw and some twine into the front seat. Several minutes later, they turned down the dirt road, and dust clouded up around them. "I don't think I've ever actually been down a dirt road. I didn't expect so much…dirt."

London laughed. "It's been dry for several months. Once we get a few good snows, it won't puff up like this." She slowed when she got close to her family's property. "There," she said, pointing several yards into the distance. "See those pine trees? Blue spruces, they make the best Christmas tree." She pulled off the road a little to the embankment so that in the unlikely event that another vehicle passed by, there'd be room. She had no plan for how she'd explain cutting down a tree, and she doubted she'd need one.

They got out of Reggie's FJ and walked along the property. London inhaled the scent of the trees.

"If only someone could bottle that smell, they'd make a fortune!"

Tate had said last year. "Oh, wait, Bath & Body Works already did that."

London had tears in her eyes, but she was smiling. Reggie was right; it was good they were doing this. It had been a family tradition, and even though her heart felt like it might pound out of her chest from missing Tate, she also felt an odd sense of peace somewhere deeper than her heart. He would've been pissed if she hadn't kept coming back here to stick it to her father.

"Psst!" Reggie called from a very round and full spruce. "What do you think of this one?"

"I think it's perfect. Good choice, baby."

Reggie glowed. "Do you want to make the first cut?"

London nodded and reached for the saw. Tate had always granted her the ceremonial first digs at the tree before he grew impatient with her slow pace and took over. She leaned down and began to saw the thick trunk of the hearty tree. About a third of the way in, Reggie took over, and London rubbed her hands together. They might not have had snow yet, but it wasn't because it wasn't cold enough. As soon as they had precipitation, the ground would be covered in a cold blanket of white crystals.

London looked down the road and saw a cloud of dust surrounding a vehicle she couldn't fully see. She assumed that the driver couldn't see them very well, and the FJ was parked so that by the time the car passed them, they'd be mostly concealed.

"Heads up," London murmured. "Incoming."

Reggie stopped sawing and looked up from her crouched position, a tiny bit of alarm in her eyes.

"I'm sure they'll just drive by," London said. "Don't worry."

But they didn't. As the vehicle came to a stop, parallel to Reggie's Toyota, London saw it was a C-Class Mercedes-Benz sedan. After a few moments, Frederick Craft stepped out of the luxury car, followed by Diana a few seconds later.

"What do we do?" Reggie whispered.

"Don't panic," London said under her breath. She strode over to the road and greeted her family. "Hi, Dad. Diana."

He paused. "Hi, Dad? That is what you have to say to me when I catch you in the act of grand theft?"

"I would've thought you'd be happy that I finally agreed to take a piece of my inheritance," she said smoothly. "Isn't that what you wanted?" She snapped her fingers. "Oh, I forgot; you only want me to get the inheritance if you can manipulate me into being a different person."

His mouth tightened. "I could call the police and have you arrested for this."

"But you won't. Because guess what would be on the front page of the *Keys Crossing Bulletin* tomorrow? Maybe not above the fold, but even below would do enough damage to your precious reputation, wouldn't it?" Reggie had joined them and slid her hand gently around London's elbow.

In an almost mirror image, Diana folded her fingers around their father's elbow. "Come on, Daddy," she said in nearly a whisper. "Let's leave them alone."

Red splotches bloomed on his face. "I don't understand you. Your mother and I gave you everything. The best clothes, the best car, the best education, and this is how you repay us? Staying away from home for years, returning only to steal from us with this, this—"

London stepped between her father's pointing finger and Reggie's face. "Don't you talk to her. Don't even talk *about* her. This is about you and me."

The blooms on his face blossomed, and anger painted his face a deep maroon. He opened his mouth, but London held up her hand.

"How dare you?" she yelled. "You say I stayed away from home? You threw me out on Thanksgiving! I spent that Christmas alone in my dorm room. You can't pretend to be the victim in this when you tossed me out of here and told me never to come back. What did you expect to happen?"

He sputtered. "Your mother couldn't get out of bed, did you know that? She couldn't get out of bed for two weeks after that Thanksgiving, and when Christmas arrived, she went back to bed and stayed there until after New Year's."

"And I'm supposed to feel what about that, Dad? Guilty? Ashamed? No. *Fuck* no. You and Mom made a choice to ostracize me. You don't get to make me feel bad about the choices you made."

"You're the one who made a choice. You and your vulgar lifestyle. How could we allow that in our home?" He shook his head. "You weren't raised like that."

"Daddy—" Diana began.

"No," London said. "I guess I wasn't. But it's the way I was made." She turned to Reggie. "Now, don't we have a tree to take home?"

Reggie glanced at London, then her father. "A few more swings with the saw, and it should be good to go."

"Perfect." She walked toward the tree with Reggie and turned back to see her father standing there, aghast. Diana stood slightly behind him, and if London hadn't known better, she would've sworn her twin had tears in her eyes. "You gonna stay and watch our handiwork? See the lesbians in our natural habitat?"

He turned on his heel and walked to his car, jerked the door open, and paused to take one last disgusted look at London before getting in and slamming the door. Diana walked much more slowly to the passenger side, not taking her eyes off her sister for a second until she too was in the car. As soon as Diana was inside, they drove off in a cloud of dust.

Reggie turned to London. "You okay?"

She nodded. "I will be. Come on, let's finish chopping down our tree and get home. I don't want to be late picking up Quentin."

They were quiet as they finished cutting the tree and mounting it on the roof of the car. Aside from instructions like "Move the tree toward you" and "Tighten the twine on that side," they didn't speak. Reggie drove home, and after they'd been on the road for a silent thirty minutes, she cleared her throat.

"Did you plan to say all that? In case we saw your dad?"

London shook her head. "I really didn't think we would see him."

"Was he really going to call the cops, do you think?"

"No. He was bluffing. It's what he does when he doesn't know what else to do with me."

Reggie paused. "What's going on in your mind?"

"Honestly, I'm thinking about Q. That night he got so upset at Compass, he basically said the whole 'It Gets Better' campaign is a crock because after almost twenty years, my family hasn't changed at all. They haven't moved even an inch toward accepting who I am. My mom is dead, my dad is old, and my sister is just a puppet. It's not going to change. He's right; it is a crock."

"It's not a crock." She covered London's hand. "They may not ever be better, but that's not what it's about. You are better; your life is better. Your biological family doesn't accept you, but your chosen one embraces every part of you. Telling Quentin or any other kid that it gets better is true because as you get older, you aren't limited to just the family you're born into."

London gave her a sad smile. "I know you're right. And of course my life is better, I know that. I'm lucky to have you, your parents, Grant, and Jasmine. I was lucky to have Tate." She rubbed her temples. She'd spent the last twenty years surrounding herself with people who loved and accepted her, and she considered them family. She knew she was more fortunate than most, but even that knowledge couldn't always chase away the loneliness of being cast out from her parents and sister. It was worse now, with Tate gone. She had a family, she knew that. What she didn't have were roots. She didn't have a childhood history with anyone. She couldn't turn to someone and reminisce about things she'd done as a kid. That was all gone, and she felt hollow from the absence of it. "I wasn't prepared for how hard these holidays were going to be."

She plugged her phone into the stereo and pulled up her music app, playing Tori Amos the rest of the way home. They pulled into the parking lot at Quentin's school and saw him come out the doors with some friends about fifteen minutes later. He stopped when he saw the vehicle with the tree on top, then slowly walked toward it.

"Surprise!" Reggie said as Quentin climbed into the back seat. "We got a tree to decorate!"

"I see that," he said quietly.

London glanced at Reggie's concerned face and turned to look at Quentin. He stared at his hands resting in his lap.

"Quentin?" she asked. "Is something wrong?"

"My parents always get a live tree too," he said. "We go to this Christmas tree farm and all pick one out together. My little sister always likes the tall skinny ones, and I like the rounder ones, so they let us take turns choosing." He used the heel of his hand to wipe a tear away. "This was supposed to be my year to pick one."

"Oh, honey, I'm so sorry," London said. "We should have talked to you about this before getting a tree. I didn't even think about it."

"Me neither," Reggie said. "We should have prepared you for it. Shit, we should've asked you if you even wanted to get a tree."

He smiled through his tears. "You said 'shit.'"

"Shoot, I meant," Reggie said.

"Nah, she meant shit," London said, and to her relief, he laughed a little. "Listen, we don't have to decorate this tree. We don't even have to take it home if it's going to make you upset. We can go dump it on the side of the road somewhere for all I care. You tell us how you want this Christmas to go, okay? Your first set of holidays without your family is rough, and there's no way around that. You deserve to decide how you want it to play out, and Reg and I will support whatever you decide. Right, babe?"

She'd been so shaken after her ugly interaction with her father, it had consumed her for the last several hours. Seeing Quentin's pain and knowing exactly how devastating it was to spend the holidays feeling alone and unloved, all she could think of now was how to make things better and happier for him.

"Yep," Reggie said. "If you say the tree goes, the tree goes. Along with anything else Christmas-related. Just say the word."

Quentin's dark eyes were wide. "Seriously?"

"Seriously," Reggie said.

He bit his lip for several moments and shook his head. "No, I want the tree. I want a Christmas."

"You're sure?" London asked. "Because we can kick this broad to the curb, literally, and never look back."

"I'm sure. Thank you, though, so much."

"No problem," Reggie said.

They got home, and the three of them maneuvered the tree into the house and set up in the stand. "Wanna help us bring the decorations up from the basement?" Reggie asked.

"Sure."

London put on her favorite Motown Christmas mix with the first song—"Twinkle, Twinkle, Little Me," by Stevie Wonder—coming on as they were arranging the lights on the tree.

"Is the music okay?" she asked.

Reggie and Quentin nodded.

"I like this song," Quentin said.

Once the lights and garlands were on the tree, they opened the new box of decorations Reggie had picked up. They were *Star Wars* themed ornaments, and Quentin was enthusiastic about each of them. "Cool, Darth Vader! Look at these light saber ornaments!"

Reggie and London smiled at each other as Quentin picked up each ornament and dangled it in front of his face before finding the perfect spot to hang it on the tree.

"So," Reggie said when they were nearly done hanging the ornaments, "any idea what you want for Christmas?"

He looked at them, his eyes wide for the second time that day. "You don't have to get me anything."

"We know that," London said. "But maybe you'll let us get you something anyway?"

"I wouldn't even know what to ask for. I thought I'd be spending Christmas at Compass and getting whatever gift got donated to me."

"Well," Reggie said, "I guess we'll have to think of something. Here, do you want to put the star on top of the tree?" She held out the tree topper, and when he saw it, he grinned.

"The Death Star?" He reached for the moon-shaped space station.

"Yep." London pulled out a stepladder she kept behind the couch. "Do the honors."

Quentin stepped to the top step and fastened the topper to the tree. "There." He came down from the ladder and stepped back to admire his handiwork.

"Looks great." London joined Reggie on the opposite end of the couch, and after a few minutes, Quentin sat between them. They sat together for a long time, looking at their tree and listening to Christmas music.

CHAPTER FIFTEEN

So, let me see if I understand all this," Ross said. "Since the last time I saw you, you were stalked by one of Tate's predators, Grant moved out, you've taken in a twelve-year-old child, Reggie moved in and the two of you are essentially together again, and you stole a tree from your father's property?"

"Yeah. But to be fair, the stealing thing happens every year, I just never told you about it." London faced Ross with a sheepish smirk on her face.

"You do love to test my counseling abilities, don't you?"

"It's always a good time."

"I see." He took off his glasses and cleaned them on his shirt, carefully folding the soft, flannel cloth around each lens and massaging it. "At the risk of sounding like a cliché, how do you feel about all of this?"

"I'm over the moon that Reggie is home again, obviously." She was still a little on edge about the reasoning behind their sudden reconciliation, but it felt so good and right to be back under the same roof with Reggie. She tried to keep her focus on how well they were doing rather than her uneasiness that they may have rushed. "We haven't really talked about the marriage thing any further since she came back; there hasn't been a lot of time for it. Grant is settling back in at his own place, but we still see him all the time. The thing with the tree…I didn't expect to see my father, but when I did see him, I don't know…It felt good to say those things to him. It's terrible to know he hasn't grown or progressed, not even a little."

"I can understand all of that," Ross said. "And Quentin? How do you feel about caring for this child, so unexpectedly?"

"It's weird."

"Weird how?"

"Mostly in how not weird it is. He's away from his parents, and it's the holidays, so he's had some triggering moments. Actually, I wanted to see if you thought it would be a good idea for us to get him into counseling. We've been working through it with him as best we can. And I really like the kid; he's sweet and funny, and we have a good time together. I was panicked when Joan brought up the idea, all the way through signing the paperwork. But we've gotten into a good rhythm. He fits."

He stared with his best neutral gaze.

"What?" she asked.

"You're considering getting Quentin into counseling?"

"It just seems like it might help him process through all this." His face was expressionless, which meant he had a lot to say. "Do you think it's a bad idea?"

"I didn't say that. But therapy, as you know, is a long-term process, and from what I understand, Quentin will only be with you and Reggie for a short while."

"Oh. Right."

"Unless you're considering having him stay with you for longer than just a month or two?"

"No. Well, yes, maybe. We signed a contract to keep him for up to six months, if need be, but Joan said she didn't think it would take more than a couple months to get him back."

"With his parents?"

"No, to Compass."

He frowned. "It's interesting that they're having him stay with you for weeks or potentially months only to go back to a halfway house afterward."

"I…I hadn't thought about it like that. When we signed the papers, we were just trying to do the best thing for Q in the moment."

He nodded. "Yes, I understand that. And unfortunately, the nature of the foster system can be a transient one for the children involved."

Now it was her turn to frown. Were they going to be putting Quentin into another painful situation by taking him in and then returning him to Compass when one of their beds opened back up again? It was something she and Reggie would need to discuss with Joan when they went back for their volunteer night. She must have ways to deal with transitions like that.

"It looks like our time is about up." He rose from the couch and walked to his computer. "Let's schedule your next appointment."

"Do you wanna schedule a few appointments?"

He turned away from his computer to look at her, his mouth shaped like a little O.

Before he could say anything, London spoke quickly. "It's just, I know you like to get a month's worth of appointments on the books at a time, and it's not really fair if I'm the only person just scheduling one. I figure it's time to start pulling my weight around here."

"Okay."

She thought she saw a glimmer of a smile on his face before he turned back to his computer. Minutes later, after they'd agreed on four days and times, he handed her appointment card to her with all the information. London looked at the card jam-packed with writing.

It had taken years to get to this point. Even though it was such a small, nearly symbolic gesture, she was as proud of it as any of the giant steps she'd taken in therapy.

"Well, look at this. My dance card is full."

London left therapy feeling good. It could be so taxing, and she often left feeling exhausted and spent, but today she just felt positive. She stopped into Stauf's to get some really good coffee, and when she left, she attempted to whistle as she walked to her car. She wasn't a very good whistler, having only the capacity to push out two or three wavering notes, but she didn't care. It was cold and sunny, and the light dusting of the season's first snow sparkled as if the ground was covered in some of the glitter from her art room at Hell.

It's like this day was made for me. She unlocked her car and got in. It was the best she'd felt in a long time. Before Tate and her mother died, before Reggie had moved out, before the landscape of her world had changed.

A few minutes later, she pulled into her parking space and walked up to her door, still blowing that ugly whistle. She opened the door and yelled, "I'm home!" Hanging her coat on the hook by the door, she peered into the living room and stopped short.

Reggie, Quentin, Detectives Harper and O'Connor, plus a man she didn't recognize with salt-and-pepper hair and a fancy suit, were all sitting there looking at her.

Harper cleared her throat and stood. "We need to talk."

"Okay." She stayed motionless, frozen in place.

The man with the fancy suit also stood and crossed the room, his outstretched hand reaching to shake London's. "I've been meaning to meet you in person for some time, Ms. Craft." His clear baritone voice made her think he was probably a pretty decent singer. "My name is Kyle Brown, and I'm the prosecutor in charge of the case against Tate's attackers."

London shook his hand. "London Craft."

"Yes. Ms. Craft, could we sit down?" He held his hand, palm up and fingers extended toward the living room, and Reggie and Quentin scooted apart to make space on the couch for her between them. Harper and O'Connor sat in the club chairs adjacent to the couch, and Kyle Brown moved a stool from the eating area into the living room. Everyone looked up at him, and he resembled a teacher about to give a lesson.

"First," he said, in his soothing voice, "London, let me please extend my condolences to you, for the loss of Tate Morgan. I understand he was much more than just a friend to you, and losing a family member in such a terrible way is devastating."

"Thank you." Her ears were ringing a little bit, but she stayed focused on the man on the stool.

"We're preparing for trial, which will take place at the end of January. We are cautiously hopeful that, based on the evidence against the perpetrators, we will be able to obtain convictions on at least the most serious charges."

She realized that he'd paused, expecting her to speak. "That's good news."

He nodded, apparently pleased with her answer. "Indeed. Now, what you may not know is that we ask family members to speak out at trial, give the jury and judge a window into the life of the victim. Who they were, what they meant to the people around them. They get a chance to speak about what they've lost as a result of the crime." He folded his hands and raised his two index fingers to make the steeple in the old nursery rhyme. He pressed the steeple to his lips, then lowered his hands, folding his steeple back in to become part of the congregation.

"The thing is, Ms. Craft, we haven't been able to find anyone in Tate's biological family who's willing to speak. And this isn't the thrust of our case, you understand, not at all. Judgments are made based on evidence, which is substantial. It is, however, customary to have people speak, and it can affect the severity of the sentence for the perpetrators. And after all, we don't want this to look like a crime of no consequence." Her mouth dropped open, and he rushed his next few words. "Not that there's any such thing, of course. I know that, and you know that."

She had a feeling that he did not, in fact, know that. She'd never had the distaste or mistrust of lawyers held by so many. Her friendships with people like Grant and Thomas had given her insight into some incredibly decent, compassionate, and warm-hearted attorneys. Hell, even Larry Kopp was a good guy; it was his clients that had caused her so much turmoil. But this short conversation with Kyle Brown gave her a hefty helping of a smooth-talking, unfeeling lawyer, and she didn't know how much longer she could stomach it.

"Look, we're aware that this was a devastating loss for a lot of people. I've come to you today to ask if you'd be willing to speak on Tate's behalf. The detectives have assured me there was no one closer to Tate than you. In fact, they urged me to come to you from the beginning." He had the courtesy to look sheepish, although it was clearly an orchestrated move. "I was sure we could find someone in his biological family who would do it. His mother was the obvious choice. I was wrong."

"What did she say?"

"Pardon me?"

"Tate's mother. What did she say when you asked her to speak?"

He looked at the detectives, who glanced at each other uncomfortably. "Ah, I don't think we need to go into that—"

"Tell me." She knew whatever it was would be unbearable, yet she had to bear it. *Had* to.

Detective Harper left her chair, knelt in front of London, and grabbed her hands. London had never seen her up close like this. She was really striking, like a young Natalie Wood.

Harper's lovely dark eyes filled with concern and compassion. "She said they did her a favor. She said Tate killed her daughter over a year ago, and they did her a favor murdering her daughter's killer."

A sharp gasp to her left made her turn. Quentin was crying. She wrapped her arms around him and turned to Reggie. "He shouldn't be here for all of this."

"I told him that. He wanted to be here and wouldn't take no for an answer."

Quentin put his head on London's shoulder, and she rested her head on his, rocking him as they both cried. Aside from their sniffles and occasional sobs, the room was silent. After several moments passed, London wiped tears from her cheeks, keeping one arm around Quentin. "Of course I'll speak for Tate. And I'm sure I won't be the only one. Reggie?"

"You know I will. And Grant will too."

"That's good to hear," Mr. Brown said. "I'm very sorry to have upset you like this, and I wouldn't have bothered you in your home if I didn't think you were the best person to do it."

She nodded.

"Well." Mr. Brown stood. "Detectives Harper and O'Connor can get your contact info to my office, if that's all right with you. We'll reach out to you to work out the details in the coming weeks. Thank you again for your time. We can see ourselves out, can't we?"

He put the stool back where he found it, and he and Detective O'Connor, who hadn't said a word, gathered their coats and gloves. Detective Harper hadn't moved from her spot on the floor by London's feet before she stood and thanked them.

"You still have my information, if any of you have questions about this. I'm not an attorney, but I've seen enough of these—too many, honestly—to know how things go. And I'm in regular contact with Kyle, so I can liaise between you if you'd like." She touched the shoulders of Quentin and London, who were still resting on each other, and shook Reggie's hand. "Call or text me if you need anything."

And suddenly, London, Reggie, and Quentin were alone in the living room.

❖

London lay awake for a long time that night. Reggie had held her until she fell asleep herself and rolled over on her other side. London stared at the ceiling for over an hour before accepting that she wasn't going to sleep for quite some time.

She turned the events of the day over and over in her mind. Detective Harper had told her she could contact her if she had any questions. Using the light from her phone, London read the phone number on Harper's business card and entered it into a new text screen. She typed and deleted the same few words three times before finally finishing the message and hitting send. London gazed into the darkness around her for several more minutes, then reached into her nightstand and felt around for the familiar piece of construction paper, closed her fingers around it, and got out of bed.

She went into the living room, thinking she could look at the letter by the light of the Christmas tree, but when she walked into the living room, she found Quentin sitting on the couch watching *The Twilight Zone* with the volume turned almost all the way down.

"I thought you were asleep." She joined him on the couch.

"I thought you were too."

She shrugged. "Guess we were both wrong."

"Yep." He looked at the paper in her lap, the mint green a stark contrast from her black terry cloth robe. "What's that?"

She handed him the paper. "It's a letter I wrote to my future self when I was ten years old."

He read the letter carefully, then looked up at her. "Wow."

"I know. When my mother died, she had her lawyer give this to me and said she'd leave me one hundred thousand dollars if I started living this way. Then a few weeks later, my father added another fifty thousand to the pot."

He studied her. "Are you gonna try this? For the money?"

"No! Hell no." She sighed. "Well, not for the money. And not everything on the list. I've been trying a few things on to see how they fit, but it's more...I just want to understand who I was then."

"Why?"

She shrugged again. "I figured it might help me understand myself now."

"And is does it? Help you understand yourself, I mean." He handed the letter back.

"I'm not sure yet."

She thought about what she knew for sure. She knew, and had almost always known, that she wouldn't fall in love with a man. She knew volunteer work was important to her, and she was happy to be making it a larger part of her life. It was becoming clearer that she'd never had a corporate job because she wasn't cut out for that.

There was still the question of marriage. She glanced at her bedroom door and could almost hear Reggie's soft snore on the other side. Did she still want to get married? Did London? It was the last thing on the list about which she was uncertain.

They were quiet for a while, watching the nearly muted television together. When it went to commercial, London spoke again.

"Do you have any questions about today? I know I haven't talked much about Tate with you."

"Reggie filled me in a little. And so did Joan."

"*Joan?*" London cried, baffled. "Joan talked to you about Tate?"

"A little bit. The night I found out I was going to be staying with you two, Joan told me about Tate. I think she wanted me to feel comfortable coming home with you, knowing you'd been so close to someone who was trans."

"Oh. I guess that makes sense." Joan never failed to catch her off guard. "I'm sorry you had to hear all that. I'm glad you already knew a little about it, but I'm sorry you had to hear…you know. What Tate's mother said."

London and Reggie had agreed to let Quentin decide when and how much he wanted to discuss being a trans boy. Joan hadn't told them much about the circumstances under which he'd been kicked out of his parents' house, only that he'd been unexpectedly outed. They wanted to give him ownership of his gender identity and let him come out to them as he chose.

The events of today made London wonder if they shouldn't be having discussions with him about it. She still wanted to let him feel like discussing it was his choice, but she also wanted him to feel seen and accepted.

"It's okay." His voice trembled.

"It's not okay." When she realized he was crying again, she moved closer. As earlier, he rested his head on her shoulder. He didn't make any noise, but she could feel his body shudder, and soon there were warm tears on her neck.

"What Tate's mom said," he said, his voice still shaky, "do you think that's how my parents feel? That it would be a favor to them if I died?"

She shifted and held his pink, puffy face in her hands. "I don't know your parents, but if they feel like that, then they are absolutely wrong. You just might be the best person I know, Quentin, and your gender identity doesn't change that. In fact, there is nothing braver anyone can do than live out loud. Lots of people don't get to do that until they're older, but you? You have your whole life ahead of you, a whole life of living as exactly who you are."

She wiped the tears from his cheeks and hugged him to her again, wrapping both arms around him and holding on as tightly as she could. "They're the ones who are wrong," she said. "Not you. You are courageous and amazing, and if they don't know that, they don't deserve you."

All over again, she was angry at Tate's mother. Her hatred and bigotry had cut Tate to the core, and now it was too late to mend anything between them. But it wasn't just Tate's mother; it was Quentin's parents and the murderers who'd taken Tate from her. It was all the folks who hated Tate and Quentin—two of the kindest, funniest, most generous people she had ever met—simply because they were trans. It sickened her to think of a world so cruel that it had taken her best friend from her and that the sweet boy in her arms would face dangers of his own, that he'd already endured so much at the hands of those who let their ignorance rule their actions.

She held him until he cried himself to sleep. She pulled the blanket from the back of the couch onto them, and soon, she fell into a fitful sleep too.

Reggie handed London a stack of plates and silverware. "Put these on the coffee table. My parents can sit on the couch, and the rest of us can sit on the floor."

Since Quentin had been staying with them, they'd been going to weekly dinners at Betty and Herb's house, sometimes with Grant joining them, and once Jasmine and Diego had come. It was a few days before Christmas, and Betty was busy getting everything together for Christmas dinner, so Reggie suggested they come over to the condo.

"Sounds good." London grabbed the plates. "It smells amazing in here."

"It better." Reggie laughed. "I'm making lasagna the way Mama taught me, and I'll know if she doesn't like it."

"Like your mother would ever say your food was bad."

"She wouldn't, but I'd be able to tell. Her face gives her away every time."

Quentin appeared from the alcove. "Need any help?"

"That depends," Reggie said. "Did you get your homework done?"

"Yep. Even did the extra credit."

"In that case, come in here. You can help me with the garlic bread."

There was a knock at the door. Betty, Herb, and Grant stood

outside, shivering. "Come in where it's warm." London took their coats. "Did you all ride together?"

"Just got here at the same time," Grant said.

Betty went into the kitchen with Reggie and Quentin. "My babies are making it smell good in here!"

Herb sat on the couch, and London handed him the remote. "I don't know if there's any football on, but you can check." She sat beside him. "You can check for parades too," she whispered.

"I'll do that." He chuckled and turned on the TV and started flipping through the channels.

Grant sat on the other side of London. "So, how's Quentin doing?" he asked quietly.

She peered over the half wall into the kitchen where Quentin blew on a spoonful of sauce and pushed it toward Betty, letting her try it.

"He's doing pretty well. Much better than anyone could expect, honestly. He's a strong little boy."

"Mm-hmm," Herb said. "It's not often you meet a child that's so strong *and* so sweet."

"You don't meet many adults like that, either," Grant said.

"You're right." Herb stopped on an old episode of *Columbo* and settled back into the couch.

"What are your plans with him?" Grant asked.

"We're supposed to meet with Joan later this week to discuss how soon she expects a spot to open back up at Compass. Probably sometime late in January is my guess."

"You're going to send him back?" Grant's eyebrows rose.

"What do you mean? Why would you think anything different? This was never a permanent thing."

He shook his head. "I just thought the three of you had been bonding so much, maybe you'd decided to keep him for good."

She didn't know what to say. First Ross and now Grant. She was beginning to feel pretty concerned for Quentin. As much as she wanted to care for him and make him feel part of the family, she didn't want him to experience further pain when he had to go back to Compass and a life of uncertainty. She hadn't even considered adoption, but apparently, she was in the minority. She wondered if Reggie had thought about it, and if she had, why hadn't she mentioned it?

"Dinner's ready," Reggie called. "Come and get it."

London and Grant went into the kitchen and brought the serving dishes back to the living room, and the group congregated around the table, passing dishes. It was a tight squeeze, with plates knocking into elbows as they passed and every inch of space provided by the coffee table utilized.

"It looks like it's time for you to start looking for a bigger place," Betty said.

"I agree," Reggie said.

"You do?" This was the first London was hearing about it.

"Sure, I mean this place is really only made for one person to live in comfortably. It's a bachelor pad. Bachelorette pad, in this instance, and you're not living that life anymore." Reggie saw the surprise on London's face. "Are you?"

"No, of course not. I just didn't know you were thinking about it." An uneasy feeling settled in her stomach, and it took a moment for her to identify it. At first she thought she was panicking at the thought of taking that step with Reggie. She remembered all those months ago when Thomas had asked if she were afraid of commitment. But no. She wasn't scared of moving forward into an expanding future with Reggie. She just wanted to be kept in the loop.

All around her, it seemed, the people she loved were discussing potentially huge changes that could directly affect her life. Why was it that none of them were initiating conversations with her about them?

"Relax." Reggie patted London's hand. "I just started thinking about it."

"I'm relaxed," London said in a voice that didn't sound very relaxed, not even to her.

"Is there any white wine?" Grant asked.

"In the fridge," Reggie said.

Grant went to the kitchen. "London, your phone is ringing. It's Jasmine."

"Answer it."

"Oops, didn't get it in time." He brought it to her. "Sorry."

"It's okay." She looked at her phone. "Oh my God."

"What?" Quentin asked.

"I've missed six calls from her in the last ten minutes." She hit the call button and held the phone to her ear. Jasmine answered halfway through the first ring, sounding breathless.

"London! Thank God."

"What's wrong?"

"Your sister was just here looking for you."

"My *sister*?" Her voice squeaked. "There must be some mistake. Diana wouldn't set so much as a toenail in Hell."

"But she did. And when I told her you weren't here, she said she would just come to your house. I've been trying to reach you since the minute she left, to warn you. I didn't even know she knew where you lived."

There was a knock at the door.

"I didn't either," London said. "Jas, she's here. I gotta go."

"What's going on?" Reggie asked as soon as London hung up the phone. "Who's here?"

"Diana." London shifted around her guests toward the door.

"Who the hell is Diana?" Herb asked.

Betty shushed him, and Reggie answered, "London's sister," at the same time.

London opened the door, and standing there, looking as regal in her designer coat and scarf as her royal namesake, was Diana Craft. "London," Diana said.

"Diana."

"You're not surprised to see me. Did your employee warn you of my arrival?"

"My *friend* told me you were coming, yes." She wondered if Diana knew what she was doing. Her sister had a terrible knack of putting a distance between London and the people with whom she felt close. Was it mere snobbery or a deliberate move to make her feel isolated? Either way, it never failed to make hot shards of anger cut through her.

"May I come in out of the cold?"

London hesitated, then opened the door wider and stepped aside. Diana frowned as she looked from face to face around the coffee table.

"I'm sorry. I didn't realize I'd be interrupting a party."

"That's probably because you didn't call first," London said.

Reggie quickly crossed to the door. She reached out. "Hello, Diana, you may not remember me. I'm Reggie."

"Why, yes." Diana shook Reggie's hand using only the tips of her fingers. "You were one of London's friends who accompanied her to our mother's funeral. It was good of you to come."

"She's my *girlfriend*," London said between gritted teeth. The anger hadn't even begun to subside before this fresh wave hit. "Not my friend."

Reggie rested her hand on London's arm and said, "Diana, we just started eating dinner. It's lasagna. Would you like me to fix you a plate?"

Diana surprised everyone when she said, "Lasagna sounds lovely. Thank you."

"Here." Grant grabbed his plate and wine. "I've finished my food. You can take my spot."

She looked at the coffee table and the now vacant spot on the floor Grant had designated for her. She hesitated before moving.

"I'll take your coat," Grant said.

"Thank you." She removed it and handed it to him. She slowly descended to the floor, then sat, legs tucked under her and hands resting tentatively on the table.

London followed Reggie into the kitchen as Herb began to speak to Diana. "Awfully snowy night for a road trip," he said.

"What in the actual hell is my sister doing here?"

"I have no idea," Reggie whispered. Then out loud, she said, "Hand me a plate."

"This is a nightmare. And you! Why did you invite her to dinner?"

"What should I have done? Let the two of you keep shooting icicle daggers at each other with your eyes at the front door?"

"Maybe." London grabbed a couple pieces of garlic bread and put them on the plate beside the lasagna.

"Does Diana drink white or red wine?"

"How should I know?"

"She's your twin!"

"Reg, neither of us were even legal drinking age when I got tossed out."

Reggie sighed. "Fair enough." She turned to the living room. "Diana, we have red and white wine, if you'd like either one."

Diana half turned and said, "Just some sparkling water will be fine."

"Oh, ah...we don't have sparkling water."

"All right. White wine, please."

Reggie grabbed a stemmed glass from the cupboard and poured the wine.

"Not too full," London whispered. "We don't want her to get so tipsy she can't drive home."

Reggie put her hands on London's shoulders. "Breathe, baby. Breathe. Let her eat some dinner, say whatever she came to say, and then we'll send her on her way. Okay? I need you to just breathe through this night."

London took several deep breaths and nodded. "Okay." She took the plate and wine glass and went into the living room with Reggie close behind her.

As much as she didn't want to deal with Diana, London was proud of herself. Her initial instinct was to send her sister back out into the snowstorm from which she had come, but she resisted. She would face whatever tonight brought, and she would live to tell the tale.

"Here you go." London set the food and drink in front of her sister. "*Bon appétit.*"

Quentin giggled. "Bon appe-what?"

"It's French," London said. "And fancy."

"It's weird," he said.

"Well, you know me," London said, and even though her estranged sister was sitting on the floor in her living room, she couldn't help smiling at him. Something in his laugh and teasing reminded her of Tate.

Diana cut the lasagna into several tiny pieces while everyone else in the room looked on. She resembled a surgeon making the most delicate and strategic of slices. Finally, she put a miniscule bite in her mouth, chewing slowly.

"Why, this is delicious," she said once she swallowed. "London, did you make this?"

Quentin started giggling again. "London can't even cook a salad!"

Everyone laughed, including London. "It's true. If it's not microwaveable, it's not for me."

"I see." Diana took a sip of wine. "Some things never change."

"What do you mean?" Reggie asked.

"I had an Easy-Bake Oven when we were kids. One day I came home after gymnastics, and my room smelled horrible, like burning rubber. London had decided to make brownies, but she couldn't find the pans that came with the oven, so she put the batter into some ice cube trays. They, of course, melted, and in the meantime, London had gone outside to play."

As the others howled with laughter, London shook her head. "I forgot all about that."

"You've been a terrible cook since day one," Diana said with a small smile.

"To be fair, that's a terrible toy. Someone could've gotten really hurt with one of those. Who gives an oven to children?"

"I don't think they got much hotter than a heat lamp." Grant chuckled. "How much harm could they really do?"

"Tell that to the stench in my room," Diana said. "It took days to air out the smell." But she was laughing now too.

Reggie looked around the table. "With the exception of Diana, it looks like everyone is done. Does anybody want more food?" Everyone shook their heads. "I'll start clearing the plates. Quentin, Grant, can you help me out?"

"Sure," Quentin said. The three of them became a whirlwind of action, and within minutes, the table was clear.

"Oh, rats," Reggie said, returning from the kitchen with Grant and Quentin.

"What's the matter?" Quentin said in a voice that sounded rehearsed.

"Well, I forgot to get dessert, and we don't have anything here in the house."

"No dessert? That's terrible!" Grant said, and London scowled at him. He grinned back at her and winked.

"It really is," Reggie said. "Mama, Dad, would you be willing to go out for dessert? We can hit BabyCakes for some sweets."

"I wouldn't be opposed to some cake," Betty said.

"And I could stand to stretch my legs." Herb rose from the couch.

"London, I'll get your usual flourless chocolate cake." Reggie kissed London on the head even as London frowned at her. "Diana, can we bring you back anything?"

"Do they have crème brûlée?"

"They sure do," Grant said. "Best in the city."

"We'll be back," Reggie said. "Well, Quentin and I will."

Five people put on five coats faster than London would have thought possible, and she was suddenly alone with her sister for the first time in two decades.

London was struck by the divisive nature of her thoughts. On one hand, she had years' worth of questions to ask. She had half a lifetime of pain and anger stored, and tonight, Diana had appeared on her doorstep, the only time anyone in her family had come to her in all this time. She knew this might be her only chance to say everything she'd wanted to say. On the other hand, she didn't know where to start and didn't know if she had the energy to open up a conversation that had no clear beginning or end.

Diana dabbed at the corners of her mouth with her paper napkin. It was from a holiday set London designed and sold both in the shop and in New York and Los Angeles. It said, "Ho Ho Hoes have the happiest holidays." London didn't think Diana read the napkin because if she had, she would have voiced her disdain.

"This really was a delicious meal," Diana said. "Thank you for having me."

"Thank you for having me?" London couldn't help letting out a coarse laugh. "As if this is a normal dinner with family who hasn't shut me out for the last twenty years, and you're not dropping a bomb by showing up here tonight."

"Regardless, saying thank you is the polite thing to do." Her eyes narrowed.

"What are you doing here?"

Diana looked across the room at the stout tree covered in twinkle lights and *Star Wars* decorations. "Is that the tree you stole?"

"That's the one. Did you drive two hours to get it back?"

"Of course not."

"Then why?"

"He's taking back his offer for the extra fifty thousand dollars," Diana said. "And he's trying to get Larry Kopp to rescind Mother's inheritance money to you as well. I don't know that he'll succeed, and I'm sure you'll be getting a letter detailing everything. But I thought you should know."

"You came to tell me that money I've refused to accept is going to be rescinded?"

Diana paused, drank the remaining wine, and set her glass down on the table with a clunk. "The letter you wrote, the one that started all of this…may I see it? Please?"

She nearly said no. Who did Diana think she was, coming into her home and demanding to see something so private? Except it didn't really seem like a demand. More like a plea and a slightly desperate one at that. It was the nervous desperation that caused London to agree.

"All right." London rose unsteadily from the floor. She forced her racing heart to slow down with a few deep breaths and wished she could find a way to slow the thoughts moving through her mind at record speed. "I'll be right back. You can move to the couch if you'd be more comfortable."

London got the worn piece of green construction paper from her nightstand. As she always did when she picked it up, she traced some of the letters before going back into the living room where Diana waited. She was surprised to see that her sister still sat on the floor. She grabbed a bottle of wine from the counter, joined Diana, and filled both their glasses to the top before sliding the letter across the table.

Diana picked it up, and London was fascinated when she slid her fingertips across the childish handwriting before beginning to read. She sipped her wine and watched her twin. She hadn't really looked at her in a long time.

While London was a mixture of her parents as far as her appearance went, Diana could have been their mother's clone. It wasn't just her facial features—although her delicate ice blue eyes and fine lips were nearly identical to Grace Craft's—she also carried herself in the same regal manner, dressed in the same classic and understated style, and wore her hair in a similar bob that their mother had made her signature throughout most of her life. Only her hair color was different. Diana's was more platinum than their mother's dark blond locks, and London had a feeling that had more to do with visits to the salon than genetics.

It was odd to see someone who looked so much like their mother sitting before her. An achy twinge spread from her throat to her chest as she was reminded again of all the things she'd never get to say to Grace.

Diana looked up with her eyes full of questions. She pressed the old paper between her palms before setting it gently on the coffee table, careful to check for water spots or particles of food, and finding an acceptable place for it.

"Do you remember the day we wrote this letter?" Diana asked.

London gasped with the shock of Diana's question. "What do you mean, *we* wrote it?"

"I mean, we wrote it. You really don't remember?"

"No. I've been racking my brain trying to remember who I was when I wrote this. I haven't been able to figure out how I could be so different now than I was then."

"Well, to be fair, I don't really know you now. But my impression is that you aren't that different."

"How is it that *we* wrote this letter?" She took another drink of wine; it wasn't quite a gulp, but it was close. "Can you tell me that much?"

Diana took a sip from her own glass and rotated the stem in her fingers, making the liquid swirl inside it. She stared down into the glass as a fortune teller would look into a cup of tea leaves. "Ms. Watson gave us a week to do the assignment, and you forgot about it. You were always leaving your work until the last minute, and still, you were so good at school. That killed me. You were so good at it, and you barely even tried while I did everything early, studied twice as hard, and got the same grades as you.

"Anyway, you forgot this assignment, and somehow you charmed the teacher into giving you an extra day to finish it. Honestly, I think you selectively forgot it because you were in a complete panic about it. 'What am I supposed to say to my future self? I don't know who I'm gonna be,' you kept saying."

"That sounds like me," London said, and she couldn't help giggling.

"Exactly. You begged me to help you write it because you just didn't know what to say."

"And you did?"

Diana nodded. "I did. I thought of all the things I wanted to do when I was grown, and I told them to you. You wrote them all down."

London picked the fibrous paper up and stared at it. "You mean, this was all you?" For a moment, the world seemed to have fallen out from under her, and she felt as if she was floating in a whirlwind of disbelief.

A few years earlier, London and Tate had ridden Power Tower, a ride at Cedar Point that lifted its riders two hundred and forty feet into the air and dropped them back down to earth. It was the only roller coaster that had ever made London feel queasy. "Never again," she'd told Tate.

She felt now as she had then. Her stomach seemed to have risen to her throat, making it nearly impossible to swallow. She was dizzy and unsteady and felt desperate for something solid to grab on to.

"A lot of it," Diana admitted. "Although we didn't want our letters to be identical, so you thought of a few of your own things to add. The dog named Chowder was completely your idea and so was the volunteer work. Look, I know we haven't been in touch in many years, and I know…" She paused to take a longer drink. "I know it's basically my fault. I just wanted to remind you, before you got any official communication about the money being rescinded, that the terms outlined in this letter were never about what you wanted. This was the result of your procrastination in fifth grade and my attempt to dictate what I thought a proper adulthood would look like."

London looked at the letter for a long time. This document she'd been using as a makeshift map to try to navigate her life since her mother died was nothing more than someone else's version of what being a grown-up would mean. This was why she felt so lost. The letter had been her something solid, the thing she'd held on to since her mother and Tate died. She set the piece of paper down and felt a wave of sadness wash over her as she did. It felt as if she was giving up a security blanket that had seen her through some of her hardest days.

"London? Are you okay?"

"I was never going to take the money," she said. "I was actually pretty salty about it. But I have been kinda…well, pretty obsessed with this letter."

"Really?"

"Really. I just…I wanted to understand who I was then, and how I came to be so different. Different from my former self, different from the rest of my family to the point where we haven't been able to successfully be within five hundred feet of each other for almost twenty years."

"Well, we've been in the same room for over an hour with no major catastrophes."

"The night is still young."

To that, Diana raised her glass and clinked it against London's, and they both drank deeply. "You may not be very different from who you were at ten years old," Diana said, "but you've always been different from Mother, Dad, and me. It scared them, you know? They were always a little afraid of you."

"Because I'm so terrifying." She was being sarcastic, but Diana nodded.

"To our parents, image was everything. How scary must it have been to have a daughter who never cared what anyone thought of her? How terrifying to have created a person who valued expression and freedom over what was proper and accepted?"

London thought about that. "And you? Were you scared of me too? Is that why you stayed away?"

"No. I was jealous of you because their approval didn't dictate your life the way it dictated mine. Do you know, I could cross every item off the list of that letter? Well, except for the Chowder dog."

"You're married?"

"Divorced. My ex-husband left me for a much younger woman, and all our parents could worry about was how to spin it to make it look like I wasn't undesirable."

"You loved him?"

Diana was quiet for a moment before London saw tears escaping her eyes and rolling down her cheeks. "I thought he was the love of my life."

She didn't know what to say. "I'm sorry." In her anger all these years, she'd allowed herself to believe Diana lived a life free of any kind of pain or hardship. She realized how foolish she'd been to think she was the only one in her family who had earned the right to be sad, angry, or lonely. A bit of that anger drained from her now.

Diana wiped the tears delicately away with another raunchy napkin. "I'm the one who should be saying sorry. All these years I've spent being nothing but a yes-woman to our parents because their approval was how I gauged success in my life. But look at me. I'm nearly forty, divorced, and living with my father. I spent my entire life wanting to please my mother, and now that she's gone, I don't know who I'm supposed to be." Diana gazed at her. "I owe you so much more than an apology for standing with them when they shut you out and continuing to isolate you all this time. I don't know if you can ever forgive me, and I'm sure I don't deserve your forgiveness. But I wondered if we can try…"

"Try?"

"Try to learn to be sisters again."

Whoa. "I…" She paused to swallow. "I don't know if we can." When she saw Diana's crestfallen face, she hurried the rest of her words. "I'm not ruling it out, it's just…we don't really know each other anymore. If there's one thing I've learned after all these years without the three of you, it's that family is so much more than blood. If you truly want to be sisters again, you'll have to be patient with me. And you'll have to earn that title. I'm sorry, but that's the way it has to be. I don't have many reasons to trust you right now."

She didn't want to hurt her sister, but she knew herself. It would take a lot more than one night drinking wine together for her to let her guard down after all these years. Still, she was surprised at the glimmer of something she hadn't had with regard to anyone in her biological family in a very long time: hope. It was small and fragile, but it was there.

Diana nodded. Her eyes were sad, but they weren't as hopeless as they'd been a moment ago. "I understand."

"And Dad? Will he understand your new interest in building a relationship with me?"

"I don't know, and for the first time, I don't care. I think it's time I started living for myself."

This time, London tapped her wine glass against Diana's. "To new beginnings and living for ourselves."

They finished the wine with that toast. When Reggie and Quentin returned, they found London tucking Diana in on the couch. She pulled her index finger to her lips in a "Shh" motion. After she got Diana sufficiently covered in blankets, they gathered in the kitchen.

"She's staying the night?" Reggie asked.

"We drank a lot of wine, and I don't think she's as accustomed to alcohol as yours truly."

"Are you okay?" Quentin asked.

London put her hand in her back pocket, feeling the construction paper there. It was folded into fourths, the first time she'd folded it since she was reintroduced to it rather than placing it carefully back in the file.

"Yeah. I'm okay."

Long after Reggie and Quentin went to bed, London stayed up in the chair across from her sleeping sister. She felt a strange mixture of angst and relief at the knowledge that she no longer had to figure out who she was when she wrote this letter. Admittedly, it'd been like trying to put together a puzzle using pieces from different sets that were never meant to go together, and now she knew why.

Still, she was grateful for the letter and even grateful for the misunderstanding about it. It had given her something to focus on in the months in which she'd suffered enough loss to last her a lifetime, and her obsession with it had kept her just busy enough to help keep her from sinking into despair.

Tomorrow, she would need to begin to rearrange her life and priorities with this new knowledge. She would release this piece of paper from the power of defining a portion of her life. Tonight, she would allow herself some rest. The letter lay in her lap, and she fell asleep in that chair, her right hand clutching it.

❖

"London, you never cease to amaze me," Ross said the next afternoon. "I didn't think you'd top last week's session, and now here you are, the day after an impromptu slumber party with your estranged sister."

She'd seen Diana off that morning with plans to meet for lunch after the new year and several hugs—tearful ones—on Diana's end.

"Promise you'll call when you know what day will work for lunch," she'd said.

"I will."

She'd enjoyed seeing Ross so rapt as she told the story, but as she got to the end, she felt the lump of disappointment in her chest. She pulled the letter out of her coat pocket, the folds she'd made last night already a permanent part of the page.

"It could be the start of getting my sister back," she said.

"Indeed. So why do you seem sad?"

"Well, for one thing, I'm not getting my hopes up. Diana has been ruled by the whims of my parents for as long as I can remember. She may be changing. Lord knows the death of our mother has caused some self-examination for me too, so I guess it's not completely out of the question that she'd change now. Still, it'll be smart to hold back and see how this all plays out. I'm not ready to invite her over for Christmas dinner yet."

"That is your right, considering your history. It's a fine line to walk between openness and caution. And for another thing?"

"Excuse me?"

"You said that last point was for one thing. I assume there's at least one other thing?"

She sighed. "For another thing, I've spent the last several months trying to get into the head of my ten-year-old self by completing items from a letter I didn't even write. I'm back to square one on the self-discovery thing."

"Oh, I don't think that's true. You're hardly at square one. Think of all you've learned in the process."

"Enlighten me."

"You've learned that you didn't enjoy being without Reggie, and it seems like your time apart has really strengthened your relationship. You've learned that you've become so strong with your chosen family that you don't need to rush into anything with your biological one. And now that you know Diana was behind the goals in that letter, you've learned the most important thing of all."

"What's that?"

"That you are the same person you were when you were a kid, more or less. You didn't somehow drastically shift into a completely different London. Those goals were Diana's. Quite frankly, it didn't seem like you had much in the way of goals."

She snorted. "And I'm the same person now? Thanks a lot."

"London, you've accomplished a lot in your life. The success of Hell in a Handbasket, the growth you and Reggie have experienced, the building of a family comprised of people who have earned a place in your life. These things are huge. You don't have traditional goals, and it seems you never did. And when you do want something, you don't go about getting it in typical ways. It works for you, though, for the most part."

"I guess it does."

"So, where's the problem in that?"

He was right. She didn't need a letter to dictate who she was going to be. She knew who she was, and just as importantly, she liked who she was. She loved her business, her friends and family, her life. She didn't know exactly what she would have written, if she'd done that assignment herself, but she knew she couldn't have asked for a life that gave her more satisfaction or fulfillment than the one she had.

"There isn't one." She grinned. "I guess that means I'm cured."

"Nice try," he said. "I've already got you scheduled for the next month."

CHAPTER SIXTEEN

L ondon handed a stack of colorful cardstock to Quentin. "Here, tell me which ones you like."

"How many am I choosing?" He flipped through them.

"Two or three. Pick a few that pop out at you, and we'll get started."

They would be going to Compass the following evening for their holiday party. London and Reggie still volunteered once a week in the kitchen, and it gave Quentin a chance to visit his friends there. London had asked if he'd like to help her make holiday cards for the kids and staff, and he enthusiastically agreed.

She went over to the corner of the living room where her art supplies were overflowing from the steamer trunk she'd designated for her creative items. Since Quentin had been with them, she'd been working more and more from home so she could spend time with him. It'd been more than a week since she'd even been into Hell. Ohio State was on winter break, and Diego was helping Jasmine in the shop full-time.

This morning when she had her daily check-in phone call, London said she was thinking about bringing in another person to help in the shop. "I'm not there often enough to really even help you anymore."

"Oh?" Jasmine asked, and even in that single syllable, London recognized the satisfaction in her voice. "You won't be coming back in full-time?"

"I've enjoyed working from home a lot more than I expected. Despite the absolute mess I'm making of the living room. I swear, Reg is gonna kill me for this disaster one of these days."

Jasmine laughed. "You need an art room, somewhere you can

spread everything out the way you like and still be out of Reggie's way."

"Oh, not you too. Did Reggie put you up to talking to me about getting a bigger place?" She couldn't keep the annoyance out of her voice.

"She didn't have to. Everyone knows you need one."

London shook her head, exasperated. "Anyway, you're not opposed to bringing someone in, are you? You can have full discretion as far as the interview process goes since whoever it is will be primarily working for you. And while we're on this topic, it's about time you got a raise and a better title."

"No," Jasmine said, "that's not necessary."

"Maybe not, but it's the right thing to do. Jas, you run that place. It runs smoother with you in charge than it did when I was the one managing it. You should be called the executive manager with the salary to match."

"But—"

"No buts. This is good for me too, you know. With you in charge of the store, I'm free to do my creative work and deal with operations outside of Columbus. It will free up so much time for me. And it's what you've basically been doing for the last year, anyway."

"Well…if you're sure."

"I am. I'll come in next week and we can iron out the details."

It had been wonderful to give that news to Jasmine. London had relied heavily on her for such a long time, and she realized during this time working from home that this was a gesture that was long past due. She was only sorry she hadn't thought of it sooner.

Now she struggled to find the paints she was looking for among the piles of paper, fabric, jewelry findings, and writing instruments.

"Aha!" she said at last. "Found them." She made her way back over to the kitchen counter where Quentin sat. "Any luck?"

"I think I've decided." He handed her three cards: a silver one, a gold one, and metallic hunter green one. "Are these okay?"

"They're perfect." They cleared all the other papers away, cut the number of cards they needed for their project, and assembled them and got the paints and brushes set up. London got on a stool beside Quentin, and they began their work, sharing the paints between them. They worked in companionable silence for quite some time.

"Thank you for letting me help," he said shyly. "I used to do a lot of painting before my parents kicked me out."

"You don't have to thank me. I should be thanking you; you're doing a great job." She frowned. "You're not taking any art classes in school?"

He shook his head. "My parents wanted me to focus on academics. They thought art was silly."

She pondered this. "It can be. It can be silly or malicious or devastating or glorious. It can be one hundred percent honest and pure fantasy at the same time. That's what makes it so great."

"Yeah. You're right."

"We can see about getting you into some art workshops. There are so many avenues to take classes, some really good ones if you like."

The smile faded from his face. "No. No, thank you."

"Okay." She almost didn't ask but couldn't help herself. "Why not?"

"Because I'm not going to be here much longer." His voice was so quiet, she had to strain to hear. "And when I go back to Compass, I won't be able to keep taking those classes. I'd rather go back not knowing what I'm missing than have that amazing experience and have to give it up."

"I see. Is that how you feel about being here, with us? That you would have been better off not knowing what you were missing?"

He didn't speak. He dipped his brush in water and watched the tendril of black paint swirl around in the clear liquid.

"I'm sorry. I'm sorry if I was insensitive."

"It's not your fault."

"Quentin?"

"What?"

"Will you tell me what happened the day your parents kicked you out?"

He was silent so long, she thought he wasn't going to answer. She set her brush down and reached over to rub his back.

"I'm sorry," she said again. "You don't have to talk about it if you don't want to." She bit her lip. It had taken her years of sad Christmases to talk about the pain of why she was without her family on the holidays. A big part of her felt as if she could have sped up her healing if she had spoken out sooner, and she wanted that for Q. What she didn't want was to make things worse.

He took a long, jagged breath and turned to face her. Except he kept his eyes on his lap. The deflated tone of his voice when he finally began talking nearly broke her heart. "I have a Chromebook for school.

Everyone got one from middle school through high school. We use them for homework, class projects and stuff. Most sites that aren't academic are blocked, but you can petition to have access to certain web pages if you can convince your teacher why it's necessary for school.

"In science, we had a chance to do a project where we could pick the topic ourselves, as long as it related to something we were studying in the class. I decided to do my project on the biology of transgender beings—humans—and animals. Did you know there are lots of examples of trans animals?"

"I did. But only because Tate told me." There hadn't been a single day since Tate died that she hadn't longed for him, hadn't missed his jokes, his candor, and the very familiar rhythm of their easy conversations. But never had she wished he was still here more than she did in this moment. No matter how hard she tried, she couldn't give Quentin the kind of support he needed, not the way Tate could have.

"Right. So I requested access to a few different pages. One of them was this doctor who specializes in gender reassignment surgeries. I got really excited reading about that, you know? It was the first time I felt like maybe I wouldn't be stuck being a girl forever. Like there was hope for me."

She squeezed his shoulder. "Of course there's hope for you."

"I sent an email to the doctor's office, asking a lot of questions. Some of them were related to school, but some weren't. I asked how old you had to be to start taking testosterone and have surgery. I thought maybe I could start saving now for it. I babysat a few of the neighborhood kids, and my parents said I could start a dog walking business when I turned thirteen. They didn't know what the money was for. I guess they thought I was saving for college."

He took several more deep breaths. They weren't as jagged as before, and London hoped that was a good sign.

"I was babysitting the little girl next door one night, and when I got home, my parents were sitting at the kitchen table with my Chromebook open, looking at the email I sent. When I filled out the contact form, it asked for my address, and I put it in there. The doctor's office contacted my parents asking if they wanted to bring me in for a consultation.

"The form I filled out asked if I was a minor, and if so, did I have my parents' consent to speak with them. Like an idiot, I put yes to both.

I didn't know they were going to call. I thought I'd just get an email back."

"What happened?"

"My mom started screaming that I was a demon. She said I was evil, that only a demon would insult God by trying to change my natural form from what He intended. And my dad...he didn't say anything. He used the buckle of his belt to get his point across."

She shuddered and pulled him closer.

"After I took the beating, they put me in the car and drove me downtown, dropped me off outside Stonewall. They told me I could go get the other fags and trannies to help me. My dad started driving off before I even got all the way out of the car. That's the last time I saw them."

"Jesus, Quentin. I am so, so sorry they did that to you." This child was, without a doubt, the sweetest human being she'd ever known. As long as she lived, she would never understand how a parent could do something like he described. He'd drawn back, and she had to fight the urge to wrap her arms around him again. Everything in her wanted to form a protective shield around this little boy, to spare him from ever being hurt like that again. She realized what was holding her back was what he'd said about not wanting to know what he was missing. How protective could any embrace or word or action from her be if she was just going to send him back into this cruel world to fend for himself?

"Me too." He paused. "I'm glad Reggie was able to get me in at Compass."

"Wait. Reggie? You met Reggie before the night you came home with us?"

"Yeah," he said, seeming surprised. "You didn't know? I thought that's why I came home with you guys, because she'd met me before. She even came to Compass a couple times to say hi and check on me."

Waves of confusion, disbelief, and anger washed over her, and in those waves, she couldn't catch her breath. What did this mean? And why hadn't Reggie said anything?

"London?" His voice brought her back into the moment. "You okay?"

"Oh, honey, I'm an ass, I'm sorry. I should be asking you that question."

He shrugged. "I'm still here."

"I can't tell you how grateful I am for that."

"Can I ask you something?"

"Of course. Anything."

He picked up his paintbrush and fidgeted with it. "Remember when you told me the story of your first Christmas without your family and how hard it was?"

"Yes."

"Well, how did that get easier? How did you get over it?"

She thought for a moment. "Time and space from a traumatic event works some pretty major miracles. This will be my nineteenth Christmas since that happened, so you might say I've had some practice doing the holidays without them."

"Okay. What else?"

"Therapy has helped me a lot. It's helped me learn about distinguishing between things that are and are not within my control. I can't control the way my family reacted to who I am, and I've had to learn to let that go. And saying that makes it sound easy, which it's not. Simple, yes; easy, no. I can control how kind and forgiving I am to myself, and to others. I can control the levels at which I accept and love myself."

He nodded, his lips pressed together.

"And I've built a family of my own, as you've seen." Her voice wavered, and she had to pause for a moment. It was Tate who'd helped her through those first few Christmases when it was just the two of them. She glanced at the stolen tree and wiped a few tears away. Her heart ached with missing him. "I've made new traditions with people I love and who love me. That makes a big difference. It's hard for you now because you don't have the same luxury at your age to decide who's going to be your family. But someday you will, and I hope, when you get there, you won't accept less than people who embrace all that you are and love you without condition or apology. Those are the kinds of people who deserve to be your family. You'll get there."

"I hope so," he said, resting his head on her shoulder. They sat like that for several minutes. London got up and made some hot cocoa, and they resumed their art project almost as if there'd been no interruption. That companionable silence had been replaced with an uneasy one, though, and try as they might, they couldn't go back to the contented atmosphere they'd started with.

London wondered if she'd done the right thing asking Q about the circumstances surrounding getting kicked out of his parents' house. She watched as he focused on one of the cards, his tongue stuck out while he concentrated on painting. He'd been through so much, and she worried about him holding all those bad memories inside. She knew all too well how toxic emotions had a tendency to fester inside a soul, and she didn't want Quentin to lose even a tiny bit of himself to that.

She looked back over at the tree and thought of Tate. Lots of people believed that their loved ones watched over them after they died and that a part of them lived on, aware of earthly goings on. London had never thought much about it before, but now, she desperately wanted to believe that was true for Tate. *If you're there, help me figure out what's best for this little boy. I don't know how to do this without you.*

❖

Betty called and asked if they'd like to come over for dinner that night.

"Sure. Did you ask Reggie too?"

"I texted her, and she said it was fine but to check with you."

"Sounds good." London had an idea. "Betty, would it be okay if we left Quentin with you for an hour or so after dinner?"

"Of course, darlin'. Is everything all right?"

"Yes," she fibbed. "We just have some last-minute Christmas shopping to do, shopping we can't do with him around."

"I understand. That sweet boy. He deserves a beautiful Christmas after everything he's been through."

"I agree. Can we bring anything tonight?"

"Oh, if you'd like to pick up something for dessert, that would be wonderful."

"Will do."

Several hours later, Reggie drove the three of them to her childhood house on Sumner Street. When they arrived, Herb was shoveling the walkway to the door. Quentin ran up to him. "Why don't you let me help you?" Quentin asked.

Herb rested the base of the shovel in the small snow mound next to the walkway and clasped his hands around the handle. "I'll tell you what, if you finish the walkway, I'll pay you. How does twenty dollars sound?"

Quentin laughed. "It sounds like twenty too much for a job I offered to do for free."

"Well, that's my final offer, my good man, although your impertinence does tempt me to go up to twenty-five."

"Okay, okay." Quentin held his hands up, palms out. "You've got a deal."

"Good." Herb handed over the shovel. "And when you're done, just set the shovel over by the garage. Then go over and water the plants across the street like you did the other day." He fished around in his coat pocket, pulled out a key, and handed it to Q. "Betty's making hot cocoa, and we'll have a cup waiting for you when you get back."

"Oh, Mama's cocoa," Reggie said. "I'm ready for my cup!"

"Well, come on in."

London looked out the front door at Quentin, already hard at work clearing the sidewalk, before following the others into the kitchen. "It smells good in here." She set the apple pie they'd purchased from Giant Eagle on the counter. "I didn't even bother to ask what was for dinner because I know whatever Betty makes is going to be good."

Betty hugged her. "Sweet-talking me about my cooking always was the way to my heart. It's just a good old-fashioned pot roast."

"Yum." Reggie had a marshmallow mustache from taking a large gulp of cocoa. "I can't wait for Q to try this."

"He'll love it," Herb said. "Although I'd hate to meet the monster who didn't like your mama's hot cocoa."

Betty chuckled. "Oh, listen to the three of you. This is how you get out of helping me in the kitchen."

"Yes, but it's all true." London grinned.

Nothing could turn her mood around like spending time with Herb and Betty. She'd been hollow with the absence of Tate today and had been unable to shake the feeling that she was on the verge of being lost, of floating away from herself and her life like a balloon someone neglected to tie securely to a child's wrist. Ten minutes with Reggie's parents brought her firmly back to the ground, and the earth felt solid under her feet again.

"So, whose plants is Quentin watering?" Reggie asked.

"The Smiths are spending another winter in Florida. Although, last I heard from them, they might be moving there for good."

"Wow," Reggie said. "They've been here since before we moved in, haven't they?"

"Yes, but their kids grew up and moved away, and they really enjoy themselves down there. Looks like they'll come back in the spring to put their house on the market, and when it sells, that will be that."

They heard the front door open and Quentin stomping the snow off his boots. Betty poured a fresh cup of cocoa, adding some marshmallows and setting it on the table at the seat beside Reggie just as Quentin entered the kitchen.

"Quentin!" Betty rushed over to squeeze him to her. "You just get more handsome all the time."

Quentin smiled and thanked her. He was almost as tall as the tiny woman. *Has he grown since he came to live with us?* It didn't seem possible, and yet, she was sure he hadn't been this tall last time they saw Betty and Herb.

Soon, they all sat down to a dinner of Betty's pot roast. After they'd passed the serving dishes around, poured the water, soda, and wine, and Quentin led them in a prayer at Betty's request, they began to eat.

"Oh," Betty said, turning to Reggie and London, "when you go out to run your errands tonight, I wondered if it's all right if we take Quentin to look at Christmas lights. If you think you'd like that, Quentin?"

"I'd love it!"

"Our errands?" Reggie stopped with a forkful of roast beef and carrots halfway to her mouth.

"Yeah," London said. "I let your parents know we have some last-minute Christmas errands to run, and they said they'd like to hang out with Q while we go." She held her breath and hoped that Reggie would go with it without a fuss. If she had to come clean with Reg, she would, but she preferred to go into the evening without any preconceived ideas.

Reggie looked at her with blank eyes, then shrugged and put her food in her mouth. After dinner, Herb and Quentin went to the living room to watch television. Betty looked in on them on her way to the kitchen where London and Reggie were loading the dishwasher.

"He just loves that little boy," Betty said. "We both do."

"He's easy to love," Reggie said.

"That he is. Now, you girls go along. You've cleared most of the dishes, and I can do the rest."

"Are you sure?" London asked.

"Of course. Get on out of here. Quentin is in good hands until you get back."

When they stepped out on the front porch, Reggie said, "I didn't remember us having any errands to run tonight."

"That's because I made it up." London grabbed the keys from Reggie's gloved hand. "I'll drive."

CHAPTER SEVENTEEN

"What are we doing here?" Reggie asked. They sat in the Compass parking lot.

"We have a meeting with Joan." She stepped out of the car, bent over, and peered at Reggie, who was still sitting inside. "Coming?"

Reggie had given up trying to guess where they were going less than five minutes into the ride.

"You'll know once we're there," London had said before turning the radio up and singing along with the newest song from Tegan & Sara.

They stepped inside, warm air surrounding them in the small vestibule. They hung up their coats and went toward Joan's office. On the way, they bumped into several kids, said hi to Bernadette and Jacob, and waved at Michael and Doris who were training newbies in the kitchen. Finally, they reached the office and found Joan reading through some papers at her desk. London knocked on the heavy wood of the door frame, and Joan looked up.

"Hello." She set down her papers. "Please come in."

Reggie and London filed in and took the same chairs as last time. It had been only a month ago, but it felt like a lifetime to London. She'd been so unsure and panicky about taking Q home. She couldn't believe how quickly he'd become a part of her life, her family. This room suddenly seemed smaller, less daunting, as if forging her relationship with Quentin had made her larger.

"How can I help you this evening?" Joan asked. "You were cryptic on the phone today, London."

"That seems to be the theme of the day," Reggie said. "What's this all about, babe?"

London took a deep breath and exhaled slowly. For good measure, she did this two more times before she spoke. "I'd like to know the truth about Quentin."

Joan frowned. "I'm not sure I know what you mean. What is it you'd like to know?"

London laced her fingers together and set her hands in her lap, "I found out from Quentin today that he met you," London turned to Reggie, "on the night his parents kicked him out. In fact, he was dropped off at Stonewall, and you were the one who got him to Joan." She paused, surveying the look of surprise on Reggie's face; she relished it. *Good, let her be surprised. I'm tired of being the only one blindsided by people's secrets.* "Why didn't you tell me? If not when I started volunteering here, at least when we brought him home. Did you think it wouldn't come up someday?"

"I thought it would take longer than it did," Reggie said. "I didn't expect him to share so much so fast with you. I figured it would come out naturally, and I did plan to tell you, but I thought I had more time."

"I don't understand. More time for what? Why didn't you just tell me you knew him?"

"Maybe I can help a little with this," Joan said. "If I may?"

"Please," London said, and Reggie nodded.

"It was clear, so many months ago when Regina brought Quentin here, that he was an incredibly special little boy. No child deserves to be cast out, as so many of the ones who come to us have been. But Quentin? He's all sweetness. He's not wild or rebellious or hard to handle; he's just a compassionate, loving child."

"Okay," London said. "I get all of that. But why the secrecy, Reg? Q said you came here to visit him a couple times, and the night we brought him home, you never mentioned it. You acted like that was the first night you met him, and I want to know why."

In all their years together, London had never known Reggie to lie, not even by omission, to her or to anyone else. It was one of the things she loved most, her inability to be anything but truthful. The question that had been in her mind since Quentin told her he already knew Reggie surfaced again. Why would she start now?

"I just loved him," Reggie said. "We've been talking for years about adopting, but I never got a firm answer from you. I knew if I begged, you might go through with it, but I didn't want to beg. It shouldn't be like that."

"What does adopting have to do with you meeting Quentin?" Moments after London said it, things added up in her head, and she gasped and stared. How foolish she'd been. Everyone else had seen this coming; everyone had known on some level that this was the plan. She hadn't been able to get her mind around it because of what she knew— or thought she knew—about Reggie. Reggie, who was always honest and direct, hadn't breathed a word about adoption, and so she hadn't thought it was on the table. London didn't know which was worse, realizing Reggie betrayed her in ways she never thought possible or how inexplicably stupid she had been about the whole situation.

Joan stood. "Why don't I give you two some time alone. I'll go see the kids." She slid around the desk and left, closing the door gently behind her.

"London—"

"Is that why you asked me to marry you?"

"I asked you because I want you to be my wife. But, yes, it's easier to adopt when the couple is married. Especially when it's a lesbian couple."

London kneaded her forehead with her knuckles. "So, you met Q a few times, decided we should adopt him, and you and Joan concocted this whole plan together? This is why you steered me toward Compass when I became interested in marketing work? Did you know what was going to happen when we came here on Thanksgiving?" She'd just realized Reggie lied, and now she had to come to terms with the way she'd manipulated her. That hurt so much worse than the lies. London had spent her childhood and young adult life being manipulated by her parents and always felt as if her thoughts and emotions were being twisted in an attempt to get her to bend to their will. Never could she have imagined Reggie might be capable of something like that. Her head pounded, and her heart throbbed with this new knowledge.

Reggie tried to speak and stuttered a few nonsensical words.

"You did know. Jesus. You've been pulling my strings since September, and I've been the good little puppet, going along with every scene you've set up for me to perform in."

"It's not like that."

"How is it, then?"

"Please," Reggie said, "give me a moment to explain."

London crossed her arms. Six months ago, she would have gotten up and walked out, but they'd been through so much together recently.

She was keenly aware of all the ways Reg had shown up for her, and all the concessions she'd made for their relationship, and for that reason alone, she stayed in her chair.

"Like Joan said, the moment we met Q, we knew he was special. He made me think again about adoption, brought it back to the front of my mind. At first, even though he was the catalyst, it wasn't even him I was thinking about. We've always talked about adopting a baby or a toddler, a child we could raise from the beginning who would only know us as parents.

"At the same time, my birthday was coming…my fortieth birthday. I have my career, my finances, my friends, exactly as I want them. And I have you, but I wanted more with you and for us. I wanted you to be my wife. I wanted us to have a family. Suddenly, with my birthday looming over me, I just…"

"You just what?"

"I realized that I don't have an unlimited amount of time to have the life I dreamed of. You and I have been together for six years, and I knew I wanted to marry you and have kids with you three weeks in. I thought you'd eventually come around, but all these years later, I wasn't so sure. I've spent all this time giving you space to come to the same conclusions—that we would be married, with a family—and I realized you may not ever get there. And I decided to give you a nudge."

"A nudge." The room swirled, and she clenched the armrests to steady herself.

"Yes. I thought, I'd ask you to marry me, and if you said no, there'd be no harm done, you know? That if you said no, nothing would change, and we could just keep going as we had been because married or not, kids or not, we had a beautiful life."

"But when I said no, you left me."

"I wasn't prepared for how much it would hurt. I wasn't prepared for how brokenhearted I was when you turned me down."

London didn't know what to say. She was sorry she'd hurt Reggie, but she'd already made all of her apologies for that, and besides, she was too furious about what she'd discovered tonight to feel sympathy right now. "So, steering me toward Compass. That was all a ruse to get me close to Quentin?"

Reggie shook her head. "It really wasn't. I sent you here because I knew Joan, and I knew she would put you to work. I thought this place would be good for you."

"And the night we took him home? You knew?"

Reggie hesitated. "Joan contacted me the day before Thanksgiving and told me the situation here. She said we were her first choice for Q. I told her I was for it, but it was going to ultimately be up to you."

London felt tears prickle her eyes, but she blinked them back. "We got back together that night."

"London, don't you see, this all happened for a reason. My sending you here was the start of us restarting our life together, a life that Q can be a part of." Reggie reached for her hand, but she yanked it away.

"We got back together that night, and it was just another manipulation in a long string of manipulations to get us where we are now." She stared down at her white-knuckled hands, still clenching the arms of her chair, unable to look anywhere near Reggie. In their time apart, she had waited for Reggie to see they were meant to be together and come back. Despite her unease with the circumstances surrounding their reconciliation, she'd let herself believe Reggie had come to her senses. Now she felt as if it had all been a means to an end, and she was shattered all over again.

"Baby, please," Reggie said. "I was trying to do what I always did after the proposal. Lay out the options for you and give you space to do what you wanted to do organically. To come to whatever terms you felt were best for you, that's all. I learned my lesson after I proposed. I've always known you're someone who can't be pushed, and I pushed when I proposed because I wanted so badly to marry you. I didn't want to make that mistake again."

"So you lied to me?"

Reggie raked her hand through her hair. "I thought it was something we'd laugh about someday after it all came out."

"After we got married and adopted Q under false pretenses."

"What false pretenses? We love each other, and we both love Quentin."

London stood. "It's not that simple, and you know it."

"Where are you going?"

"I'll take a Lyft to Grant's house. I can't be with you right now; I need to think tonight. Tell Q I'll pick him up tomorrow to come here for the holiday party."

London rushed through the living area, grabbed her coat from the vestibule, and stepped outside. She moved to the front of the building, stood on the sidewalk, and ordered her Lyft. Then as an afterthought, she texted Grant.

You home? Less than thirty seconds later, he responded.

Yep.
Good. I'm on my way over, and I need to crash on your couch.

❖

London woke the next morning to the sound of Grant making coffee. She sat up on the couch and looked between her fingers around the sun-filled room.

"You need curtains in here," she muttered.

"What?" he called from the kitchen.

"Good morning," she called back. Moments later, he arrived by her side with a steaming cup of coffee. She accepted it and inhaled the rich smell before taking a sip. "God, I forgot how good your coffee was."

"Reggie doesn't make coffee like I do?"

"She makes it, but you make it stronger. I can practically feel my eyes flexing their muscles when I drink your coffee."

"Mission accomplished." He took a sip. "I have to start getting ready for work after I finish this cup. You're welcome to stay as long as you want."

"Thank you."

"Sweetie, that's my way of asking how long you're staying."

"Oh. Just today, I think."

"Really?"

"Yeah. I'll go home tonight. I just needed space away from Reggie last night. I needed to process."

"Did you come up with any decisions?"

"I did. But I'll tell you more about them later, okay?" The worst of the sting from last night had subsided, but she was still tender about the situation. It had taken most of the night to calm her feelings enough to think reasonably about the whole thing, and she wanted to stay in that logical space until she had a chance to talk to Reggie.

"Okay," he said. "I'll be here. In the meantime, is there anything you need from me before I leave?"

"Can I use your computer? I have a few emails I need to send out and work to do today, and I didn't anticipate the need to bring my laptop with me last night."

"Sure, I'll get you set up before I jump in the shower."

She sat at the desk in the corner of his living room, looking around. The fresh pale blue paint was lovely and gave the apartment a tranquil feel. That combined with the Asian-influenced décor, made her feel positively Zen. She hadn't been back to Grant's since Thomas moved out, she realized, feeling a little guilty. Granted, he'd moved in with her after his breakup, but he'd been back here for a month, and she hadn't been over once. *Is this what parents go through? Getting wrapped up in their own lives and their kids to the point of neglecting their other loved ones?* Maybe.

She realized she was thinking of herself as a parent and Quentin as her kid, and she waited for the familiar panic to flood through her, but it didn't come. Instead, she felt a nearly crippling love for him. It stunned her, leaving her unable to move for several moments. She loved him, and that love filled spaces in her heart she never knew existed. It was as if Quentin had access to a place she'd never visited, but all the same, that place was home. She had to shake herself a little to remove herself from her thoughts, and she deliberately focused on business.

She turned to the computer and began sifting through emails. It amazed her how many could accumulate in the evening after she signed off for the day. She opened a message from a prospective art buyer whose shop London had been trying to get into for over a year, asking for some of her summer samples. She looked around Grant's impossibly clean desk for paper and a pen so she could jot down a few ideas before emailing him back.

"How can anybody work like this?" she asked under her breath. She opened the top drawer and found some pens and a notepad. When she went to close the drawer, she noticed a set of four photos in a long strip, the kind from a photo booth. She pulled it out and gasped at who was in the pictures with Grant. How could he not have told her?

Footsteps behind her made her whirl around. Grant was approaching the mirror on the other side of the room, straightening his tie and pushing a few loose strands of hair back where they belonged.

"I'm gonna leave a spare key so you can lock up in case you need to leave before I get home." He caught a glimpse of her in the mirror and stopped his primping. "What's with the face?"

She held up the pictures. "I was getting ready to ask you the same thing."

He squinted, turned around, and walked a few steps toward her before realizing what was in her hand. "Oh."

"You've gotta say something besides 'oh.' How long have you been dating Michael? And when were you planning to tell me?"

"We've only been on a few dates."

"A few dates? And you're already taking photo booth pictures?"

"We went to see the Christmas lights at the zoo, and the booth was just right there." He ducked his head. "And I planned to tell you. I just wanted to see if it was going to stick. And because...well, it's not even three months since Thomas and I split and even less time since I gave up hope he'd come back. I don't normally move on this fast, but we hit it off and started staying in touch, and...he's a great guy. I would've told you once I was sure there was something to tell."

"Fair enough." A part of her felt as if this was another secret kept from her, another lie of omission. The more sensible part of her knew Grant was cautious, and probably had good reason to be wary after his break up with Thomas.

He glanced at his watch. "Listen, I've got to run. I'm leading a big meeting this morning, and I need to get to work to set up. Text me if you need anything, okay? I'll be at Compass tonight for the holiday party, so I'll see you there."

He kissed her on the cheek and hurried out the door, grabbing his coat and putting it on as he left. London looked at the happy faces in the four photos, then put them in the drawer and got back to work.

She got her second and much larger shock that day when she opened an email from Thomas's law firm. She expected it to be the communication Diana had warned her about. What she found instead gave her a jolt that made her feel as if her blood was racing through her body at record speed, and she shook her head and read the message again, and a third time. She leaned back in the chair and twirled around in it.

"Well," she said to the empty room, "I didn't see that coming."

❖

"Did you have a good time at Grant's?" Quentin asked as he and Reggie got in London's car.

"I did," she said. "I'd forgotten how long it had been since I was last at his place. He'll be there tonight, by the way. He's excited to see you."

London texted Reggie when she was on her way to make sure Reggie was still coming. Reggie had seemed surprised London still wanted her there. *It's the holiday party*, London had said in her text. *You should be there.*

Quentin, excited about the party, talked nonstop all the way to Compass. London was happy to let him do all the talking she and Reggie didn't want to do, and she was glad he was so enthusiastic about tonight.

It had been lightly snowing when they left the condo, but in the ten minutes it took to drive to Compass, it turned into nearly a whiteout. London felt relieved when she pulled into the parking lot, having spent the last several minutes straining to see past the billowing clouds of snowfall that pushed toward the Jeep's windshield. They walked in a clump to the door to ward off the wind. Inside the vestibule, they felt the familiar blast of hot air as they took off their coats.

"Quentin!" Bernadette called when they walked into the living room.

"Hey!" He waved. "Can I go give my friends their holiday cards?"

"Of course."

He joined the other kids, hugging them and handing out the festive cards he and London had made together.

London felt a hand on her back and turned. Grant stood there in a dark red sweater with a plaid tie peeking out the top. "Hey stranger." He hugged her, and after a brief pause turned and hugged Reggie too.

"Thanks for keeping my girl company last night," Reggie said.

Grant lifted his eyebrows. "It wasn't exactly under the happiest circumstances, but you're welcome."

"I know it. I'll make it up to her." She turned her apologetic gaze to London. "I'll make it up to you."

"Yes, you will." She was beginning to forgive Reg for what she'd done after spending the night trying to see things from her point of view, but she wasn't ready to share that info yet. She would forgive, and they would move on, but not before they had some serious discussions about trust and communication. Reggie's eyes widened, but she didn't say anything else.

"Hey, you three," called Doris, her gravelly voice cutting through the chatter around them. "Get over here to the kitchen and make yourselves useful." They joined Doris and Michael in the kitchen and exchanged hugs. London watched Michael and Grant kiss each other's cheeks and embrace, and she grinned when Grant caught her staring. She gave him a brief thumbs-up before anyone else noticed.

"Since we all know what a hazard I am in the kitchen, I'm sure none of you will mind if I excuse myself for a minute," London said.

"Where are you going?" Reggie asked.

"To talk to Joan." She squeezed Reg's outstretched hand. "I won't be gone long, I promise."

"She's in her bedroom," Doris said, "not her office. Just go right through the east sleeping area, and you'll find her."

"Thanks."

She found the doorway of Joan's bedroom. It wasn't what she expected at all, so different from Joan's office and her personal aesthetic. It was a cozy room that looked as if someone had attempted to try to make it shabby chic but had only achieved the shabby part. Frayed blankets draped the double bed and the back of a worn armchair, and chipped paint covered the single nightstand. There were old black-and-white portraits on the wall: one of a couple on their wedding day and another of the same couple holding a baby wearing a christening gown.

"Those are my parents." Joan stepped out of a room off to the side that London hadn't noticed. The vanity and shower curtain led her to deduce it was Joan's bathroom. "And me when I got baptized." Joan was putting an earring through her lobe and fastening it.

"Where are your parents now?"

"They died many years ago. I used my inheritance to build this place."

"I'm sure they would've been proud of you for that."

Joan chuckled. "They would've called me a fool. But that doesn't really matter, does it?"

"Most days, it doesn't."

"Come on in." Joan sat in the armchair and gestured to the bed until London sat gingerly on the edge. "What can I do for you this evening?"

"I had a few questions for you." When Joan nodded, she continued. "First, I wondered if you'd given more thought to the prospect of me working here in some marketing capacity. That was, after all, my reason to come to you, and despite my desperate fails in the kitchen, I wanted to follow up on it."

Joan held London's gaze for a moment, then reached into the pocket of her bright red blazer, scooped out the other earring and began to fasten it. "Truthfully, no."

"No?"

"I haven't given more thought to you working here. And that's not to say that you won't someday teach art classes or serve in some sort of artistic capacity, as I know you're very skilled in that area. There's a far smaller chance you'll ever be in marketing, but I think you know that."

"I do. Which leads me to my next question: Reggie sent me here because she had the professional connection to you, and she thought it would be a good place for me to start. That's what she told me, and I believe her."

"I believe her too, for what it's worth. To my knowledge, she never cooked up sending you here for any reason other than wanting to help you achieve a goal you were determined to accomplish."

"And you? Was that ever something you thought was possible?"

"No, I never saw you rising in the ranks to become our next great marketing executive. It was never about that."

Knowing the answer already, London asked, "What was it about, then?"

"Quentin."

"You knew from day one he'd be coming home with us."

"I hoped. I knew the two of you showed enough promise to get you involved and see where it would go. I caught a glimpse of what could be when Reggie brought him here the night he was so scared and beaten down, devastated by what the world and his family had done to him. And then, when you came here...it just seemed like all the stars may have been aligning, but of course, I had to vet all of you to be sure."

"And now? Are you sure?"

"Well, now, I'm afraid, it's not my job to be sure. That is up to you, and not just you. You, Reggie, Quentin. You have to be sure, sure of each other and sure of yourselves. I can give my opinion on it, and when the time comes, I will. But as it stands right now, it's not up to me."

London pondered that. Now that she'd gotten her bearings and made her decisions, it was scary to think that so much was still beyond her control. It hadn't occurred to her that Reggie or Quentin might not want the same thing she now wanted, and the thought made her throat tighten. She got lost in her worry until there was a knock on the door.

Quentin stood there, smiling and holding out a sparkling gold card. "Is it okay if I give you your holiday card now, Joan?"

Joan smiled, and it encompassed her entire face. She crossed the room with outstretched arms to hug Quentin, and he hugged her back ferociously. When she pulled away, Joan put her hands on his shoulders. "You look good," she said. "You're taller. Now, where's my card?" Quentin handed it to her, and she opened it and read:

"Now and always, know that you are loved and sacred. May the spirit of the season hold you and fill your every moment." Joan turned to Quentin. "And it's got this beautiful painting in the background!" She touched the shimmering peace and infinity symbols Quentin had artfully woven together.

"London and I made them together," he said. "She did the calligraphy for the words, and I did the painting. We came up with what it was gonna say together."

"Sounds like you two make a perfect team. I love it; thank you so much." She put the card on the very front of her dresser, center stage in the midst of a dozen other holiday cards. "Now, we should probably be getting out there, shouldn't we? I bet dinner is almost ready."

"Yeah," he said. "Reggie sent me to get you guys; she said it would just be a few more minutes."

Moments later, they all stood behind their chairs, heads bowed as they prepared to eat their holiday meal. "Quentin," Joan said, "we haven't heard from you in quite some time. Would you like to speak tonight?"

"Okay. I'm thankful tonight for friends I've made, for love I've shared, and wishes I'm starting to make again. Especially that last one. You know things have gone wrong in your life when you stop making wishes. I don't know what's going to happen in the next few years or even the next few months, but I know there are good people in the world, and I know again that not all my wishes are wasted." He cleared his throat, and through tears, London realized he was crying. That newly discovered maternal love swelled in her, and she was struck by an overwhelming urge to hug him as tightly as her arms allowed. She gripped the back of her chair instead. "That's it," he finished.

The rest of the evening went by in a flurry of shuffling chairs, heavy food and sweets, lots of laughter, and a few more tears. When London went to bed that night, she realized she could barely remember the food or conversation, but she felt she would never forget what Quentin said before they sat down to eat.

CHAPTER EIGHTEEN

L ondon woke early the next morning and lay awake, staring at the ceiling in the dark. Reggie was off work until after Christmas, and of course, Quentin was on winter break, so they'd both be sleeping in. Quentin had gotten up at his normal time the first few days of break, but he'd been sleeping later and later. It was December twenty-third, and London had a lot to do today. She waited until almost six a.m. and slipped out of bed to shower and dress.

Before leaving the apartment, she peeked past the screen into Quentin's alcove, finding him sleeping soundly on his stomach, his legs tucked under him and his butt up in the air. She covered her mouth to keep from giggling. She wrote a quick note to Reg and Q, letting them know she was out running errands and would be back with lunch and dessert, grabbed her coat, and tiptoed out the door.

As a small business owner, London made it a policy to patronize other small businesses as much as possible, and this included coffee shops. She mostly stuck with Fox in the Snow, which had, in her opinion, the best coffee in the city. But it was very early, and Starbucks was not only open, it had a drive-thru. She made her second and probably last trip to Starbucks for the year and got a salted caramel mocha, venti-sized, to match the tasks she had in store for the day.

She'd drained nearly half the cup when she arrived at Thomas's office fifteen minutes later. She waited only a few minutes before the pretty receptionist told her she could go on back. She looked at the time on her phone and saw that it was barely after seven. She knew Thomas arrived early, but she was surprised to see administrative staff at this hour. Hopefully, the receptionist made a lot of money for her trouble. London was still barely coherent this early; she couldn't imagine having to be friendly and fully coiffed with a full face of makeup and attentive attitude to match.

"London." Thomas opened his office door and waved off her extended hand to pull her into a hug. "Sorry to keep you waiting."

"I've only been here a couple minutes."

"Good. You look well."

She laughed. "You know damn well that looking well doesn't happen for me before nine a.m. But thank you."

He chuckled and pulled one of the chairs facing his desk back, giving her space to move in front of it. "Please sit down and make yourself comfortable." He shifted back behind his desk and sat, pulled something up on the computer screen, and nodded. "I know you have an idea why you're here today since you got my email."

"A vague idea, yeah."

"Again, I have to apologize for the delay in relaying all this to you. Tate had initially set all this up through a different attorney before he had his surgeries. After we met and became friends, he wanted to start transferring things over so I'd be managing his funds, but we were in the midst of that when he died, causing delays. Due to the nature of my friendship with him and with you, I fought to be the one who took care of all this. It wasn't about the money for me; I want you to understand that. I made next to nothing and let the previous attorneys keep most of the fees. I wanted to do one last thing for Tate."

"I understand." She was touched. Tate had impacted so many people, and she was pleased Thomas wanted to honor him. "I appreciate that, and I know Tate would've loved you for this."

His eyes clouded. "He was very special."

"Yes, he was."

He shook his head. "Now, let's get down to business." He looked again at his computer screen, clicked a few times, and London heard the buzzing of pages being filtered through the printer behind him. He grabbed the sheets and swiveled back to lay them on his desk. "Tate was very successful at his job. He was also very frugal, spending only the minimum needed for living expenses throughout his career. He had nearly no debt, and what little he did have has been paid off already, as have his funeral expenses. What's left goes to you." He slid one of the papers across the desk. "Did you bring your bank account information?"

She nodded, unable to speak. She got out the checkbook she'd gotten for free but had never used—*who writes personal checks* _anymore?_—and wrote "VOID" in large letters across one of the checks, ripping it out and handing it to him.

He took it from her, grinning. "You could've just let me copy the info I needed. You didn't have to waste a check."

She shrugged and shook her head.

He wrote the information on two different sheets of paper. "Okay if I shred this?" he asked, holding up her voided check. She nodded again and watched him shove the small paper into the machine that ate it up. He then asked her to sign the bottom of both sets of papers. When she was done, he handed her one set to keep.

She stared at the sum Tate left her. It came with no conditions or ultimatums. She wasn't required to live someone else's life or reach someone else's goals. He'd given this gift in death as freely as he'd given acceptance and unconditional love in life. Even now, he was finding ways to tell her she wasn't alone, that she had family, and she was loved.

"One more thing," Thomas said. "Something I didn't mention in the email. I wanted to talk about it in person."

"What is it?"

He pulled a plain white envelope from his desk drawer, the kind used to mail a bill. "He wrote you a letter when he was getting ready to transition in case something happened to him."

She swallowed hard. Another letter. Her deceased relatives certainly had a way of speaking to her from beyond the grave. With shaking hands, she hugged it to her chest. "Have you read it?"

He blushed. "Yes. It wasn't entirely my business, although I could pretend I needed to read it to make sure there was no pertinent legal information inside. Honestly, I just wanted to…to feel him again, the way he was. I'm sorry."

"Don't be. I get it." She stood, gathering her paperwork, and once again, he stepped around the desk to hug her.

"Don't be a stranger, okay?" he said.

"I won't." She moved to leave, and as she reached for the door, Thomas spoke.

"London?"

She turned. "Yeah?"

He paused, biting his lip. "How's Grant?"

She smiled. "He's good. Really good. Do you want me to tell him you asked about him?"

"No." He shook his head. "I just wanted to know he was okay."

She nodded and left, closing the door behind her. She checked the time on her phone and saw that her appointment had taken much less time than she anticipated. Given what her next errand was, she thought it was positively divine intervention that allowed her to have this brief interaction with Tate. Hoping it would fortify her, she walked the few blocks from Thomas's office to Schiller Park and read his letter.

The nervousness she'd felt all morning was gone. Tate's letter was tucked into the left breast pocket of her coat, and as she walked into the jail, she put her hand over her heart and felt the reassuring crinkle of the pages.

Detective Harper met her at the entrance and gave her a concerned smile. Since the night London texted her requesting to speak to Amanda Alexander, Detective Harper had been trying to talk her out of it.

"The prosecutor will never allow you to visit. We can't take the risk that anything you say could affect the outcome of the trial. If it looks like we let you intimidate any party involved, it could ruin our chances at a guilty verdict."

It had seemed as if that was the end of it until yesterday, when London received a call from Kyle Brown informing her that Amanda had made a plea deal agreeing to testify against her friends in return for serving less time. She would be incarcerated for only eight months with credit for the time she'd already spent behind bars.

"I want to see her," London said to Kyle. She kept her voice low and steady, not wanting him to hear a trace of the rage she felt at the news that this woman would be spending only a few months in prison.

Kyle had paused. "Yes, Detective Harper mentioned you've been interested in speaking to her. You'll have the opportunity to face Mr. Morgan's attackers in court, and I think that would be the best way—"

"She came to my store." She struggled to maintain her composure, but her anger was so thick that it felt like an erupting volcano. Hot rage bubbled through her, and she heard her voice waver. "After what she did to Tate, she figured out where I work and came to find me. I need to know what she had to say."

Several phone calls and texts later, she got word that she'd be given twenty supervised minutes with Amanda, and she couldn't discuss the specifics of Tate's murder or Amanda's plea deal. And now she was emptying her pockets and going through the metal detectors, her eyes fixed on the ugly gray doors in front of her. Once past those doors, she'd be face-to-face with Amanda Alexander.

She thought maybe she'd be talking to Amanda on a telephone, with a thick layer of glass separating them. Instead, she was led to a small room with a few tiny circular tables. Amanda sat at a table in the center, her cuffed hands resting in front of her.

"Twenty minutes." Detective Harper sat at the table nearest the door and pulled out her phone.

London sat across from Amanda. Even with her tan jumpsuit, unkempt hair, and dark, bruise-like circles under her eyes, Amanda was very pretty. They stared at each other without speaking for nearly a minute.

"I know you're not allowed to talk about what happened the day you murdered my best friend," London said.

"I didn't—"

"You killed him," she growled. "You may not have thrown a single punch, but you are as responsible as the ones who beat him."

"London," Detective Harper warned. "Remember our agreement."

She closed her eyes for a moment to gather herself. "How did you know where I worked? And why did you come to Hell that day?"

"I'd heard about your success with your store on the news a few times, so when Tate talked about you, I knew exactly who you were. I thought it was cool he was so close to you." She cleared her throat nervously. "He…he told me he'd bring me there someday to meet you. So you were easy to find."

"I see." London shifted uncomfortably. The fact that she'd been so easily located by someone involved in Tate's death was unnerving.

"And as far as why I came…" Amanda pinched her lips together for a moment, and tears filled her eyes. "You have to understand, I'm not a monster. Everything happened so fast that day, and I didn't mean—"

London held her hand up. "I didn't come here to listen to you tell me you're really not a bad person. If that's all you have to say, I'll just go." She stood, and the chair moving against the linoleum floor made a high-pitched screech that hurt her ears.

"No, wait!" Amanda reached across the table, not quite touching London with the tips of her fingers. She stayed that way, with her cuffed hands outstretched until London sat back down.

Amanda pulled her hands back to her body and held them up to her chest with her fingers woven together in a pleading gesture. "I had something of Tate's. I was bringing it back to you."

London shook her head. "I don't understand."

"Before our date, Tate raved about all the awesome playlists he had on his phone and how he had the perfect one for our road trip. When I told him my car was older, and I didn't have a way to hook it up to my radio, he said he'd make a CD for us to listen to."

London swallowed the lump in her throat. That was exactly what Tate would've done.

"A few days after the…after Tate died, I realized the CD was still in my player."

"Where is it?" London startled at the sound of Harper's voice. The detective had moved directly behind her.

"I left it in the store. I thought London would find it and think maybe Tate forgot it there or something."

"*What?*" London gasped. "Where did you leave it?"

"On the rack of postcards, tucked between a few of them."

"I take it you haven't found the CD," Harper said. "I'll need to send an officer over to the store right away."

"But why?"

"It's evidence until CPD and the prosecutor's office say it's not."

London was crushed. Before she even had a chance to process the fact that she had something in her possession from Tate's last day, it was being yanked away from her.

Detective Harper looked at her watch. "Time's up." Only seconds later, an officer came in from the hallway to escort Amanda away. She barely had time to cast a glance over her shoulder, catching London's eye for the briefest moment, before disappearing from the room.

London was starting to wish she hadn't come. Until today, Amanda had been a monster who had lured Tate to his death. Today, she'd proven herself to be human, and that made it so much worse. It was easy to understand how a monster could be responsible for her best friend in the world being gone forever, but Amanda was a woman who'd tried to return a meaningful possession. In that moment, London knew it would probably take the rest of her life to understand the flaws and limitations of humanity.

CHAPTER NINETEEN

It snowed all night," Reggie whispered. London barely opened her eyes to check the time on her phone. Six fifteen a.m.

"What?" she mumbled.

"It's Christmas morning," Reggie said, "and it snowed all night. Come see."

London got out of bed and went to the window where Reggie had the curtain pulled back. Glistening snow covered the city in great, round tufts. There had to be at least six or seven inches.

"Let's go tell Q!" London grabbed her robe. Reggie followed her into the living room, and when they got there, they both stopped short. Last night after Quentin fell asleep, Reggie and London had put a bunch of gifts under the tree for him, giggling and shushing each other the entire time. Now, he sat near the tree with two gifts in his lap wrapped in paper they didn't recognize.

"Merry Christmas." He stood and hugged them both, handing them the presents. They opened their gifts to find that Quentin had framed two large pictures. Reggie's picture was of the three of them at Betty and Herb's in front of the fireplace, and London's picture was from when they stood in front of the big Christmas tree at the center of the city in the Columbus Commons. In both photos, they were all smiling broadly, and in the one in front of the tree, Quentin was laughing.

"How did you do this?" Reggie asked.

"Herb helped me," he said. "He took both of those pictures, and I asked him if I could do chores to earn money to print them out and buy the frames so I could give you something for Christmas."

London and Reggie looked at each other, and London saw the tears in her eyes mirrored by Reggie's. "They're just beautiful, Q. Thank you." London reached over and squeezed him, and Reg moved to the other side of him to hug him on that side. She could never have imagined that someone she'd known for so short a time could become so precious to her so quickly. Quentin had lived with them only a month, and already she couldn't picture her life without him.

"You really like them?" he asked.

"Very much," Reggie said. "We love them."

"Oh, good," he said, and the relief in his voice broke London's heart, but not as much as what he said next. "I thought it would be a good way to remember the time I spent here with you once I go back to Compass or to a foster family. I got copies for myself so I can remember too."

London looked over Q's head at Reggie, and mouthed, "Now?" Reggie nodded and guided Quentin over to the couch.

"We need you to start opening your gifts." London moved to the far side of the tree where a package was tucked behind all the others. "We were going to save this one for last, but I think we're both too excited." She sat on the couch next to Quentin and handed him the gift.

He smiled as he unwrapped the shiny paper, carefully setting each piece on the coffee table as he went. When he opened the thin box and saw what was in it, his smile froze and turned into a look of puzzlement. He picked up the top sheet of paper—a form that hadn't yet been filled out—and showed it to them as if they hadn't seen it before.

"What is it?" he asked.

"They're adoption papers," Reggie said.

Quentin's mouth dropped open. "Adoption?"

"Yes," London said. "They're blank until you tell us whether you'd like to be part of our family."

"We've gotten Joan's blessing," Reggie said. "As of yesterday. She printed out the paperwork herself. If this is something you want, we'll go forward. You can think about it as long as you need to."

Quentin's mouth popped closed and he shook his head. "I don't believe this."

"What's wrong?" London's heart was in her stomach. She tried to figure out how to prepare herself for taking Quentin back to Compass and saying good-bye to him. She couldn't imagine it. Everything in her felt heavy and cumbersome, as if her hope of adopting him had become an anvil.

"I just can't believe you'd think I would need time to think about it," he said, cracking a smile, and London's heart, an anvil only seconds before, now felt filled with helium.

"Really?" she asked. "You're sure?"

"Sure, I'm sure!" And even as he smiled, Quentin started to cry. "I thought you guys would never ask me!" They held him and let him cry. As he was winding down, he gulped and sat up straight.

"What is it?" Reggie asked.

"What will I call you?"

"Call us?"

"Like, am I gonna call you Mom or something?"

They laughed, and London patted his hand. "You can call us whatever you want, my love."

Once they dried their tears, they began opening their other gifts, but when any of them looked back on that day, the only gift they would remember was the first one that Quentin opened. The gift for all of them.

❖

That evening, they braved the snow to have Christmas dinner with Betty and Herb. They waited until dinner was nearly over to share their good news. Betty rushed to Quentin, who was still seated, and hugged his head so tightly, they could barely hear his muffled laughter. Herb pulled a handkerchief from the front pocket of his sweater and wiped his eyes, his smile bigger than London had ever seen it.

After they cleared the plates, Herb handed keys to Reggie. "Can you go over and water the plants? I want to play Scrabble with my grandson."

Quentin beamed. London, Reggie, and Betty stood in the doorway, watching them set up their Scrabble board.

"I just can't imagine a better Christmas." Betty sighed.

"Well, I guess I better walk across the street and water some plants," Reggie said.

"I'll walk with you if you'd like some company," London said.

"Your company? Always."

Betty went to the coat closet and pulled out their coats. "Just be careful out there, girls. There are sure to be some slippery spots."

"We will."

The night was clear and sparkling with a bright, fat moon. Downtown, they rarely saw more than a handful of stars even on the clearest of nights, but here, they were just far enough from the city that the sky seemed positively packed with dazzling lights. London and

Reggie's gloved fingers intertwined as they made the short walk across the street.

Reggie flipped the light switch just inside the front door, and they set to work getting the watering cans filled and the plants watered. Between the two of them, they were done in less than ten minutes. London waited as Reggie took a final look around the living room.

"I think we got them all." When she turned, she visibly took in a gulp of air.

London had gotten down on one knee, reaching out. "Come here." Her outstretched hand was steady. "Please?"

Reggie took the three steps across the room and took her hand. London reached into her coat pocket, took out the folded construction paper she'd been carrying around for months, and handed it to Reggie. She'd thought it might be hard to let it go when this moment came. She'd thought she would have to fight down the feelings of panic and fear that had always blocked her from committing to her own happiness. Now, staring up at her love, all she felt was calm and the absolute understanding that she was finally ready to embrace her life with open arms.

"Reggie, I love you so much. When I think about my future, it's filled with images of you. You're the one I'll be coming home to, every time I come home, forever. You make me so happy, you make me crazy, you make me honest, and you make me feel.

"I talked to the Smiths in Florida. This house is ours, if you want it. I negotiated with them—if you can call it that, considering they wanted what they bought the house for in the sixties—so we can move in after they get back in the spring and get all their stuff out. All I want is you and Quentin in a place where we can grow old, and he can grow up. Will you marry me?"

A long silence. "You bought this house?"

"No. But I will if you want me to. Everything is in order; just say the word."

A twinge of a smile passed across Reggie's face before it disappeared. "We don't have to get married to adopt Quentin. Grant said we'll have to jump through more hoops, and it'll probably take longer, but it'll most likely go through without marriage given how long we've been together."

London stood. "I know. That's not why I'm asking."

Reggie bit her lip and ducked her head. "I thought you didn't want to get married."

"I thought so too. But these last few months I've taken a hard look at what I want and what I'm scared of. I've spent all this time trying to reconcile who I am to a letter that I didn't even write. I've been focusing on the wrong things. I always associated marriage with my parents' world, the world of rules and institution and doing things because you're supposed to. I hated that world even before I got kicked out of it."

"I don't understand. Now you want to be a part of that world?"

"Of course not," London said. "But you're not a part of that world, and you want to get married. Your parents aren't a part of that world, and they've been married, what, forty-six years? It took me this long to realize how many reasons there are to get married that have nothing to do with my parents or their life. I want to be with you, I want us to be a family. You, me, and Q. I want it to be official, all of it. If you still want to marry me."

Reggie looked at the letter. "Why do you still have this thing when it doesn't mean what it thought you meant?"

"I'm giving it to you. I've made some changes I think you'll like."

Reggie unfolded the letter, and the longer she looked at it, the larger her smile grew. The list of goals now looked like this:

1. *Wear business suits every day. *No. I look better in jeans and combat boots.*
2. *Get a job in marketing. *I already have a job I love.*
3. *Fall in love with a really awesome boy. *I did, his name is Quentin.*
4. *Get married. *Now, that I can do.*
5. *Volunteer at least once a week to help people in need. *Done.*
6. *Have a dog named Chowder. *Name is negotiable.*

Reggie looked up, tears glistening in her eyes.
"Yes."

Epilogue

Shortly after the murder trial ended in February, London agreed to speak at Compass about Tate. She arranged for Joan to have a CD player in the main living area when she arrived, and London slipped Tate's road trip mix into it. She was all nerves. She'd practiced and practiced her speech and got emotional every single time. A few tears were okay, but she really didn't want to have a total breakdown in front of these kids. She had thought about calling and canceling but couldn't bring herself to back out. So here she was, anxious but hoping for the best.

She pushed play and turned to face the room filled with kids. Many she recognized and some she didn't, and she was grateful that Q and Reggie sat at the back of the room, smiling at her. The opening chords of "Beautiful Day" by U2 played, and London began to speak. She told them stories from when they were kids, detailed Tate's transition, and finally, discussed his death and the trial. It was satisfying to let them know that Karl McCoy and David Witcher had been convicted of second-degree murder and had both received the maximum sentence of twenty years in prison.

"I'm always more inclined to talk about Tate's life than his death," London said, nearing the end of her speech. "But I've gotten to the point where I can tell Tate's story, his *whole* story. As much as I'd love to only tell the good parts, that wouldn't be honest. Tate was very honest. I think if he were here, he'd like me to tell you to live. Live carefully, yes, but live fully and bravely too."

It was at this part where she tended to lose control of her emotions, but she surprised herself. Rather than breaking down in uncontrollable sobs, she felt a warm sense of calm. She believed Tate was there with her, maybe right next to her, guiding her through it.

London peered at Reggie and Quentin and smiled broadly. "Finding your family can take a while. Take your time getting to know people before letting them close to you, but once you let them in, love them with everything you've got. Someone I love very much once said, 'Not all wishes are wasted.' That's true. It can feel like you're wasting your time and effort, but once you find your people, let them in. Let them love you. Live out loud. Life is too short to do anything else."

As it turned out, the Smiths' house wasn't a good fit for their family. While they loved the neighborhood, and obviously it would've been great to live so close to Betty and Herb, it was far from Quentin's school, and they didn't want to make him change districts; plus, it was far from work for London and Reggie. Besides, the city was where they'd always belonged.

"You were so keen to get me to marry you, you almost moved us to the suburbs," Reggie was fond of saying.

They found a large, prewar house near Franklin Park that suited all their needs. It was on the edge of the city rather than in the middle, but they loved the area, and the house gave them more than enough space. London even had a dedicated room for work and art, the door of which Reggie insisted stayed closed at all times lest she be tempted to go in and organize it to suit her own excessively organized taste.

It also gave them plenty of space for the enormous, two-year-old German shepard mix they rescued, a dog the people at the shelter called Biscuit.

"It's not Chowder," London said, lying on the concrete floor of the shelter the second time they visited Biscuit, where her voice was muffled because the dog had his front paws on her shoulders and was covering her face in sloppy dog kisses. "But it's pretty darn close." They'd taken it as a sign that the dog who chose them also had a name that was food oriented.

Their lives were filled with these changes in the months after that fateful Christmas, and more than that, they were filled with adoption filings and court dates and wedding plans. The court dates they found especially stressful, even though Grant assured them that everything would end in their favor.

"These things always take time," he said. "And I have a feeling they'll speed up at least a little once the wedding happens."

They didn't waste any time in that aspect, either. Not just because it would help adoption proceedings, although that definitely stayed on all of their minds, but because they knew what they wanted: small, simple, and sweet.

On a chilly, slightly overcast day in March, twenty-five of London and Reggie's close friends and family gathered in Schiller Park, their white wooden fold-out chairs facing the stage of the amphitheater. Black and gold ribbons hung from the back of each chair, and a thick, gold-flecked black cloth swept down the aisle in the middle.

Two small white tents in the back held the brides as they got ready and waited for the ceremony to start. Reggie had her father in her tent, Grant kept London company, and Quentin passed messages between the two. When London peeked into the crowd, she saw that Diana sat beside Betty in the front row. How times truly did change.

She was grateful she'd been able to have her twin back in her life. Their reconnection hadn't been fast or easy, but the tears they'd cried together seemed to have watered their roots and strengthened them. That Diana was at her wedding made her hopeful for their continued relationship.

London looked in the mirror and adjusted her hair for the dozenth time.

"You look great, babe," Grant said. "Beautiful."

"Thank you."

Q popped his head in. "Reggie says she won't cry if you won't."

"Tell her no promises," London said. Quentin grinned and popped back out.

"It's about time for me to head out there," Grant said. "You'll be walking down the aisle in less than ten minutes, so I should take my place."

London hugged him. "Thank you for performing the ceremony." She was determined not to cry before it even started, but it was a struggle. "You have no idea what it means to me. To us."

"I think I have a bit of an idea. Thank you for asking me." He turned to leave, then stopped. "By the way, Thomas is out there. He told me to tell you the papers you had drawn up are ready to sign."

"That was fast." she paused, blinking back tears for the second but probably not the last time that day. "He'd be proud, wouldn't he?"

"Tate? Yes, he'd be proud. And I have to believe he *is* proud, wherever he is. He'd be proud of what you've done, and so happy for you today."

"Yeah." She looked at the ceiling in an attempt to keep the tears from escaping. "I think you're right." It didn't take away the pain that Tate wasn't here the way she wanted him to be. She'd felt all morning like she was forgetting something. She'd checked and rechecked everything she needed until she realized she'd made herself late. In the car, she realized nothing was forgotten, but missing Tate had made her search for something she wouldn't find.

London had been working with Joan to create a subgroup under the Compass umbrella called TransConnect, dedicated to resources for the trans community. Everything from counselors to medical doctors to legal advice. That was what she'd decided to do with the money Tate left her. The idea had sparked in her mind the moment she saw the large sum on the bottom of those legal documents, and it had been quite the undertaking.

"You might end up being an executive after all," Joan had joked.

London had laughed. "I'm not cut out for that, and you know it. I just want to take this money and put it toward something I believe in. Once we get it set up, it's all yours to run as you see fit."

Grant pulled London into another quick hug, interrupting her reverie. "I'll see you out there," he said, and then, in a gesture that would've tickled Tate, he smacked her butt.

London sat carefully on a little chair in the corner. She reached into the sleeve of her dress and pulled out the letter Tate had written.

Dear London,

Are you okay? Of course you're not. If you're reading this, I've gone to the great big boobs in the sky. Remember when we thought heaven was made of boobs because that's what clouds looked like? If that's the case, I'm sure I'm doing great, and I'm sure you're having a tough time.

I've thought a long time about what I wanted to say to you in this letter, as I'm getting ready to become the person I always wanted to be. I have no idea how I'd go about living my life without you, so it doesn't seem right to give you advice on how you should live without me. I'm not gonna do that. I don't think there's really a right way to handle situations like that anyway, except to do the best you can, which I know you always do.

Mainly, when I've thought of writing this, I've been

searching my brain for anything I'd like to tell you, things I haven't told you before. That in itself has been weird because we tell each other everything, don't we? Almost. Nearly everything.

If there's one thing I haven't said, or at the very least, haven't said enough, it's thank you. Long before I thought transitioning was something that could ever happen for me, you knew it could. When I thought it was just a dream, you spoke about it as if it was a certainty, and if you hadn't been so sure, I don't know how many more years it would've taken me to get to the place where I made the decision to live, truly and honestly, as the man I've always been.

In the last several weeks, I've planned my funeral and gotten my affairs in order on the off chance that surgery gets the best of me. I'm not afraid of death. My main fear during all of this has been that you will somehow feel responsible if anything happens to me. That you will mistake this gift of surety and encouragement you've given as the reason that I'm not in your world anymore. Maybe you won't feel that way, and please, I hope you don't. These last few months I've been taking testosterone and seeing my body transform have been the most exhilarating of my life, and even planning these surgeries has been exciting because it gets me where I need to be.

What you've given me—not only in terms of transitioning, but always, our whole lives—is the freedom to just be myself. You've loved me so dearly and unconditionally that I always knew I had a place to be me. You taught me what family was, and have continued to teach me every day since I've known you. No matter what happens, no matter how my story ends, I will always be grateful to you for that.

You've already done so much, but I want to ask for just one more thing: always give yourself the freedom and space you've given me. Find your dreams and pursue them as fiercely as you've helped me pursue this. Be you, always, no matter what shape that takes.

I'm not sure how to end this because I know that if you're reading it, this is going to be a good-bye, and you know I'm no good at those. I guess I'll just say see you later.

*I'll see you later, London, and I know you'll have some
badass stories to tell when I do.*

Love you.

Tate

*P.S. The only other thing I never told you was that I tried on
your bra in seventh grade after you fell asleep at my house.
It was way too big, and the lace made my boobs itch. I don't
know why I never told you before.*

A few tears spilled from London's eyes, and she grabbed a tissue
to blot them away, even as she giggled at that last part of the letter, as
she had every time she read it. She tucked it back into her sleeve and
patted it.

After months of carrying the construction paper around, London
hadn't wanted to replace it with another letter. She'd had enough of
getting her courage and identity from a piece of paper in her pocket.
But she did bring Tate's letter with her on certain occasions when she
wanted to feel his comforting presence. She'd had it in her pocket for
all of their adoption court appearances. And she couldn't leave him out
of today of all days.

"Love you too," she said.

Quentin reappeared. He looked so handsome in his tuxedo with
the shimmering gold tie. His usually unruly curls were slicked back
into a modern pompadour.

"You look great." She straightened his tie. "The perfect man to
walk me down the aisle. Don't let me fall, okay?"

He laughed. "We're in trouble. I was gonna tell you the same
thing."

She heard the first strains of "Don't Dream It's Over" by Crowded
House, and her spine straightened.

"Okay, here's where I need you to help me. You have to peek out
and watch Reggie and her dad go down the aisle, tell me when they
make it to the end, and that's our cue."

"Got it." He peered outside. After several moments, he turned
back to her. "It's time. Are you ready?"

She took a final look into the mirror. The woman in the reflection
looked calm and happy, dressed in a lovely black gown. It had been a
journey to get here, but she'd made it. She could step out there and walk
toward her future knowing she was exactly where she was supposed to
be.

Six months ago, Reggie had proposed, and London couldn't have imagined herself ever submitting to the oppressive institution of marriage. The very thought made her feel like an animal trying to escape before it would be irrevocably trapped. But she'd explored who she really was, beyond her fear of being anything like her parents, and realized that marrying the love of her life wasn't oppressive or archaic, and it was nothing like her parents' relationship because she and Reggie were nothing like them. That had been the thing that had finally changed her mind, she realized. She and Reggie got to decide what their marriage would be together, and she believed in their marriage because she believed in them. As London smoothed her dress down a final time and turned toward the opening of the tent, where her future waited, what she felt, more than anything else, was free. She took Quentin's arm.

"I'm ready."

About the Author

Nan Higgins wrote her first book—a seven-page ghost story about the rickety old Victorian farmhouse she grew up in—when she was ten, and she has been writing ever since. She majored in music theater and puts her schooling to use by singing and dancing much more often than her friends and family think necessary. Nan is the cohost of *Stalled*, a podcast about the victories and struggles of two writers who got a late start turning their passions into their profession. She is also the creator and host of the new podcast *A Gay with Words*, in which she explores the labels and language utilized in the queer community.